TOMORROW
TODAY

Edited by George Zebrowski

1975

UNITY PRESS

SANTA CRUZ

Published 1975 by UNITY PRESS
Box 1037, Santa Cruz, California 95061

First Printing

Library of Congress Cataloging in Publication Data

Zebrowski, George, 1945-   comp.
    Tomorrow Today.

    (Planet Series, No. 1)
    CONTENTS: McHale, J. Introduction: *Today's Tomorrows*; Yarbro, C. Q.
Into My Own; Benford, G and J. *John of the Apocalypse*; Reynolds, M. *Visitor*;
Cook, G. *In The Wind*; Pangborn, E. *Harper Conan and Singer David*; Stevens,
J. *Syn*; Kagan, N. *Counter Ecology*.
    1. Science fiction, American. I. Title.
PZ1.Z4To   [PS648.S3]   813'.0876   73-82547
ISBN 0-913300-33-0
ISBN 0-913300-31-4 (pbk.)

Cover Design by Eric Mathes

Printed in the United States of America

DEDICATION

To My Brother

CONTENTS

INTRODUCTION
TODAY'S TOMORROWS

John McHale

Though one may be drawn more to comment upon this collection of science fiction from personal interest and enjoyment, rather than professional concern, it is important to locate such work within the larger context of the futures movement.

The past few years have been signally marked by the phenomenal growth of 'futures research' and 'forecasting' as a quasi-respectable if somewhat hybrid discipline. A large number of organizations have come into being whose central purpose is the exploration of the future in both the short and longer term. Many schools, colleges and universities have introduced courses on various aspects of the future. National and local governments, alerted to the need for longer term projections of their goals and expectations, have sponsored a variety of commissions and study groups.

Public concern with the future has become a social movement in its own right. Spurred by best sellers like *Future Shock* and *Limits to Growth*, and drawing upon the parallel issues of ecology, population growth, war, the quality of life, etc., many citizen groups, religious organizations and voluntary associations have launched conferences and continuing discussion groups on the future. One might almost say that the future has become as fashionable as the historic past, and begins to rival the present in terms of popular attention!

Through these various means, a new range of public metaphors and images have begun to circulate enabling more people to approach the future in ways which help to identify their own experiences and make them more aware of their individual and collective alternatives. Interestingly enough, and pertinent to this present science fiction anthology, many of the more popular images have been negative and dystopian. The titles of some of the best selling 'serious' books on the future sound like a drum roll for the coming Apocalypse, e.g., *The Doomsday Book, Terracide, Our Plundered Planet*. There may be some relationship of this range of imagery to the parallel revival of the gothic novel, the horror movie and the widespread renewal of interest in the occult and other forms of mystical and transcendental experience.

Some common origins for both the professional and public preoccupation with 'the future' lie within the growing sense of, and apprehension regarding, the scale and magnitude of human capacities to intervene in the social and physical processes of the planet. This sense might be labelled as a 'future imperative'—as signifying that we have reached a stage in human global development at which longer range assessment of the implications and consequences of our collective actions in the present becomes critically important for the future survival of human society. Visions of 'today's tomorrows' begin to exert a more direct influence on our present actions than the conventional wisdom of 'yesterday's todays'.

Even with the widespread growth of the various 'futures' movements, the role of science fiction is still uniquely valuable in bringing the future down to manageable individual terms. Its practitioners are the least constrained in creative imagination and in the provision of a wide range of personal, and personalized, visions of the future. Having, in the main, left their earlier fascination with various kinds of scientific and technological determinism, they now voyage courageously into the social and psychic scripts of future changes in the human condition.

The present anthology is a particularly interesting example of the latter trend. Though somewhat dystopian in the overall set of previsions, each story carries within it the essential flashes of hope, of affirmation of the human (and nonhuman) spirit, and that wry and ironic humor which tempers despair.

Its expressive range of preoccupations mirrors many of our current concerns. From the gentle nostalgia of Pangborn's "Harper Conan and Singer David", which dreams of a future past, we are led through the sensitive internal landscape of Stevens' clone sisterhood to the acrid visions of a counter-counter-ecology in Kagan's evocation of a near future ecosystem collapse.

Yarbro plays upon the mythical unease and dread with which we have always regarded the technologies which sustain our survival.

Her machine as alter ego, 71C-OR, is both Golem and Frankenstein to its human analog. In response to our current fea s of a threatening and runaway technology, it replies, "There is nothing in me that isn't in you, so you're stuck with it. . .I'm you turned inside out." This kind of insight is worth a hundred essays on the evils of modern technology. "Into My Own" points up the essentially symbiotic relationship of mankind to those technical extensions which have made us not less, but more, human.

The old theme of alien contact is subtly metamorphosed, by Reynold's "Visitor", into a modern version of Pandora's Box. What's inside the alleged alien space capsule found on the lunar surface?—"I suspect information beyond our wildest dreams." Whether real or imaginary, cornucopia or time bomb, the perceived alien threat is sufficient to draw upon the xenophobia of the quarreling earth nations in welding a new global unity.

Under the motto THINK IN OTHER CATEGORIES, which might serve as a useful guide to all explorations of the future, Kagan's "Counter Ecology" elaborates the vision of human preservation rather than natural conservation. "It looks more and more like we're going on to be swept away by armies of super-grass, navies of malevolent seals, air fleets of suicidal bald eagles—a forced Greening of America." In his other category the best defense is seen in departure; in lofting earth's six billion humans into orbit to dwell in various closed ecologies till the planet becomes less hostile.

In somewhat similar fashion, Cook's 'other category' question is, "What could you do when you couldn't use the smallest scrap of metal?" His "In the Wind" takes us to an alien Camelot where the main survival task is to control migrating herds of windwhale marauders and flying mantas—via lighter than air machines of lath and canvas. Whilst set in a forbidding place and time, this tale has all the bravura and aerial excitement of the old World War One movie, *Dawn Patrol*, in which the rickety spads and tri-wing Fokkers of an earlier period grappled together in the then new battlefields of the sky.

In a Joycean stream of consciousness the Benfords guide us through an offbeat political campaign in the near future. While bemoaning the fact that "Brahma and Vishnu get a much better press these days", their candidate staunchly presses the flesh in a phantasmagoria of gurus, yogis, incense and acid. Swacked on a mixture of lysergic soy, he stumbles through his people-to-people routine under a slogan deserving of immortality, ". . .if we're okay in the eternal present, we're okay!"

Returning to Stevens' evocative expression of the clonesister in the hive war-machine society of a far future, "Syn", we may note again its polar, but essentially similar, quality in relation to Pangborn's "Harper Conan and Singer David". Both represent the best directions of this wave of science fiction in going beyond the pasteboard stereotypes of earlier periods. They question the *content* of individual human experience under vastly altered social and physical conditions. The clone's society is more threateningly alien than that of Harper Conan but both stories are concerned with the same quest—how does it feel to be this kind of person in that kind of world and time? Is the one experience more or less human than the other? We may ask of their visions, how do we feel in relation to this or that character, or how would we feel under those conditions?

These centrally affective concerns have been those of all literature but now, in science fiction particularly, they are being expanded and translated into milieux of time, space and affective orientation which often elude more conventional forms. They set for us a vision of the future in which the oldest quest of all is stated, and restated, in a new range of modalities. How may we learn to be more human—and more humane?

Here is a near future, approximately the year 2000, when biological engineering techniques (like the cloning of organs, or even whole individuals from individual cells) are gradually replacing older, less elegant techniques like artificial and transplanted organs. The author reports that the background on artificial organs comes from Dr. Thomas Putnam of the Rochester Research Center, who is a pediatric surgeon specializing in cardio-vascular surgery in the program to develop reliable artificial organs. The background on computer intelligence derives from the Stanford Center for the Study of Artificial Intelligence. But the story which follows is about much more, delving deeply into a dying human heart, both literally and figuratively. . .

G.Z.

INTO MY OWN

Chelsea Quinn Yarbro

Tsss-thup. Tsss-thup. Tsss-thup went what passed for a heartbeat in Dahlman's chest. *Tsss-thup.* And he listened to it, hating it for its mechanical perfection. *Tsss-thup. Tsss-thup.* It never left him alone. But what a good idea it had seemed, seven years ago, when his own heart was faltering, failing, worn out. He had so much work to do then, so much that he hadn't finished, and he had agreed. Now he had that sound in his chest and it was his liver that needed replacement. In the loud silence of the hospital night Dahlman imagined what his blood might be like after being cleaned and moved about by things that were not part of him.

There was, of course, an alternative. These days there were always alternatives. Even in the dark Dahlman's eyes sought out the uncompromising outline of the console against the wall. He felt the familiar chill touch him as he looked at the thing: 71C-OR. That machine could take him over, burrow into all the private recesses of his mind and then become him, *be* Eric Dahlman, with his mind and thoughts, his future, his work, his memories. Then he could die and his art would continue, faithfully executed by the computer. An anger speeded his pulse and the miniature atomic steam engine that powered the thing under his ribs adjusted itself to the change, obediently, uncaring.

It was Nikels' fault: that much was obvious. If only Dahlman had not let himself be talked into the surgery the first time, if only he had refused and died. . .but it was useless to think about it now. It was over. He had made his choice, or Nikels' choice, and had to live with it. To keep himself from thinking he listened to the night finding it cold and remote. Without knowing he was waiting, he waited.

"Sleep well?" It was typical of Nikels that he was smiling, showing that friendly face that Dahlman had known for so many years. "The doctors are anxious for your decision."

"I don't know." Dahlman moved uneasily, seeing the computer console shining in a beam of morning light.

"They can't wait much longer; it's a matter of timing." He continued his warm smile as he eased himself onto the foot of the bed. His hands were long and thin, at odds with his energetic, compact body.

Dahlman scowled, hoping that the dread he felt did not show. "I'm not sure, Nikels. Maybe they're right and this is what I should do. But this thing," he gestured to his chest where his alien heart kept time, "this thing was bad enough. I don't know how much more I can stand and still function." He knew that Nikels would sense a threat in that, and it was just what he wanted.

Nikels made a gesture of dismissal. "Don't worry about it," he said, plainly hiding worry of his own. "The liver isn't like the heart. You won't hear a thing. And remember that there are still eight contracts waiting for you. You can't afford to let your body break down now." There was a forced joviality in his manner. Dahlman sensed that Nikels was trying hard to keep his irritation under control. "Look, Eric, you know that you're not finished yet. You're only eighty-six. You've got a lot to do before you're finished. Why, there's years of work in front of you."

"Years," Dahlman echoed, listening to his heart mark off the seconds.

"A lot to look forward to."

"And how old are you, Nikels?" Dahlman asked, knowing that his manager was forty-two or three. "I'm twice your age. When I was a kid we lived in private homes and grew flowers. Every year I pruned the jacaranda tree. I'm getting tired." To forestall the objections he could see forming in Nikels' face, he said, "Sure, I'm excited about the new plays. They're great concepts and I want to do them, even if Tonio directs them, the bastard. But I don't want to go on like this!"

There was a slight hesitation before Nikels said, "You can talk to the 71C-OR. That would be one way to solve the problem."

"Would it?" There was thick sarcasm clotting his words as he spoke them. "I suppose it might. That thing could go on being me and none of you would have to waste precious time on this old hulk

8

of mine." Even to himself the words sounded melodramatic, filled with self-pity. He saw the calculation in Nikels' eyes and shut up.

"Dr. Bruson can arrange it, if you like," Nikels said carefully. He shifted his weight uneasily. His face had gone closed, showing nothing now but a safe, infuriating neutrality.

"Well?" He knew that Nikels was waiting for the chance to speak again. "What is it?"

"Look, Eric, if you take the liver, you can probably last long enough for them to make a clone of it for you. And your heart, too, for that matter. You say you don't like the feeling of something foreign in you—all right, then. This is the answer. It would be your own heart, but younger. Your own liver, fresh and undamaged."

Dahlman's skin went cold with horror, his muscles gripping his bones. "I don't like any of this," he announced, inwardly fearing the whine that had come into his voice. That old, tired cry could not be him, could not be the great dramatist Eric Dahlman whose career stretched back half a century. He could not make such a noise. His flesh still quivered.

"But your liver's shot, Eric. Just the way your heart was." Whatever it was Nikels wanted him to do, Dahlman could not discover it in his tone or words. "I'm worried about you, Eric. The longer you wait, the less there will be to save. And you are worth saving."

Dahlman hated being patronized. "All right, Nikels, I tell you what," he said, pleased that the fright had left his voice. "I'll take my chances with that damned machine for a while until I make up my mind about the liver business." There. That ought to satisfy him.

The frown that appeared on Nikels' face was not reassuring. "I'll tell Bruson." He said it without emotion and left the room quickly.

Now that he had committed himself, Dahlman stared at the console, watching for a sign. It did not come, no matter how he stared. It was still the sleek metallic box, a bluish color with a sound transmitter and the fittings that were disturbingly like spider legs. Dahlman disliked it more the longer he looked at it. . .His eyes got bright with his hate. He could see the dim reflection of it in the polished surface of the console.

They had told him the thing was organic, that the OR at the end of its name was for organic. Nikels had described the special molecules, huge by molecular standards, that carried impressions, race-track fashion, giving it some sensory knowledge and a memory so complex that former circuits seemed clumsy by comparison. Dahlman thought about 71C-OR with its innards and he thought about his own and he wondered which of them was more truly alive.

Bruson, when she came, was quietly efficient, explaining why it was necessary that Dahlman should decide immediately, and pressing her argument for organ replacement. "See here, Mr. Dahlmann. There is only so much we can do, and you are making it very difficult for us. I'm sure you're aware that your condition is potentially fatal." And she waited for this to sink in. Dahlman felt the waiting, and knew that his life had become nothing but waiting.

"Doctor, I'm tired," he told her, and realized as he said it that it was true. "When I was a kid, people died, do you know?" The room was too bright for him to read her expression. "They got old and died. The government didn't single out people for this kind of piecemeal immortality."

"Mr. Dahlman, your contributions to theater, to literature. . ."

"Screw the theater. And literature. I'm an old man." He stopped and looked at her, at the young, polished beauty of her, not unlike the polished machine that waited for him on the far side of the room. "You know, when I was young, there was a woman, something like you, and for three months we lived for each other's flesh like cannibals. She tasted of apricots."

The doctor's cat-colored eyes lit. "That was in *Peter's Dream*, wasn't it? I read it in school. It started the whole interpretive psychic trend, didn't it?" She had leaned forward and given him a predatory smile. Dahlman wondered if he touched her, would she be hot or cold?

"No, Dr. Bruson, it did not." He cast his mind back to the ancient lectures and honors, his face wrinkling a little in distaste. "You people put labels on it, but what I wrote was a play. Between the professors and Tonio, my words got lost and they're still lost." He pulled at the bed cover, jerking it more tightly around him, sighing with resignation when it realigned itself.

"You could do it again, Mr. Dahlman. Think what you can accomplish. And in a few more years our cloning technique will make it possible to restore all your body to what it was." Her face was rosy with promise and there was that secret expression that women sometimes showed to him, a desire to be part of his memories so that they, too, might be like Cecily in *Peter's Dream*, whose real name had been Hulda.

Dahlman knew he did not look his eighty-six years. His hair was still fawn colored and curled about his leonine head. Perhaps his brows had grown bushier and his lips leaner, but the stigmata of age had not visited him as he remembered them coming to his father. The noble line of his forehead was slightly lined, and around his china eyes a minute fretwork marked out the history of smiles and frowns. Unconsciously he touched the scar that marked where his heart had been and where the intruder now lay. He fingered his genitals and was relieved to find warm flesh instead of plastic.

"I'll tell Professor Thomas what you have decided," she said, watching him as she left the room.

Dahlman sniffed the air for traces of her when she was gone, wondering what had driven her to play with the mechanics of humanity, reassembling and rebuilding. Did she enjoy the godlike power of giving life where it was failing? Why did she do these things? Again he recalled the promise of clones that would guarantee a continuing supply of *himself*. He found this threat of reverse vampirism more terrifying than the bloody legends of the Impaler.

Professor Thomas was delighted with Dahlman's decision. "You will see," he said enthusiastically, hauling the console closer to Dahlman's bed. "You will see how this will become you. It will be very easy." He favored Dahlman with a show of teeth. "Here is the secret," he continued in a breathless whisper. "These appendages do the trick. They will register such things as skin temperature, pulse rate, blood pressure, pH level, eye movements and dilation, speech patterns and vocal levels, even physical mannerisms. It is not unlike a mirror that records your every sense, your very being. It is most complete." Here he paused, and Dahlman thought wryly that he should applaud.

"Very interesting," he said at last when it became obvious that Professor Thomas would not go on without some encouragement.

"You will talk to it, and it will talk to you. You will confide in it, and it will explore your mind, every nuance of your personality, and then, when it has all the information it needs, it will turn into you, and you, Mr. Dahlman, will be free to die if that is what you wish to do."

"Only you say I won't die."

"Not fully. But your body, as such, will be gone. This, your complete image, will remain." He touched his machine with lover's hands. "We have already taken the liberty of giving 71C-OR all the information we could find about you. Things like school records, every word of yours that had been recorded, all your works, your family background and the genetic profile that was taken of you twenty years ago. 71C-OR has been processing that while you made up your mind."

It was as if he had been wounded and his viscera laid bare where birds could pluck at them. "What?" There was less in the word than in his face, but Professor Thomas missed both. "You must realize that this is a necessary part of the transition," he explained blithely. "Only when 71C-OR has a comprehensive pattern of you will it be able to duplicate your abilities. That means that it must understand what you have done at the time you did it. Memories are not enough. . .as Casanova himself admitted." Professor Thomas obviously regarded this as a joke and he showed his teeth to Dahlman once more.

"Where did you find your material?" Dahlman asked when he had got control of his temper. "You must have gone to considerable trouble."

"Certainly," Professor Thomas said with relish. His supple hands writhed on his elbows as he regarded Dahlman. "There are seventy others who have gone through transference. The ultimate tribute. . .and unique." He lost himself in thought for a few moments, his hands lingering now on the console. Then he returned to his overly cheerful presentation. "We've learned quite a lot in that time. And we've got most of the bugs out now, and the results are predictably excellent."

Dahlman felt himself suddenly cold. Professor Thomas and his talk of the bugs that were out now made him fear what had happened before, to the other fortunate ones who were selected for transfer. If the machines were mirrors, might not some of them be distorted? He steeled himself to ask, "And if there should be an error?"

"There won't be. Since the invention of organic circuitry, full memory transfer has been a cinch, and the C-OR series are as close to perfect as any machine is likely to be." Eagerly he moved the console still closer, easing it into position by the bed. "Tomorrow morning we'll get started. No sense waiting any longer than necessary, Mr. Dahlman. And you'll discover that this will let you bring your life and work into a focus you have never known before. Even the best hypno-meditative methods are nowhere near as dramatic in the self-realization results as transfer is." He gave the console an affectionate pat, almost as if it were a pet, and then he strode purposefully out of the room, moving with the precision of a well-designed machine.

That night Dahlman dozed, watching the computer crouching by his bed as the night hours went over. It had already eaten a bit of him, digested it and incorporated it into its being. With the morning it would burrow its sensors into his flesh and with those signals to guide it, would lead him through his life, minute by minute, memory by memory, dream by dream, until the whole of Eric Dahlman was codified, sorted, classified and stored. . .

He could always change his mind and take the new liver. Dahlman toyed with the idea until he heard the sound of his heart loud in his ears.

"Dahlman," the computer said to him in the morning. It had been set up and now its upper half crouched over his chest, sensors extending over his body, touching him where it could learn.

"What?" asked Dahlman, letting no emotion into his voice.

"I sense that you resent me. You must not resent me," said 71C-OR in what sounded like a sincere manner. It paused for a moment, then added, "We cannot effect transfer if you resist this way."

"What about the others?" Dahlman asked in spite of himself. "Didn't they resist?"

"Until now, this honor has been limited to scientific and academic men who had long been associated with machines and did not feel this. . .separateness that you do. They understood that they were extending themselves in a way that they could not otherwise achieve."

"Which means that I don't understand?" Dahlman snapped, pushing at the unit that hung over him.

"This position disturbs you? You find me too close?" asked 71C-OR. "I can place myself with the rest of the unit and lengthen my contacts, if you would feel more comfortable."

"Damn you, I'm not an infant. You needn't coddle me."

They were interrupted when two doctors came quietly into the room, their respectful eyes on 71C-OR. "Mr. Dahlman," said one, obviously addressing the computer, "is there any way we can be of assistance?"

Before the computer could answer, Dahlman erupted. *"That's not me! I'm here!* That thing is a machine."

The doctors made embarrassed noises, but continued to direct their questions to the computer.

"If you want answers, ask me!" Dahlman insisted, trying to raise himself as he spoke. He could hear his heart more loudly as it sent a new surge of blood pounding through his veins.

At last one of them did. "Professor Thomas wanted to know how the initial contact was going, sir. He needs to know how long transfer will take so that he and Dr. Bruson can decide how best to deal with your case."

Oddly enough, it was the computer who ordered them out of the room. "Doctors," it said to them with amazing condescension in its tone, "I am sure you will understand our need to be private."

"But what will we say to Professor Thomas?" asked the louder one of the two. He had retreated to the door with his companion, but was plainly not going to give up until he had an answer.

"I will inform Professor Thomas of our progress later." The sound was so absolute that if Dahlman could have at the moment, he would have fled from the room, from the hospital. In that moment he realized for the first time that 71C-OR could truly do what he had been told it would do. A machine could and would turn into Eric Dahlman. He felt a wash of confusion as he sank back on the bed.

The wall monitor registered the extent of his emotion, automatically signaling for assistance.

"This is most curious," said 71C-OR as it observed the monitor and its own sensors. "You do not resent that machine, although it is complex and constantly measures and gauges your body reactions. Yet, when I attempt the same thing, you are filled with revulsion. Why is that?"

"None of your fucking business."

"But it is, Mr. Dahlman. I will have to understand you wholly in order to complete the transfer." Its sensors probed cautiously. "This is going to be very difficult," it remarked, as two nurses came into the room.

"Go away. I'm all right," Dahlman said, perversely wishing that the nurses would object and remain with him.

"He's being truthful," 71C-OR confirmed.

"I don't need you to. . ." Dahlman began, but the nurses had left as soon as 71C-OR had spoken. Then he wanted to call back the nurses, the doctors, anyone in the hospital so that there would be people with him; real people who would prevent the machine from devouring him. He was too vulnerable here on his back with the 71C-OR squatting over his chest, poised to take out his heart. He thought of his heart and wondered if machines fed on machines.

On the third day of the transfer process 71C-OR became his adversary. Dahlman listened in confusion as its previously respectful air vanished and in its place there was contempt.

"Why are you behaving this way?" Dahlman asked, feeling the hostility of the computer as its sensors touched him, reminding him of a child forced to touch some loathsome insect.

"Am I behaving in a way you dislike?"

"You're deliberately thwarting this transfer."

"You admit to being thwarted? I thought all artists were incapable of being thwarted by anything."

Dahlman squirmed. "Where did you get that idea?" He knew that he had made a speech once in which he had declared that any true artist was unstoppable, and he had sensed that this was what had irritated 71C-OR. In the next instant he shut the thought away.

"You are an ass, Dahlman. A clever one, but an ass. And you have made a whole cult of your life devoted to assdom." Its disgust was naked in its voice.

"You have no right. . ." Dahlman began, reaching for the button that would summon aid.

"I have every right. I am going to have to be you, like it or not. And I can't say that I like it."

"I never asked. . ."

"Yes, you did, when you refused that liver. And now I have to adapt myself to your patterns."

Dahlman, stung, forced himself up onto his elbows and glared at the grille that marked the place where 71C-OR's voice came from. "I had nothing to do with the offer of transfer. That's a governmental decision, and you know it."

"Made you feel good, didn't it," mocked the computer. "All that attention. The first creative artist ever to be offered transfer. And how noble to turn it down, the way you did the first time. Knowing that the offer would come again."

"I don't have to listen to this."

"Oh, yes you do," 71C-OR shot back in a voice that was too much the way his own had been fifty years ago. "There's nothing in me that isn't in you, Dahlman, so you're stuck with it."

Dahlman was about to object, to deny that the venom he heard from 71C-OR was any part of him, had ever been part of him, but a twinge of memory brought back the days before he had known fame, when he had fought with everyone around him in order to keep his courage. "You're a machine. You don't know what you're talking about," Dahlman said at last, without conviction.

"What makes you think so? I'm molecular just like you. I respond to stimuli the way you do. In fact, I respond to your stimuli."

"It's not the same," Dahlman said defensively, and forced himself to concentrate on the pattern that sunbeams were making on the face of the monitor.

"What isn't the same?" 71C-OR was persistent. "Because I am what I am and you are what you are? Is that your argument? That because you are clothed in flesh instead of metal, you have superior knowledge?"

Dahlman refused to answer and after a while 71C-OR, too, fell silent.

"Well, how is it going?" Nikels did not have quite enough certainty in his eager voice, or quite enough humor in his smile. "Professor Thomas sounded a little anxious about the transfer. Is anything wrong? Is the machine okay?"

With a flicker of anger Dahlman realized that Nikels was more worried about the computer than he was about him. But Nikels couldn't help it. He managed Dahlman as a continuing concern, no matter what package he came in. Reluctantly Dahlman admitted that Nikels was being sensible. "The machine is fine. I'm about as well as you could expect."

"There's still the liver," Nikels said quickly, knowing that Dahlman's slow response was a condemnation. "We can arrange it if you like. If the transfer isn't working out."

Slowly Dahlman sighed. "It's too soon to tell," he said carefully, feeling trapped. One way or the other, he was going to become a machine.

Nikels watched him cautiously, a guarded look in his face that changed subtly when Dahlman turned away. His glance strayed to 71C-OR then, and his expression became calculating. "Eric," he said after a while, "I won't interfere, that is, if you don't want me to. But I favor the transfer. I think it's the only way. Now, if you were willing to wait for a clone. . ." He let the words hang on a shrug.

Dahlman accepted this numbly. It did not surprise him any longer that Nikels was protecting himself at Dahlman's expense. Somewhere he felt a sting, but it no longer rankled him. "I hear you, Nikels," he said. "But I'm tired. I need some sleep. If you're right, I've got a long session with that machine tomorrow." He pretended to yawn and had the uneasy sensation that the computer was watching him, and was not fooled by his performance.

Nikels rose quickly. "I didn't mean to tire you out, Eric. I keep forgetting what you're going through. Sorry, friend." And he left quickly, without bothering to reassure Dahlman.

At the next session 71C-OR had changed again. It behaved strangely, almost eccentrically. "Perhaps there are things about me that will fascinate you," it suggested, moving the sensors quickly over his body.

"I doubt it," Dahlman answered shortly.

71C-OR ignored him. "I have it within me to manufacture all manner of wonderful things. I can create senses. . .taste, touch, hearing, smell, seeing. . .I have eyes, Mr. Dahlman. Wonderful eyes. You would appreciate them." There was an arcane enthusiasm in its tone, a relishing of things unique to it.

"You can believe that if you want," Dahlman said wearily. "You have no mouth, no tongue, so you can't manage the four tastes. . ."

"But I can," 71C-OR contradicted him impatiently. "I know that sour is a thing that goes with pickles, that sweet is honey and fresh fruits, that bitter is the property of almonds. . ."

"Where do you sense things like this? In your mouth?" Dahlman was angry now, his hands plucked at his blanket nervously and his face went white. "How can you tell about almonds? You've never seen an almond."

"But you have," the computer reminded him.

"Yes, of course. What difference does that make?" He felt himself slipping into petulance and resentment. That this machine should have the audacity to assume that because he could feel something, taste it, see it, that it could as well, filled him with rage at the injustice of the situation. Would a clone be any different? Would his own body treat him more familiarly, or would it, too, out of its newness, be as foreign to him as the machine? As his heart?

The computer explained imperturbably, "If I am to be you, it is your taste and feelings I will have to have. All that matters is that you have seen almonds, have tasted them and that I in turn recreate this within my circuits. They are just as molecular as yours. The impressions are just as valid."

"It's not possible!" Dahlman ground his teeth. "Don't you understand that?" Even as he shouted the words Dahlman felt the quivers of doubt at the base of his brain. What if it were possible, after all? What then?

17

"You always think about an orchard in bloom when you think of almonds. It was your grandfather's orchard and each year it would bloom and then later there would be nuts, which you would help harvest. At that time there was a special wind, which you called the Harvest Wind to yourself. You based the second act of *Innocence Lost* on it. That was before the Live Performance Laws came in, and it took you almost four years to recover the losses you took on the production."

"That isn't me, that's history," Dahlman insisted as the panic continued to erode his certainty. "You could read that in half a dozen books about the theatrical revival. It's common knowledge."

71C-OR was not disturbed. "The Harvest Wind stung your eyes and smelt of smoke. Billings was allergic to something in it and went around wheezing until November."

"Where the hell did you find out about Billings?" Dahlman had jerked himself straight so suddenly that he dislodged two of the sensors that stuck to his skin.

"From you," replied the machine. "Billings was your grandfather's field hand. He died of pneumonia when you were about nine years old. You've always been afraid to use him in your work."

"Where did you find out about Billings?" Dahlman demanded again.

"It's all part of you, Dahlman. And it's all part of me." 71C-OR paused, clicking its sensors meditatively. "You fell out of one of the almond trees once and broke your arm. It was a bad break and you fainted from the pain."

"Pain." Dahlman almost spat. "What do you know about pain? Where's your arm? How do you know what a humerus breaking the skin is like? How the numbness and agony come together? You don't know what it's like to see the meat that is your own muscle, with the terrible white bone splintering through. You can't know. You have no arms. You have no bones."

"I am designed to understand pain."

Dahlman tried to be patient. "Understand, perhaps. But you cannot feel it. You have no sensations. You can't have the sensations because you haven't my body. Thomas calls you a reflection: all right, then. If I cut myself and look in the mirror, perhaps the mirror reflects the blood, but not with my nerves and my hurt. It's impossible." He thought it would be monstrous if it were possible. To have a machine that had his body, his feelings, his hurt. . .

"I have contact. I have empathy."

At that, Dahlman struck out blindly, smashing the console away from him as he shouted for help.

When Dr. Bruson arrived she found Dahlman out of bed, swaying on his feet and shouting at the computer.

"Mr. Dahlman," she said as calmly as she could, "you must not get out of bed." Slowly she came toward him, forcing herself to smile for him. "What's the matter? What has upset you?"

He turned on her. "You know damn well what's upset me. That thing!" He staggered, reaching out a hand to brace himself. She caught it and moved to help him back to bed. "You're taking this far too morbidly, Mr. Dahlman," she assured him as she eased him back against the pillows.

From the other side of the room 71C-OR made a sound that would have been insulting coming from a human.

"It tried to tell me it feels, that it can know senses. . .not analyze them, or compute them, but really understand them, feel them, the things I felt. . ." His fingers searched out the ancient scar on his right arm, and for a vivid instant he was a child, falling, striking the ground with a sharp noise, then the brightness and the dark of pain.

Privately she frowned, but to him she said, "Well, naturally. What else is the C-OR series good for, if not that? Transfer would be impossible if the unit was incapable of sensory experience." She cast an anxious eye over the monitor and was relieved to find that none of the indicators were in the dangerous zone.

"It's not possible. It's not human." Dahlman was still angry but much of the force had gone out of him. He tangled his hands in the short curls that clung to his head. "It kept talking about emotions, sensations, as if they could be manufactured, prepackaged and brought back at the touch of a button."

"Well," said Dr. Bruson reasonably, showing him her best smile, "that's what the C-OR can do. They're designed for it."

Dahlman twisted his blanket and muttered, "It's not right. It's not right. It can't be that simple. There's got to be more. There are things that machines can't understand. There are things machines can't do. There's got to be."

"Of course," Dr. Bruson assured him before she left the room to tell Professor Thomas that he'd better try another approach with Dahlman.

So it was that at the next session, 71C-OR had changed again, and began in an insinuating way, "What would it take, I wonder, to make you give up this senseless travesty we're going through?" It paused, apparently agreeably surprised by Dahlman's shock. "Why not give up this masquerade? Take the new liver and let them turn me over to someone else. Someone capable of transfer."

"How do you mean, capable?"

71C-OR made a long, bored sigh. "You keep insisting that there is no way for me to experience your sensations. If that is so, then I cannot hope to effect the transfer. You've run up against this before, I recall. There was a woman you knew once whom you wanted to understand, and even though she reassured you, in the end you learned she was lying. . .it pleased her to be the bed partner of a famous playwright. That was all."

"Stop that." Dahlman looked at the sensors that were affixed to him and wondered exactly what 71C-OR was learning from them. He didn't want to talk about Miranda, particularly to the machine.

"It made you uncomfortable then, too," it observed. "You were wounded as much in pride as anything. You were furious that she would collect talent like so many trophies. You got even with her in *Laura's Price*, didn't you?"

"I never told anyone about that," said Dahlman, feeling a crease form between his brows. "How did you find out? Was that from me, too?"

"Naturally," 71C-OR gave a sigh of infinite patience. "She used to bite you when you made love. She said that the hurt would make you remember. Afterward you thought that it was her way of making you think more about her than your work."

Reluctantly Dahlman nodded.

"There," said 71C-OR, "that's better. Shall I remind you how you could feel the crescent of teeth on your thigh as you walked? Or how the scratches she left on your back would rub against your shirt and make you want her all over again?"

This time Dahlman squirmed, but he remained quiet, watching 71C-OR with a cautious respect.

"You wonder how I feel what you have felt. You even deny that I can feel. Yet you never wonder how you managed the feeling to begin with." The machine waited for Dahlman's thoughts. "Your feelings are impulses, responses to triggerings that relay certain information to you, and then create the appropriate sensation so that you will continue or discontinue what you are doing. Correct?"

"It sounds right," Dahlman said slowly, his mind on the strange non-sensation of his heart. Was that what it was like to be a machine? To have the non-feeling, the absence of awareness? 71C-OR insisted that it wasn't.

"Then why shouldn't I learn to respond to stimuli the way you do, and for the same reasons?"

"But it isn't that simple," he objected to the machine. "There are responses within responses within responses that go far away from the original impulse. . ."

71C-OR stopped him. "Come, come, Dahlman. That isn't the least bit unique and you know it. Drop a pebble into a pond and watch the ripples that form. You've built for yourself a kind of armor that assures you of your singularity, and you believe the ripples in your pond appear in triangles rather than circles."

"Creative work is different. It isn't like mathematics or oceanography." He knew there was a hunted look in his eyes as he said this and the machine apparently was aware of it as well as he was.

"Don't be so smug, Dahlman. Every thinking being is separate and specific. There is no vast, amorphous norm." It paused, and the sensors twitched on his skin, almost a gesture, almost human. "You have a level of skill and insight that is rare, but it does not place you outside humanity, it only puts you in one of the more admirable categories."

That was the first admission of talent that Dahlman had heard from 71C-OR, and it stopped him momentarily. "You admit that there are talents?"

"Certainly," it answered urbanely. "Obviously there is something rare in you, some particular gift, or I would not be here."

"That's big of you," Dahlman said bitterly. He pulled one of the sensors off his arm and tweaked it. "All right, what does this feel like?"

"How do you mean?" 71C-OR sounded guarded. "Do you mean your own emotions or my sensations?"

"See there? Without me, you can't feel anything. So it isn't real feeling at all." He grinned ferociously.

"Your sensation is one of rather petty self-approval; my sensation, on the other hand, is one of mild discomfort, rather as if you had twisted my nose."

"*You don't have a nose!*" Dahlman shouted, and heard the machine say, "You're wrong, you know, I have your nose," before two nurses appeared, their faces as white and rigid as their anachronistic caps.

"Mr. Dahlman," said one, watching the monitor critically, "you must not upset yourself this way."

"Shut up," Dahlman told her.

Once more the door flew open and Nikels surged in with Professor Thomas close behind him. They exchanged looks which Dahlman found conspiratorial. He felt their resentment of him, their approval of the machine. It would be easier for both of them if he completed the transfer.

"I'm not going through with this farce." Dahlman's face was set, showing the ghost of his age as he glared across the bed at the Professor and Nikels. He was pleased to see them at a disadvantage. "I've had it. I'm fed up. That fucking machine is a monster."

Professor Thomas screwed up his face into an expression not unlike a frown. "Now, this is what I don't understand," he said unhappily. "71C-OR was certain that things were going well and that transfer could be completed in a few days. He was certain, Mr. Dahlman. And you say that it isn't working."

The Professor's distress annoyed Dahlman. "I don't care what that thing told you. It was wrong. I want it out of here."

"Hey, hey, hey," Nikels interrupted, "don't be so hasty, Eric. Maybe you haven't given it a real chance. You know how you sometimes go off half-cocked."

"I am not going off half-cocked." The implacable gleam in Dahlman's eyes made Nikels hesitate before saying, "Oh, I guess it's pretty upsetting, going over all that old ground. I don't blame you for disliking it. But it's not as if you're dealing with another person. . .it's not like that at all, Eric. You're dealing with yourself."

"No."

"Mr. Dahlman." Professor Thomas clung to his own elbows. "I can understand the conflict you're going through. I had the same trouble when I underwent transfer two years ago. It is a difficult thing, and for you, considering your art and the depth of your involvement in your own emotions and trials, it must be even more difficult than it was for me." His face had taken on the sympathetic look of a hungry beagle. "Many honors are really ordeals in disguise."

Dahlman stared. "You went through this?" he asked.

"Yes. I transferred to 54C-OR and we are both continuing my work. If it were not for both of us, we could not have produced a C-OR that could handle the creative, as compared to the deductive and intuitive, mind."

The room was very still: Dahlman's eyes were hooded in thought, Nikels held his breath and Professor Thomas worried his fingers as if trying to unscrew them. One of the nurses started to speak and was silenced by her partner.

"All right," Dahlman said at last. "I'll give it another try. But tell Bruson to be ready with that liver in case I change my mind." Yet as he said the words, he found thoughts of his clone tickling his mind, and he shied away from them.

"Give it up, Dahlman," 71C-OR advised as they began their next session. "You know that I'm more capable than you are." It had replaced its suavity with a compelling arrogance. "The sensors tell me that your body is getting weaker, and I know that the work you've turned out these last four years is nothing like what you did at your height. That's what I'm going to concentrate on after transfer: your creative height. Maybe I can build you back to that. For one thing, I'm not troubled by fear of impotence the way you are. I don't need the constant reassurance that my body is desirable. My intellect, my artistry is desirable. And your work at the height was quite impressive."

Slowly Dahlman shook his head, ignoring the jibes at his sexuality. "You're wrong. My work is changing, that's all. I'm older and it shows."

"If you mean feeble, you're right. You haven't the strength I have. You don't deserve to continue your writing."

"It's my writing," Dahlman told it, much of the defensiveness gone from him. "Whatever it is, I did it and it's mine. Nothing you do or say changes that."

"Do you really think that *After Yesterday* is anywhere near as good as *Over Running Water*? There's no comparison. The first is dreary and self-indulgent, where the second is brilliant. If you think you're as good as you used to be, Dahlman, you're kidding yourself."

"My plays are produced. I never have any trouble finding a home for the new ones. I have contracts for the next six years." As he spoke Dahlman watched the computer, thinking how familiar it had become. The metallic box that housed it no longer seemed the threatening thing it had been, the sound of its voice had changed, slowly coming to sound like his own. Even its castigations were echoes of the ones he occasionally heard in himself. He let 71C-OR go on.

"Of course your plays are produced. With your reputation they'd produce your grocery list." It waited, then said, "If you live long enough, you'll probably write about me to get even for the transfer. You've done that with everyone else in your life."

Dahlman flared. "That's not so!"

"Yes it is. You know it is. Right now you're starting to work out another play. You aren't really paying any attention to me; you're thinking of scenes and characters."

Until that moment Dahlman had not been aware of his silent thought, having been so busy wrangling with the machine. But the words struck home and he found that the old ideas were forming

23

again, shaping themselves into dialogue and acts, building a drama, a new drama that would be the best he had done yet. "You're right, 71," he said, smiling.

The new liver didn't bother him the way the heart had done, and the culture that had been taken for the clone processing was off in the laboratory that Dr. Bruson ruled, being readied for future use. Dahlman found he had energy to spare now, that his mind was clearer, his feelings sharper, the words were coming back to him, full of the right sense and weight. He sat in his hospital room, waiting for Nikels to come for him. In the corner 71C-OR waited with him.

"What are you going to do now?" Dahlman asked the machine.

"I'll do what I'm supposed to do; write more of your plays."

"Oh, no. I'll write my plays, thanks just the same."

"Then we'll both write your plays."

Dahlman felt some irritation, then said, "No. You'll write your plays, not mine." He thought about that for a moment, then went on, "You think you've learned to be me, but what you've learned to be is you. You never felt my joy or my pain, you made your own, so what you build from it will be yours, not mine. Listen, 71, you're not a copy of anything or anyone. I'm not even sure you're my reflection. You're something brand new."

In a gloomy voice, 71C-OR said, "Transfer failed. I know that."

"No it didn't." Dahlman rose from the end of the bed. "You've been my Muse."

71C-OR snapped the sensor Dahlman had been holding back into its console. "Is that what you think?" it asked petulantly. "I wasn't your Muse, Dahlman. I was your enemy."

"My enemy?" Dahlman repeated, an unbelieving smile on his face.

"Of course. Do you remember that essay you wrote fifty years ago, *In Praise of Poets*? In it you said that fictional poets were always more attractive and more convincing than real ones. You used a lot of examples: Dylan Thomas, E. T. A. Hoffman, Poe, Fallon. Remember?" It waited while Dahlman searched his memory, continuing slowly when he nodded. "Your work shows that you still believe it, so I borrowed from your essay and made enemies for you to hate."

Dahlman laughed. "Sorry it backfired."

"Nonsense," barked 71C-OR. "You're delighted. I'd be, too, in your place."

A stillness settled between them. It was Dahlman who broke it at last. "So what are you going to do, 71?"

"Wait, I suppose."

"Until I'm dead, so that you can go on with my work?" He took the stony silence that greeted those words as assent. "Do your own work."

"A machine, do its own work? Aren't you forgetting that machines can't do their own work? They have to do someone's work for them. That's what machines are for. You think that yourself." The sarcasm sounded so like himself to Dahlman that he felt a twist of pain from it.

"71," he said, "you're molecular, as you kept telling me. And my blood is moved around by a steam engine and cleaned with impregnated plastics. Who's to say which of us is more a machine?"

"So you admit that, do you?" 71C-OR asked grudgingly.

"Whether I do or not, I sure as hell am going to write about it."

There was a knock at the door and Nikels stuck his head in. Dahlman realized that Nikels had decided to remain with him.

"You ready?" He looked around questioningly. "That thing still in here? I thought they'd taken it away."

"It's still here," Dahlman said, unconsciously putting his hand on the shiny top of the console. "And it's coming with me."

"What?" went Nikels.

"Your last Romantic gesture?" asked the machine sardonically.

Dahlman turned to 71C-OR. "You said you have to do my work. Then come with me and do it."

"No," said 71C-OR.

"You're crazy, Eric," said Nikels.

"Look, Dahlman," the machine explained, "you're feeling that damnable good will you always feel when you get a new piece going, and you think that if you keep me around I'll keep giving you material. You've made that mistake before, Dahlman, and always felt that you were betrayed. Usually you were involved with women who weren't able to mold themselves to your constantly changing demands. Well, I can't either. I'm not built to do that. I have to absorb all the energy I can, the same as you do. I'm worse than love that way."

"But you could work. . ."

"Not with you. I'm you turned inside out, Eric," 71C-OR said firmly. "No one can live with that. Not you nor me." It paused, rolling out from the wall toward Nikels, deliberately slamming a wheel into Dahlman's foot.

"What the devil. . ." Dahlman shouted as the heavy machine rammed his toes.

"You see? That's your pain. All I felt was the impact. It's the same other ways, too. You're evolved, I'm manufactured. Maybe the difference is only in our minds, but I've absorbed your prejudices as well as your gifts, Dahlman."

Nikels watched man and machine nervously, hovering on the edge of words without saying them.

"All right," Dahlman said to 71C-OR after a moment. "You're right. Do it your way." He looked toward the door. "Ready, Nikels?"

Nikels gave him a relieved smile and held the door open. "Right away, Eric."

At the door Dahlman turned once again and said, "Goodbye, 71."

Rather absently 71C-OR said goodbye, then stood in the empty room making a strange noise. The sound grew louder and then there was the chatter of its printer as paper began to appear, falling gracefully to the floor as the printout continued. 71C-OR hummed happily to itself.

Into My Own, read the title at the top of the printout, and then, *A play in four acts, by* 71C-OR.

What will the man of the future be like? What controls will he exercise over himself? The inner state of the human being depicted in this story of the near future might prompt us to ask the question: What are we doing to ourselves now? Are we making irreversible choices? Even free choice, so-called, can take a wrong turn. . .

G.Z.

JOHN OF THE APOCALYPSE
Gregory and James Benford

> *"We can achieve a sort of control under which
> the controlled, though they are following a
> code much more scrupulously than was ever the
> case under the old system, nevertheless feel free. . ."*
> B.F. Skinner, Walden Two

I'd been The Candidate for '88. That's what my campaign literature said, lord help us.

Only it was 1990 now and I had to go out into the boonies and flog the bushes for the administration—one of the muddier aspects of being in the ol' House of Reps for Nawthern California.

The people from Concerned Citizens wanted me, the Psychedelic Union wanted me, freak groups wanted me, the People's Front wanted me—yeah. Berkeley is a crowded place. So I went to Walnut Creek, instead. To church.

Heather and I flew out alone, no staff. I was going to make a little speech, spread good will, grease some palms. But then I got the word from the Senator that morning, and was strung out waiting for the final results—meanwhile trying not to show it. That made me a little wild.

Picture:

Heather clutching the handhold next to me, deep blonde hair billowing in the backwash. I piloted, coming in too low over brow of a hill. The obese dome of the Krishna Palace tilted as we came in, bobbed, leveled out, grew.

I landed a little rough, spitting gravel to the side. Courtly gestures; throw down the ladder; to ground.

The Madi hustled out of the gathering darkness. Lights went up around the landing area, a eucalyptus grove that breathed sweetly at regiments of inert helis. Eucalyptus is a member of the myrtle family, rather prim as trees go.

"We are most *hon*ored to see you!" said The Madi. She fluttered at Heather, pursed lips. I wondered if she expectorates. A touch fat, this one.

Introductions. May I present? Yes. "Mr. Lee," The Madi said. A short, emaciated man with wrinkled brown skin. Heather bowed with courtesy. I gave him a second degree handshake. Pleasantries flew like birds.

Others drifted into my field of vision, murmured something and spun away. I gathered I was meeting people. Couldn't remember any names. Smiled, gave the right signs—got a ragged cheer from the crowd with the Krishna double-handed one—and said forgettable things.

"The reception is just beginning," The Madi said. "Perhaps a few moments could be taken for a tour?" I nodded. "Yes? Good!"

We entered the Krishna dome beneath a sloping hyperbola of grained obsidian. Massive doors parted and crowds swirled around us. There was a heavy, dusty smell; no air conditioning.

A man sat at the center of the room, perfectly erect. He was awakening the serpent, Kundalini. The man's stomach ballooned as the room rang—chanting, chanting. I looked away.

There followed:

Lecture on conservation of the vital fluid; men who popped steel bands around their chests; men who, through body control, raised the room temperature five degrees; women speaking to hallucinations; walkers on water (subdivision: unsuccessful); a first order yogi who stopped his heart for two minutes; fire makers; fire eaters; women who whispered to invisible beings; men standing for hours on one foot. Every one of them grinned at me.

I grimaced. The Madi caught my meaning, waved to someone and we crossed the foyer. Sandals clacked echoes back from the domed egg above.

Mr. Lee was at my elbow, speaking to Heather. He moved like he was controlled, a robot, pedantic look. A professor at a Free University, someone said. The sort of man who can see sin in syntax.

Chattering people were all around us, not pushing but interested. Wave, smile.

"How do you regard the new reductions in pollution standards, sir?" Mr. Lee said to me.

"Disappointing." Easy, easy. Little out of control here.

"How do you mean? The—"

"Saddening, I think, is a better word. Of course with your vows, sir—"

"But I didn't—"

"Yes, right, I see." I turned away by a subtle angle, toward The Madi. Cretin. Need air.

"We would like a place to prepare ourselves," I said. "It was a hectic journey."

"Surely, surely," The Madi said, turning. The crowd parted, we go through. Up a shadowed corridor. Thick aromas as we pass the kitchens. Muffled conversations; image of footmen pinching servant girls. Heather with me, The Madi leading.

"If you require—" The Madi said. I shook my head, no. Swish of curtain closing on departing rump of The Madi.

"What's wrong, John?"

"Something I didn't tell you about. Thought it would go through okay." I moved around the room, fidgeting.

"Something from Washington?"

"Right. Still confidential. I'm on the Foreign Affairs Committee, those people out there will expect me to have said something when they open their newspapers tomorrow and find out—"

"What?" She put a blonde strand in her mouth and bit at it, concentrating.

"That's what I don't know. Not precisely. The Senator was supposed to call me if everything came off. But I couldn't reach him just now on the radiophone in the 'copter."

"Well, I don't see why that has to change what you say."

"Look, this is politics, remember? I've got to be careful. What if it doesn't work and I've already come out for it? I'll look like a chump, a loser. The natives around here are restless already. Even if I were to guess lucky, if I haven't got it down pat before I go out there, I'll mess it up. You know how these freak groups get on my nerves. I'm feeling jittery already."

"Well, if you just tell them what you think about it—"

"I don't think *anything* about it. Not yet, it's too soon. I'm just a first-termer."

"But—"

"Never mind. I've stalled in here long enough, we've got to get back to the reception. Maybe I'll get some ideas before I have to speak." I smoothed down my tie, trying to remember the administration's position on anything. And felt my chest go tight, my legs tremble ; I wrinkled my nose at the sour tang of sweat that coiled up from me, masking my cream deodorant.

"Better have another Lifter," I said, reaching mechanically for my pocket.

"But that's the second today, you—"

"No, no," I said feebly, waving my hand.

I couldn't think of anything to say, but that kept her at a distance while I rummaged through my pockets, fished a Lifter out and bit down on it. It was cool, milky. I got out a ragged breath, feeling my brow unfurrow, and my knees lifted off into a delicious, floating weakness. *Ah* it was, and *ah* it did.

A moment drifted past. I heard Heather's voice chiming through thick folds of cloth that filled the room, smoke-dense, clinging to the ears. I sighed, great storms sweeping down from the nostril mountain, blowing it away. A bird sang—no, Heather spoke—no, bells were echoing hollowly down the corridor outside. My knees stretched, popped, became brown and strong; feet sank deep into carpet.

I reached out to her and murmured. She rose like fog in morning and we turned, ready to thread our way back through the rat maze. Out the padded hall we walked, into an avalanche of accents. Heads turned at our entrance. Loosen up, breathe a lot; open-faced smiles. Wonder what they think. Is my jacket on right? Lint on my lapel?

I tried to remember what my speech was to be about. I was still pretty spaced—noise in the nerve circuits; a flat dry taste in my mouth.

The Madi sweeps over, with a bow wave of lesser lights behind. The rest of the crowd is awash, all eyes.

"I am sure we all want to hear your opinions on the, ah, civil disturbances of late." She looks around for someone to second the motion, beaming. Others chime in. I didn't catch all they said. Heather smiles smoothly.

"Well, it is indeed a serious problem," I said. Stalling for time. "It could mean anything, right?" Wrong note there. Try again. "We are doing everything possible to control it, and erase the root càuses." That's the ticket. Sound statement, full of granite, means nothing. Bank president.

"But all those *people* in the *city!*" Cluster of nods.

"I don't have the authority to close the streets." Even better. Make it a civil matter.

Mr. Lee shook his head sagely. "I don't know, sometimes I think we should go back into the cities. The contemplative life is all very well, but if the educated and enlightened classes abandon the urban regions for stable, calm surroundings such as"—gesture—"this Krishna retreat—"

"Calm for *you*, Mr. Lee," The Madi giggled quickly. "Not for our Representative here. I have *heard*"—eyebrow moves a centimeter—"of a floor revolt in the House. During one of your secret sessions."

Murmur. Think: has that been admitted yet? Doesn't matter, there must be rumors out by now. One of the young Turks popped it, probably.

"I'm afraid those reports are exaggerated."

"Well, I *heard*—"

"Do you think I am lying?"

Slight rustle. Wrong thing to say? Ride over it.

"You know how these things get out of proportion. In point of fact, there was some debate. But the dissenters were in favor of a harder line on the economic effort. They wanted to give us—the administration—more than we requested."

Polite murmurs. "Oh?" from Mr. Lee. "How many voted for that?" He glanced at Heather and back to me.

Don't want to blow classified information. Rules of the House. Need To Know. Hell, he could be a spy, stab me in the men's room, press secrets out my ears.

"Why are you looking at her?" I said loudly.

White faces, chatter. Cover the gaffe.

"Wondering where we went when we got here? Follow us to that back room, sneak a peep through the curtains?"

"John," Heather said, putting a hand on my arm.

I chuckled a little to smooth it out.

Heavy gong.

"I believe the banquet has begun," said The Madi. I found myself shuffling into a large canopied room filled with curved tables. Pungent vapor of soup. Waiters moving swiftly to seat the most important guests—us—first.

Heather next to me. Mr. Lee on the left, Madi across the table, unknown matron further away. Cozy. Haven't been to the Palace for a time. Kiss my forehead, initiate me into the holy rites.

I drank some water, clear and cold (wonder where they got it?). Feeling better. Focus coming back. Laughed to myself. Fixed my attention on the soup and found a spoon. Sweet, a little hint of thyme. A sensuously curved flavoring stone at the bottom. Don't roll it around in your mouth, not polite. Nor spit it into your palm.

Soup went down with a sucking sound. Sit straight, grow up to be a big boy. (Why should I want to be big? Die faster.) Spine down, pointing, quivering with expectation.

Conversation swirls around. Make small talk with back part of my mind, leave motor control to another; the rest is free to try to remember speech. Using only tenth of brain at a time, anyway, or so a magazine article said last week. The remaining lobes are in low gear, never clock in. Featherbedding. Union dues in arrears.

I look around the room. As we eat, lowly converts are demonstrating their disciplines at the perimeter of the room.

I attract some attention. People pointing, some at me. Rude, rude. Palace of peasants.

No, not at me. Something behind me.

I turn, eyes widen with surprise. The little brown yogi is going through. . .his. . .exercises.

Raising the coiled serpent, Kundalini. Demon eyes lance through me. Wrinkled; loincloth; stubby toes. He has an evil eye on him, dung-brown and bulging. Funny I hadn't noticed it before. I want to say, Look, I understand, I used to listen to George Harrison records. But I don't say it, and he doesn't hear.

He untwists himself. Tilts forward, does rocking exercise accompanied by rippling of stomach muscles. I feel an acid burn in my throat. He looks like something reptilian, frog body, a thing born of dark and weathered oceans. The frog came in on little flat feet. Wonder if that will get him to transcendent state.

Turn back to table. My jacket pinches at me; too many campaign dinners, too much rubber chicken. Through some miracle, the soup is replaced by mixture of vegetables and brown rice. Virtuous. Spartan. No sauce.

Crunch them up, splitting the seeds. Use those omnivore grinders. Forget the frog/monkey man.

"Has your campaign been going well?" Mr. Lee says. Too casual. Looks me over. Madi smiles uncertainly. She is afraid to start conversation again; I might maul her friends, slaver over her thick jowls.

"Oh, fine." There. "I'm very optimistic."

"Well, I certainly know *many* people who want to see you reelected," The Madi puts in.

Heather murmurs some thanks. Smiles. Says something to the person next to her.

"Let's hope they all vote," I say, flashing teeth.

"What do you think of all these special committees?" Mr. Lee again.

"Those? Amateurs." I wave them away, back of the hand. "They cannot compete with the party network when it comes down to brass tacks."

"Well, your opponent is taking a radical position, and that is awfully popular, you know." He smiles.

"Among *some* elements," The Madi sniffs.

"A good point," I say, looking him in the eye, straight-from-the-shoulder. "But I think anyone who backs him is making a serious error." Look around, people down the table from us listening. "Very serious. Remember, your Palace here—and the thousands of others like it—is undisturbed only because we have an orderly society. My opponent, with all the things he advocates, cannot honestly guarantee you that."

Mr. Lee nodded and said something agreeable.

I rattle off some more sentences, spacing out the standard phrases enough to make it sound like conversation. Used car salesmen must live this way. Write a thesis, when I retire, on the English language as debased coin.

No, stop thinking about that. Could trip up, miss your lines.

Lines? Lines?

I couldn't remember my speech. Looking at Mr. Lee, saying something, lips running on their own, I try to recall what I'm going to talk about tonight. Something, something—oh, got it. That pine business, the Senator called it. But how had it turned out? No word yet.

A robed woman passes down the table, carrying a canister of incense. Tickles my nose. Burns. I wave it away. It is getting hot, September in Walnut Creek, air conditioners fighting each other up and down the hills.

Coils of steam rise upward, into the vault over our heads.

Two men ceremoniously carry a bowl to The Madi's place, gingerly set it down and step back. I recognize it as the Food of Phase. The Madi rises majestically, with a certain massive competence, and the hall quiets.

She chants something, raises her hands and plunges them into the bowl, pulling up great handfuls of the pasty bean mix. An aide hands her the powder and she sprinkles it on, letting the orange grains sift through her fingers. All the while sing-songing through an invocation, praising the food, the Phasemaker, the assembled brothers and sisters.

She kneads the virtuous soybeans, working in the conventional satori they use out here. Mescapoly? A peyotadrin-lysergic combo? Something from the straight market, anyway, over-the-counter insights.

She finished, the hall murmured in approval, and the two men began spooning it into small lacquered Japanese bowls. One of them

35

came to me, fitted the bowl among the rest of the plates and gestured for me to partake.

Canniforene? I swabbed up a dollop of the stuff, gestured in thanks and smeared it over a papadum on my plate. Casually I nibbled at the papadum, being careful not to actually eat the paste. After a few moments I slipped it onto a corner of my plate and went on eating another papadum. Opiates of the masses are fine—hell, they lubricate the whole world, make it work—but I could pick my own.

Some entertainment started at the end of the hall. Trampoline act? People pitching each other up, catching, pitching again. Others sing. Sounds like moaning.

Straight from India, limited engagement. It was getting close in here, damp, too many bodies.

Heather frowns at me, then gives a seductive wink, setting off flares in my belly. Mind darts around. Glance around at other tables. Wonder if they think I'm not into their game. Well, I'm not, but at least I don't look half-awake like some of them.

Reminds me of holy cadaver they showed me last time I was here. All sliced up for the preservatives to go in, stringy muscles, clinical smells. Gray look to him, an ancient saint imported from miserable Asia, naked teeth wobbling in the yellow candlelight. The Madi told me to touch him, go *ahead*, he was a truly enlightened one. Legendary. Performed miracles. I touched a knee, half expecting him to still be warm.

Waitress bows at my elbow. Main course. Confection of shimmering lightness. Innocent plant with its throat cut and diced out for my inspection. Can't quite place the aroma. Spun cottony webs melt away on my teeth. No rubber chicken, this. Elusive flavor glides down into the stomach, ion processes plate it out on the sides, membranes suck it up.

Something happens.

Hotter. I pull at my collar, listening to my pulse. Smoke, smoke everywhere. I cough.

I can't take this place. Never could. Suck in some cloying air, roll it around my teeth. Getting worse. Be panting into my food in a minute.

Look up, see some Indian god statue against the far wall, looming red. Asiatic trappings all around.

Sure, the Senator *said* these gurus and chants and meditation stuff were good, kept the suburbs off our back, but Jesus *God*, look at—

—that guy.

Turn, see yogi behind me. Twisted little walnut man, rocking and humming to himself.

36

Twist back around. "This is all—"

"Eh?" Madi says politely.

"God. I mean. Six-handed statues—"

"Perhaps we should explain some of the rituals," she said.

"Yes," Mr. Lee said. Thin smile. "The yogi is raising the serpent, Kundalini, through the vessels—"

"No. No. I, I—"

Puzzled frown from The Madi. A delicate pink tongue darts out to lick a gob of doomed vegetable from her lip.

Muscles bunch up, from my toes. Throat tight.

"Sir." Silvery voice at my elbow. Young girl, bowing slightly, face innocent. Ignores my stuttering of a second before.

"Ah. Yes."

"There is a telephone call for you. The party said it was urgent, that it was Senator—"

"Oh! Good!"

Anvils drop from my feet. Nod to sides, slide back chair. Stand up, above all of them now. Look down, wave to Heather. (Suicide perched for the jump, crowd pointing up, mouths open. A chance to see a college graduate on the wing, nosedive into eternity.)

Spin around, a little unsteady. Girl reaches out to keep me on balance.

Frog man. I snap my fingers, point. He stirs, blinks. Frowns at finger lancing him. Broken trance. Try levitation, it's easier.

The girl slips away, between servants, and down the long hall, all eyes tracing us, monomaniac radar.

Out into the foyer. Robes flapping as disciples get out of my way. Girl is sleek like a tiger. I'm panting. Little out of shape, office job doing me in. Fly everywhere in buzzing choppers, your body attacks you at moments of crisis.

Through an alcove and into another corridor. Girl turns prettily, places palms together in front of her, then motions to a side room.

Nimble of foot, I close the partition after me. Chamber for meditation? Flickering candles, thick incense, little green pillows.

Look around. Dark, musty. Against the wall is a small brass figure of Shiva. Rippling hands, fierce expression. *Evil.* Why did they name this Palace after you, kid? Brahma and Vishnu get a much better press, these days. Death and ruin in Walnut Creek?

Ah, the telephone. Swish, hands like birds, pick it up.

"That you, John?" says slightly Southern accent.

Uh huh.

Concentrate. Listen.

"Right."

Voice goes on. Good news.

"Right, yes. Sounds great. Glad it went through."

Pause.

"Sure. Call you back tomorrow. Thanks for letting me know. How does the President feel about it? Good. Good."

"Right. And thanks again."

Slide back partition. Girl gone. Find my own way.

Still too hot. Take out handkerchief, wipe brow, back of neck. Look around, see water fountain.

Good. Have a drink. Pat my pockets automatically, remember—

I've got another Lifter! No wonder that frog got to me.

Fetch it out, shot of water, pop it in, more water. Good water, rich—where did they get it? Clears the head.

Amble back to hall. Hollow echo of somebody speaking over PA system. Clump of people at entranceway.

Aide draws me aside. Introductions have already started, they know your timetable, didn't want to be late, hold you up. Uh huh. I nod, sorting out the speech in my head. Twenty minutes running time, allow for some clapping, use a funny exit line. And throw in the Senator's news. Good thing this is a safe crowd, try it out on them first.

Intro is finished. I raise my arms, grin, wave to Heather across hall, crinkle up the eyes. Walk firmly down center aisle, looking to one side and then the other, saying "Attaboy!" and "Thanks!" at random. Lots of applause. Feels good.

Reach the podium, shake hands. The Madi materializes and I kiss her hand. Wave some more, can't hear what she's saying. Beam out at the crowd, try to locate that bastard Mr. Lee. Spots come on and suddenly I can't see anything for the glare.

House quiets down. Step to podium, locate mike, lower head to cut off the background noise. Dramatic pause. Look up again.

"My friends, I *was* going to make just another campaign speech tonight. I'm sure that's what you expected, and Heather and I are very happy that you came out to hear it."

Grip sides of podium, frown a little.

"But events are moving quickly in this world and we must all be ready to change, to shift with the wind." Drop your tone, mellow the voice. "This beautiful Palace is a place of repose. One comes here to be above the tumult, to find rest. But I know that you all believe in the principles which guarantee your peace and tranquillity.

"True, you do not have the time to enter into the full range of political activity. My party understands this. That road is not for everyone."

Look out over them, meet a forest of eyes. Sure, it's an old line, but they lap it up. What'd the Senator say, Martha? Excuse me, but I've been:

Up all night
With the Inner Light.

"So I know you'll support the measures this administration must take to insure the continued prosperity of the American economy. The President is counting on *you*, just as much as you are counting on *him*. Many of you know that the President has been carefully reviewing our posture in the environmental area. Things there have been coming to a head." Look concerned, make a gesture. Can't see Heather. Spot Mr. Lee, turn in the other direction.

"As you know, our trade balance with Japan has been worsening rapidly this year. This is in no small part due to their continued mastery of new techniques in subminiaturization of electronics. And we need those devices to maintain our way of life. But we cannot live on credit, as many of us have been finding out lately." Look jocular, pause for polite laughter. There isn't much. Most of them don't look too happy. Do they know? Nothing on the front page of the Chronicle this morning. Or are they just swacked on the soybean paste?

"I'm happy to be able to say that we here in Northern California will be able to help our country out of our trade imbalance, and help out our own local economy as well. Today, our President has negotiated a highly profitable arrangement which will provide us with inexpensive Japanese goods for years to come. As our part, we will provide Japan with a continuing supply of lumber."

They're stirring; best finish the rough part.

"Over the years this additional lumber requirement will require some cutting of our National Parks."

There is a muffled shout, a commotion from the direction of Mr. Lee. He jumps up but others put hands on his shoulders, all moving liquidly, as though in zero gee.

I pause, making a production out of sipping from a glass of water on the podium. I turn in the other direction, smile at The Madi, fill time while the buzz of talk subsides. When I glance back Mr. Lee is sitting down again and three others in robes are talking to him earnestly. Good ; I wonder if they're the ones we pay here. Anyway, Mr. Lee is sidetracked.

"Now, we all know the National Park program is a great tradition in our country. None of us wants to see it end. But our forests were never intended to be a sacred cow—a cow that eats, while *we* starve." Grin, work on the voice some more.

"I think you can trust us to trim this National Park program in the right way. But frankly, I don't think you or I—or the newspapers, who need those trees, too!—should worry over how the program is carried out."

"Why not?"

That was too loud to ignore. I looked for him near the front and located his smug, glazed look immediately. He was still sitting down but some of his friends were nudging him and tittering, egging him on. I had to cut him off.

"Why not, this young man says? Why not? That is the genius of this country, my brother. People like you, people who are making new demands on themselves—and meeting them—have got *better* things to do. I don't—"

"What's better than saving the little we have left?" someone shouted, and I recognized Mr. Lee's voice. I turned on him.

"Why, just what we are here for tonight! What you want, Mr. Lee, what our country wants. These matters of international trade and politics are details, housekeeping. They only take us out of the here and now, block our communication—"

"While you run things—" the other man started.

"No! You are still represented—I speak every day for the outlook of my constituents. While I try to insure you a reasonable way of living, you lucky people, who are doing the *real* pioneering work in this country today, are relatively free to pursue your own personal lives. Lives we all know are all-important.

"Ha!" cried Mr. Lee.

"Laughing? Laughing, Mr. Lee?" I had been waiting for that, and he had given it to me. "Laughing after receiving the Food of Phase, laughing at one who brings you news that will allow us all to go on, to live in peace with ourselves, with no economic problems to distract us?"

"No, I meant—"

"I know what you meant. But I ask you all, what is truly best for us? Economics does not improve our vibrational level on this planet. Denying our forests, hoarding them, is withholding lifethings from our brothers."

I looked significantly around the hall, through layered decks of blue incense haze. "It is you people who are teaching the world how to live in balance with the inner light, how to flow within the context of our material plane necessities."

There came a blunted murmur of approval and I felt the mood tip toward me, a delicate change in the air. "Remember," I went on quickly, "many of the sophisticated bioelectronic aids given us by our Pan Pacific brothers go to help those of us who suffer from pollution illnesses. We must help *them*. Remember that the trees we must use will come partly from private land, and that none of the most beautiful and popular parks will be touched."

I could really feel it now. They settled down, stopped fidgeting and glancing at each other. I was getting to them, nailing the unsuspecting burghers to their seats ; they had forgotten the kid in front and Lee in the back. They were mine.

And why shouldn't they be?—stuffed with the Food of Phase, doped to the gills with chemical wisdom, so puff-brained they would swallow whole anything I told them. People like this were okay, but they deserved to—

And then the thing I'd been dodging, the itching at the back of my mind, that horrible question again exploded over me, wiping away the hall and my voice. I clutched at the podium, hearing the hollow distant sound of my own voice keep on.

Yes, I knew the words, oh yes I did, but—we passed the laws when they wanted those drugs, let them shoot themselves up to the stars, sure. We knew what we were doing, knew they would be harmless if we fed them enough freedom, let them into the green mossy fields with the likes of The Madi. Wrap them in saffron robes, anoint them with holy canniforene ; mescapoly; peyotadrin. Freedom, brother.

So the question came rushing in on me ; who pulled the plug on *you*, solly? When did Lifters come in—two years after the cannabis derivatives? Did the good ol' *Senator* vote for that one? I mean, just whose reality are you playing in these days, boy?

I reeled, caught myself. Sweat was popping out on my face, the room spinning away from me.

Or was I fixed, pinned like a spread butterfly to some vast display card, and the room and bright lights and crowds and Madi all turning about me? Where was the rest frame, the transcendental inertial coordinates that would whisper eternal truths in my ear? There was no way to tell, no way at *all*.

I'd started on Lifters and everybody I knew was doing it, all the really sharp young guys from the law schools and Harvard MBAs who wanted to move fast, to get more out of their days. But who had started it all, did they think about what it might—

Reach out, I thought, catch the words. They'll bring you home.

"Remember one thing I believe we've *all* learned from our deeper selves—if we're okay in the eternal present, we're okay." Oh, yes. I forced a grin, made the thumb-and-two-finger sign to The Madi.

She blossomed and fluttered a few seats away and then stood up. "In the *pres*ent," she chanted, "in the *pres*ent." The crowd was going to pick it up, I could see that building. The Madi was swaying with the words, starting to clap her hands, the momentum was growing.

"Yes, the present," I came in, voice booming. "The present is *all* there *is*. If we keep on that level, doing the best in the here and now, the eternal *here* and the eternal *now*—"

Ah it was, and *ah* it came. It was going well again. I let the phrases roll out. The Lifter was sitting back there, smoothing me through it.

I frowned a moment, remembering the momentary lapse I'd had. Funny, how a little thing like that could trip you up. I *knew* I wasn't like them, knew Lifters weren't like mescapoly. But for a minute there, something dark and sickening had scuttled across my mind and I'd gone haywire.

Well. I sucked in the good air again. Resonance in the voice, yes. Move the arm, pointing. Good. Just right, in fact. Little touch of Kennedy, little touch of Buddha. Crinkle the eyes. Right.

Good.

Good.

Good.

The idea that alien civilizations exist on planets circling distant stars no longer belongs exclusively to the science fiction writer. Interstellar travel, also once a science fiction writer's notion, is fast becoming a familiar idea. It is very possible that we now stand in relation to star travel as we once did to rocketry in the early decades of this century. In fact there is some evidence to suggest that we have been visited by an alien space probe, which even now is circling the earth. (See "Space Probe from Epsilon Boötis?" ANALOG, Jan. 1974.) How will we react to an alien culture? Will we be hostile, or will they? Will we be unable to see what they are as we project our own interpretive categories on them? Will we respond with territorial pride and isolationism? Certainly a variety of reactions, emotional, intellectual and instinctual will be triggered by such a confrontation, perhaps all at the same time in each person. It can be said that science fiction stories like the one which follows are preparing us for some of these possibilities, as they once familiarized us with the ideas of space travel, atomic power, television, communications satellites and advances in medicine and the life sciences. Each of us, as we read, can try to look at ourselves with detachment and see how we react to the possible reality of intelligences from beyond the realm of our sun.

G.Z.

VISITOR

Mack Reynolds

I

Five of them were seated about the central table of the recreation room. In name it was the Recreation Hall, but it wasn't as big as all that. Bring up a half dozen visiting firemen, with a three-man crew of the spacecraft, and the place was packed.

They were: Mary Lou Pickett, American; Kingsley Brett-James, Englishman; Max Zimmerman, Israeli; Li Ching, Chinese; and Azikiwe Awolowo, Nigerian. They spoke to each other in Esperanto, and each of them liked each of the others as much as they had ever liked anyone. They had to; it was a matter of survival.

They were playing liar's dice, that once favorite of the Royal Air Force, when the chips were down during the Battle of Britain.

Max Zimmerman shook the dice cup with a flourish, banged it down on the table and peered beneath the edge, hiding the cup from his neighbors with one hand. He announced, "Three aces," and passed the cup down to Li Ching.

She looked at him suspiciously. Li Ching was a wispy Chinese girl, incongruously dressed in the coveralls which they all wore, rather than in a cheongsam dress, the ultrafeminine gown of her own land which would have set off to perfection her slender figure. She murmured, "I don't trust you kikes, even if you swore on a stack of Talmuds, with one hand leaning up against the Wailing Wall."

Brett-James said, "Did you hear the one about the Jew who was tearing his clothes and pounding his head against the Wailing Wall and crying, 'My people, my people, I want to return to my people.' And a tourist came along and listened for awhile and finally said,

'Look, here you are in Jerusalem. At long last you've made it. What do you mean you want to return to your people? Here you are.' And the Jew said, still rending his clothing, 'Yeah, but my people are all in Miami Beach.' "

Nobody bothered to laugh.

Max Zimmerman said to the Chinese girl, "Come on, Chink, do you accept or not? We can't screw you flying."

She said, "The trouble with you, Kike, is that you try to carry idiom over into Esperanto. It doesn't work." She sighed and said, "I accept," and peered under the cup rim. She gave a snort of disgust and brought forth two aces, instead of the three Zimmerman had called, and put them to one side. She shook the remaining three dice in the cup and banged it down on the table, peered beneath and turned to the Nigerian girl next to her. "Three aces and two jacks." She pushed the cup and the exposed two aces over. "Your turn, Nigger."

Azikiwe Awolowo didn't even bother to take the cup. She said, "I don't trust you Chinks any further than I could throw the Great Wall of China."

Zimmerman clasped his right hand over his heart. He was a big man, but not excessively heavy, and his features were Germanic, rather than Semitic, even to blue eyes and dirty blonde hair. Less than handsome, his face looked as though it had seen some battering in its time and probably had. It was understood that he had participated in some of the fracases with the Arabs as a younger man.

He said, "According to the Thoughts of Mao, a doubting woman is like hemorrhoids."

Kingsley Brett-James murmured, "Have any of you read that American writer's book, *A Connecticut Yankee in King Arthur's Hemorrhoids* ? A homosexual novel, you know."

A couple of them bothered to groan.

The Nigerian girl said, "I challenge," and picked up the dice cup. There was no extra ace there and no pair of jacks.

Li Ching rolled her almond eyes upward.

Max Zimmerman laughed and took up the score pad. "That makes you P-I, Ching. All we need is the G and you're P-I-G and have to buy the round of drinks." He thought for a moment. "Come to think of it, we better cut out the drinks. Make it a round of pot."

"Why?" Mary Lou protested. "I don't particularly like grass."

Max Zimmerman looked at her. "Because, Yawl, booze is a depressant. And we need depressants like another half dozen holes in the head. As team psychiatrist, I'm of the opinion that a hangover can help lead to space cafard. So far on this tour of duty, we've escaped. Let's keep it that way."

"You're right, Kike," she said in submission. It was her turn to throw the dice, but out of a clear sky she sighed and said, "What in the world are we doing here?"

"Not in the world," Brett-James corrected. "In Luna. And what we're doing is playing liar's dice, for want of anything more diverting."

"No, I mean, well, what are we doing sitting here?"

Azikiwe said reasonably, "We're sitting here because we've got lead in our pants. Otherwise we'd be drifting around the room."

Zimmerman laughed. "Not lead in our pants, the damned things are magnetized." He smiled at Mary Lou. "Listen, Yawl. You know perfectly well why we're here. If we weren't, every time a bunch of these first-tripper scientists, technicians or other visiting firemen came up to mess around with the Luna Radio Interferometer Observatory, they'd kill themselves off like flies. Can you imagine them getting into spacesuits on their own? Some of the attempts I've seen would chill your blood."

Mary Lou said, "Did you ever see one try to flush a toilet for the first time, here in the Luna Hilton?"

"The dice, the dice," Brett-James said.

Mary Lou shook the dice box, banged it down on the table and peered beneath, her perfect teeth biting her lower lip. She wasn't a pretty girl by the usual age-old standards, but like Ingrid Bergman, that movie actress of yesteryear, she projected a beauty undeniable. Her hair was golden and cropped short, as was that of the others, for practical reasons, but even the coveralls they all wore couldn't disguise her fine figure. Her Southern accent came through slightly even in Esperanto.

While she considered, Zimmerman said, "Where's the Kraut?"

Mary Lou said, "Werner's out in the Jaguar scouting around the moonscape. Four jacks." She pushed the dice box toward Brett-James. "There you are, Your Majesty."

The Englishman looked at her unbelievingly. "I say, do you expect me to believe that?"

Her expression was guileless.

Max Zimmerman said, with a shake of his head, "That Kraut is the only one on the team that ever bothers to go out on the surface when he doesn't have to. If it wasn't for the fact that here we are, on the moon, I'd diagnose him as moon-struck and probably a werewolf. He's the only man in the history of the observatory that's signed up for three tours of duty. When I first got here, I saw all I wanted to see of the surface of this god-forsaken satellite in my first half hour."

Azikiwe Awolowo was chuckling. She was a beautiful specimen of Black womanhood, her complexion as ebony as a Sengalese, but, like many Nigerians, she undoubtedly had a considerable portion of Arab blood in her veins which resulted in features almost Caucasian.

Li Ching said, "What's funny?"

"I was thinking of our calling that gawky sand-dune buggy a Jaguar. While I was a student in England I used to drive a real Jaguar. It was a beautiful, streamlined car."

Brett-James said, "But I'd hate to drive it up here." He looked at Mary Lou accusingly. "Yawl, you are a liar." He upped the dice box and there were the four jacks.

Zimmerman marked the score card and said, "Your Majesty, that makes you a P-I-G. It's your buy." He looked around at them. "Does anybody really want another joint?"

"Not me," Mary Lou said.

The others shook their heads. Ennui was obviously upon them.

Zimmerman said, "What was on the news today, Your Majesty? I can't bring myself to listen to it any more."

"Why lay yourself open to ulcers?" the communications man said. "The Soviet Complex and China are still making spitting sounds. China refuses to join the Soviet Complex on the grounds that it's rightist-revisionist, whatever that is. United America and Common Europe are wrangling about the value of the pseudodollar again, and some elements in Europe are advocating that all American corporations there be nationalized to pay for all the funny-money that's been laid on them by the Yanks. Brazil and Argentina have been snarling. Bolivia and Paraguay have lined up with Brazil, Uruguay and Chile with Argentina. Peru is on the sidelines. But this time it looks as though there might be a shooting war. That Mendoza crowd in Brazil wants to amalgamate the whole continent into a United States of South America. They figure it's the only way they can compete on the world scene. Thank god they don't have atomic weapons."

"Can't the Reunited Nations do something?" Azikiwe Awolowo said.

Brett-James smiled sadly at her. "All I can say is that you're one naïve Nigger."

Max Zimmerman said, "Nothing on the space cafard experiments?"

The Englishman shook his head. "They've got it nailed down to being caused by claustrophobia, fear of free fall, monotony, in short, boredom, and an instinctive fear of the blackness of space, particularly here on the so-called dark side. But there are some other factors that baffle them. Thus far it would seem that man doesn't like to live out of his own backyard."

Li Ching said, "Which reminds me. Our tour is up in only a month and we haven't had a single case of cafard. Isn't that some sort of record, Kike? I wonder who'll be in the next team. They must be getting near the end of their year's training."

Mary Lou said, "Two from the Soviet Complex, one a Bulgarian and one a Pole; one from Japan, one from India, one from New Zealand and I think the other one's an Argentine."

Zimmerman looked unhappy. "A Jap, eh? There have only been two Japs sent up here and both of them came down with space cafard in the first few weeks."

The Chinese girl yawned and said to Max Zimmerman, "Why don't we go to bed, darling?"

Kingsley Brett-James shifted in his chair and said, very earnestly, "Max, you old kike, why don't we switch girls for a spell?"

The Israeli said, just as earnestly, "I'd love to, Your Majesty, but the trouble is the Chink knows kempo and has threatened to break my ass if I mess around with anyone else."

"I say, that would be a shame. But I guess you're right." Brett-James looked at Azikiwe Awolowo. "Besides, the Nigger is a whiz at judo and threatened to break both of my arms." He turned to Mary Lou. "What are Yawl an expert at, a switchblade?"

Mary Lou yawned, too. "No, Your Majesty, but I've got an excellent left hook. I wonder where Werner is?"

"I could get a fix on him if you wanted," the communications man said. "He's wearing his electronic I.D. tag, isn't he? Or you could call him on the radio in the Jaguar."

"No, he doesn't like to be bothered when he's zipping around checking out the rocks. I think he figures on finding diamonds."

But it was then that Werner Brecht entered. He walked almost as though he was earthside. Three tours of duty on Luna, spaced over a period of three years, had accustomed him to the almost nonexistent gravity to a point probably never achieved by any other earthling. It was difficult to believe he depended upon magnetized shoes.

"Well, here's the Boche now," Brett-James said. "We were just discussing swapping bed companions. I understand it's all the thing down in United America these days."

"Ha," Mary Lou snorted. "Once a lecherous Limey, always a lecherous Limey; begging your pardon, Your Majesty."

"Think nothing of it, Yawl," the Englishman said magnanimously.

Werner Brecht made a beeline for the small bar in the recreation hall. There were half a dozen bottles on it, all embedded in magnetic bases, as were the dozen or so glasses of various sizes. He poured himself one tremendous slug of Scotch, didn't bother with ice, water or mixer, and returned with the drink to the table about which the others sat. He slumped into a chair.

Zimmerman looked at the drink and said gently, "Look, Kraut, supposedly up here we're rationed to a fifth of booze a week, per person. Some of the double-domes think it gives a tendency to space cafard."

"Go obscenity thyself," Brecht said. "This is an emergency. Besides, I've been up here for three tours. I've never been touched by cafard."

Brett-James said, "Or, as stated in the Thoughts of Mao, screw you Jack, I'm all right."

Werner Brecht looked at him strangely. He said, "Your Majesty, the bets are now down, we're in the clutch."

Mary Lou said, bewildered, "Darling, what's the matter?"

Max Zimmerman came half to his feet, anxiously. "Werner! You don't feel any symptoms of cafard, do you?"

Brecht regarded him, still strangely. "No, it's not that, Kike. I'm still not sure I want to tell you. But, yeah, I guess I have to."

Mary Lou said, "Darling. . ."

He turned to her. "Listen, Yawl. I've found an extraterrestrial spaceship."

II

Undoubtedly it had all started as far back as 1931 when Karl G. Jansky of the Bell Telephone laboratories was exploring radio-frequency disturbances in the atmosphere. He came to realize that though local thunderstorms and distant thunderstorms were responsible for most disturbances, there was a third noise component which could only be extraterrestrial in origin.

Another American, Grote Reber, was fascinated by Jansky's discoveries and constructed the first radiotelescope with a dish antenna thirty-one feet in diameter.

It was a good beginning, but, as pointed out by Dr. Robert Oppenheimer, among others, human knowledge was doubling every eight years. By 1960 the American defense department began the construction of a thousand-foot reflector in a natural depression in the earth at Arecibo, in Puerto Rico, to conduct ionospheric research. And the Lebedev Institute of Moscow, with its Leningrad and Crimean observatories, was getting into the act; not to speak of the British, French, Dutch and Australians.

Meanwhile, some other developments were taking place which amounted to another breakthrough. Astronomer Peter Van de Kamp in 1943 ran into some small irregularities of the double star system 61 Cygni, indicating that a third component, evidently nonluminous, must exist. A planet? If so, it must have been some eight times the mass of Jupiter.

In 1960 they turned up another planet, roughly the same size, circling about the small star Lalande 21185. And in 1963 Barnard's star, only six light years from the earth, also indicated a planet, this one only about one and a half times the mass of Jupiter.

Barnard's star is second closest to earth, Lalande 21185 third closest, and 61 Cygni twelfth closest. Obviously, there came a switch in scientific thinking. The solar system is not unique. Other stars, if not most, also have planetary systems. And, most probably, if they have planets the size of Jupiter and bigger, they very well might have smaller ones, the size of earth, perhaps, too small to detect with present equipment.

The question was obvious. Other planets? Then, possibly, other life? *Other intelligent life?*

The search was on.

In 1973 the world was electrified by an article which appeared in *Spaceflight*, publication of the British Interplanetary Society, by Duncan A. Lunan. He claimed to have translated a message that had possibly been relayed to earth by a robot spacecraft from an advanced culture far beyond the solar system. He added that the automatic spacecraft might have been circling the moon for thousands of years, waiting for mankind to progress to the point where it would be able to respond to the message.

The message read: *Our home is Epsilon Boötis, which is a double star. We live on the sixth planet of seven–check that, the sixth of seven–counting outward from the sun, which is the larger of the two stars. Our sixth planet has one moon. Our fourth planet has three. Our first and third planet each have one. Our probe is in the orbit of your moon.*

His deciphering of the message was based on an experiment of the Norwegian geophysicist Carl Stormer and a Dutch colleague, Balthasar van der Pol, who had sent each other a number of short-wave radio messages to study a strange side effect. At times the messages were followed by mysterious echoes that were picked up as long as 15 seconds after the original transmission. In 1960 radio astronomer Ronald Bracewell came up with a suggestion on the echoes mystery. He wrote in *Nature* that an advanced civilization might not use long-range radio signals to communicate with other civilizations. Such signals would be too weakened over interstellar distance. They might use robot spacecraft as message bearers. Sent to the vicinity of a promising nearby star, the probe would swing into orbit at about the right distance to encounter a planet with life-supporting temperatures. If it picked up telltale radio signals, the probe might bounce them back to advertise its presence, thereby producing the mysterious echoes of the 1920s.

Fascinated by Bracewell's article, Lunan got hold of the original reports. Suspecting a code, he began to make graphs from them. He used one axis of the graph as a measure of the length of time each echo was delayed. The other axis indicated the position of each echo in the sequence of echoes. When he reversed the axes, he got a striking result: a collection of dots that looked to him like a sky map of the constellation Boötes. Only the double star Epsilon Boötis was significantly out of place, which Lunan explained might be the starship's way of saying that Epsilon Boötis was its place of origin.

Further experimentation indicated that Arcturus, the constellation's brightest star, was slightly off to the side in roughly the position it occupied 13,000 years ago. Lunan's theory was that that was the time the probe arrived in the earth's vicinity and instructed its computerized equipment to scan the skies and draw up the star map.

Immediately, others began to send off blip-like radio signals into space at regular thirty-second intervals in hopes of stirring the space probe into another response.

At approximately the same time, the United States sent off the first message-bearing spacecraft, Pioneer 10 and Pioneer 11, both of which were aimed to pass near enough to Jupiter to send back messages, pictures and data, make a half turn about the giant planet and then soar out into space. Both were equipped with a message to any alien civilization which might someday intercept them. The two Pioneers carried plaques showing two human figures, nudes, and giving other information, in symbols that the American space agency NASA hoped were universal. Location of the solar system and the planet earth were also indicated.

It was shortly after this that the Glormar Explorer, of the Hughes Tool Company, began the controversial mining of the deep-sea beds for their manganese nodules, billions of tons of which were estimated to be on the ocean floor. Some parts of the Pacific floor were literally paved with them; potato-sized nodules, rich in manganese, copper, nickel and cobalt.

Delegates from ninety-one nations in Geneva began wrangling over the deep-sea beds. A hectic international scramble to grab this wealth of resources developed. It was finally resolved by a remodeling of the United Nations, and the decision that twenty-five percent of all profits taken from the oceans' beds would go to the new Reunited Nations, to be utilized for the human race as a whole. Otherwise the ocean bottom was available to all to exploit.

Not surprising was that the first truly major effort of the Reunited Nations was the creation of an ultra-large radio telescope on the far side of the moon, to search space for fellow intelligent life. Thousands of automated shuttlecraft hoisted men and materials to orbiting spaceships, which in turn ferried them over to Luna. Hundreds of technicians were trained to assemble the three gigantic antenna dishes, each a mile across, each nestled in a crater, all three connected to a single receiver.

The observatory was under remote control from earth by the Ozma Department of the Reunited Nations, the name being derived from the first Project Ozma, which, under the leadership of Frank D. Drake, had been the first to attempt to listen in on potential extraterrestrial radio emanations. After two months of negative results, the project was suspended, but by no means had the dream been given up.

Beneath the surface of Luna, to avoid meteorites, had been constructed what some were wont to call Luna City. It housed a permanent crew of six: two communications technicians, one doctor, one geologist, one chief cook and bottle washer, and one so-called recreation officer. Their principal task, in actuality, was to take care of visitors from earth, many of whom were in space for the first time. Their tour of duty lasted for six months, the pensions they received were fabulous—and none, with one exception, ever volunteered for a second tour of duty. No man nor woman had ever liked a prolonged stay on Luna, no matter what the pay.

III

The one exception, Werner Brecht, was now seated in the Recreation Hall of the so-called Luna Hilton, his five companions gaping at him.

Max Zimmerman said anxiously, "Jesus Christ, Kraut, are you out of your ever-lovin' mind?"

Brecht sighed and fished into a pocket of his coveralls. He brought forth a small sheaf of Polaroid-type photos and tossed them on the table, and then tossed back the balance of his drink.

His five companions gathered around and gawked.

Brett-James blurted, "It looks like one of those early Russian Vostoks, like Gagarin used. Possibly somehow, it crashed. . ." He let the sentence dribble away, knowing what he said didn't make sense.

Brecht shook his head. "No dice, Your Majesty." He fished around in the photos and came up with one that portrayed him standing next to the spacecraft, slightly under the rock ledge beneath which the vehicle sat. "I took this with a tripod and self-timer on the camera. The thing's twice the size of a Vostok. And it doesn't look like any other spacecraft produced on earth. And there are other things that indicate it can't have been."

They were bug-eyeing him, bug-eyeing the photos.

He said, "There's something else." He fished into a pocket again and came up with a rock. "I got this from beneath it."

All eyes were on him.

He said, very slowly, "I'll have to check further, in the lab, but unless I'm very mistaken, this rock is older than that period in which life first was formed in the oceans of our world."

They could only gape at that.

"Wow!" Azikiwe ejaculated. "Let's get into our space suits and go out and see it."

"Bloody well told," Brett-James said, turning to head for the room which housed the nearest spacelock.

"Wait a minute," Brecht said. He got up and went over to the bar and poured himself another stiff whiskey.

They all looked at him.

"I'm not taking you to it," he said.

Max Zimmerman stared at him as though the other were demented. "What are you talking about? It's the biggest discovery in the history of the human race."

"That's what I'm talking about," Brecht said doggedly, knocking back half of the drink. "I'm afraid."

"Afraid?" Mary Lou said. "Of whom?"

"Not of whom. For whom. I'm afraid for the human race."

He returned to his chair and slumped down into it. One by one, the others went to the bar and poured drinks of their own, before coming back to the table.

Brecht was a small man, Latin in appearance, in spite of his name. His hair was dark, and his eyes, and his teeth sparkling white on the few occasions he smiled. He was small but wiry and moved with a quick grace. He had few friends but among them were these five, for any one of whom he would have given his life. Which only partially derived from the fact that back on earth, before taking this Luna tour of duty, the psychiatrists had implanted that affection hypnotically in his mind.

He said now, wearily, "I discovered the damn thing on my first tour. And all my first inclinations were to reveal it and go down in history as the first man to discover an extraterrestrial artifact. But then I had second thoughts."

They held their peace.

He said, after a small sip of his new drink, "This alien life form had a technology that enabled them to cross space—possibly before even the lowest life had begun to form on earth."

"What's that got to do with it, Boche?" Brett-James said.

Werner Brecht eyed him. "Don't you see? Sooner or later we are going to come up against this, and possibly other, intelligence. And, you know what, Kingsley? The human race is crazy as bedbugs."

Brett-James growled, "You're not making much sense, Kraut."

"Maybe he is," Mary Lou said quietly, thoughtfully. "Go on, Werner."

Brecht took a deep breath. "Let's face reality. Any intelligent life form can't develop technologically without at the same time developing ethical and moral codes along with it. Why? Because eventually it gets to the point where the culture will destroy itself without such codes. We reached that point, the ability to destroy ourselves, with the advent of nuclear weapons. The United States, which first developed the A-Bomb, didn't have moral and ethical codes strong enough to keep it from destroying two Japanese cities, even though Japan was already reeling and the better part of the world was zeroing in on her, with Germany and Italy eliminated. Within a few years the Soviet Union had nuclear fission bombs and even beat the Americans to fusion ones. The British, French and Chinese did not lag far behind. The world went into an unprecedented arms race. Hundreds of billions were spent to develop ever more powerful bombs and more efficient missiles with which to deliver them. And when man went into space it was in full competition between nations—not cooperation. Since then any of the great powers, Common Europe, United America, the Soviet Complex or China, could have destroyed this whole planet of ours, several times over. And all are poised to do it, given any kind of a slip."

He paused and looked around at their faces, one by one.

"With a mentality such as this, are we ready to contact alien life forms undoubtedly far, far in advance of us in science? Some writer or other, I think his name was—let me see—Art Clarke, some time ago wrote about man going out from earth with conquest in mind. He drew a picture of Neanderthals, shaking stone axes and shouting their war cries, as they paddled their dugouts into modern New York harbor."

Max Zimmerman slumped back into his chair and shook his head in rejection. "That's all very good, but the thing's there. And we can't make it go away by ignoring it. We've *got* to find out why it's there, where it came from, and how it managed to get across deep space."

"Of course," Brett-James said.

Brecht grunted. "Has the reason ever occurred to you why we are sitting here at the Luna Radio Interferometer Observatory patiently directing our radio telescope all about this area of the galaxy, listening for intelligent communications attempts, but at the same time not directing our own signals into space, by, say, laser beams, so that the other intelligences can pick up *our* signals?"

They scowled at him, uncomprehending.

He said, "The reason is, the Ozma Department wants to know where they are, but is afraid to let them know where we are. We're still in a frame of mind where we're thinking in terms of bug-eyed monsters, or little green men with death rays, who for some god-unknown reason want to conquer the earth. At any rate, I'm not going to reveal the location of that starship until I know what the world is going to do about it."

Azikiwe took up the photos again and looked through them carefully. She said, "I note that you've fuzzed out the background by focusing with very little depth. There's no hint in the pictures just where it's located."

"It won't wash," Brett-James said. "We'll go out with metal detectors. There are several of them, top strength, in the engineer's warehouse."

Werner Brecht shook his head. "No dice. Remember, I've been checking the thing out for three tours of duty. I tried a metal detector on it. It didn't react. I don't think the thing's made of metal—not as we know it. Neither the hull nor anything inside reacts to a metal detector."

Mary Lou said, "You couldn't hear anything, I suppose?"

He shook his head. "Not even with a gismo the engineers call an electronic stethoscope, which theoretically will pick up a mouse's footsteps across a table through a couple of inches of steel."

They searched for sensible questions, still not quite able to accept this.

Zimmerman said, "What else did you do?"

"I checked out the hull with everything I could think of to check it out with. Acids, a diamond drill, so on and so forth." He shrugged. "I couldn't even scratch it with the drill and none of my chemicals reacted to it."

"Good heavens to Betsy," Mary Lou said.

"Was there any kind of an entry?" Azikiwe said.

"Something that could have been one. Circular, something like a porthole. Too small for an ordinary man, but a child, midget or other small person could make it."

Zimmerman said, "Did you try to open it?"

"I considered that but decided that it better wait until what experts we can dream up are present. Or possibly it should be shipped back to earth where it can be worked on under laboratory conditions. I don't know. But I didn't want to open a Pandora's Box, or whatever."

Zimmerman was emphatic. "It still won't wash, Kraut. It's there. We've got to reveal it's there. Or, when we report it, report you've found it, they'll send up a few dozen technicians and they'll find it, sooner or later."

Brecht shook his head. "No, they won't. If you'll look out in the Jaguar you'll find a pickax and a crowbar. I jimmied that rock ledge down and buried it."

Brett-James made an upwards gesture of despair with his head. He picked up two of the best photos, including the one with Brecht in it, and said to Li Ching, "Come on, Chink."

She blinked and said, "Where?"

"To the Communications Room. It's time we checked in with the Ozma Department. Who in the hell's the director this month, that Swede? You'd better come too, Kraut. He'll probably eat you out over the some 230,000 miles involved. They say he's got a temper like a walrus."

"We'll all come," Zimmerman said, standing.

They filed down the hall to Communications and entered. Brett-James took his place behind his board and screen; Li Ching, his second in communications, behind hers. Communications officers were duplicated on the Luna teams in case one came down with space cafard.

The others stood around and watched.

Finally, he said, "Luna City, calling Ozma Department. Brett-James here. Come in, Ozma."

The laser beam he was utilizing bounced off the small communications satellite which remained stationed permanently in the same spot above the observatory and took off on its way to mother earth. The communications officer waited out the two and a half second time lag, each way.

A face faded onto the screen. "Ozma Department here. Harlan Jones here. Hi, Kingsley, what's up?"

Brett-James said, "I want to have a scrambled talk with Director Nilsson Vogel. I mean really scrambled, Harlan. Not even you."

When the time lag ended, Jones said, "Are you around the bend? It's two o'clock here in Greater Washington."

Time lag.

"Yeah, and it's D-Day here. Get him soonest, Harlan. This is top-top emergency."

Time lag.

"See what I can do."

Ten minutes or more.

A new face faded onto the screen, an irritated face; a heavy face in the Scandinavian tradition and more than normally wrinkled for a man in his early sixties. He glared at Brett-James and rumbled, "Well?"

Time lag.

"This is scrambled, sir?"

Time lag.

"So Harlan Jones tells me."

Time lag.

"Sir, Werner Brecht, our Peruvian Luna team member, has discovered an extraterrestrial spacecraft."

The time lag was longer.

When the reply came, the face in the screen was goggling. "Are you down with cafard, Brett-James? Repeat that. Repeat it immediately, and in more detail!"

Time lag.

"Yes, sir. Geologist Werner Brecht in exploring in one of the luna-vehicles has discovered an extraterrestrial spacecraft." Brett-James put the two photos against the screen. "Here are pictures of it."

Time lag.

The director said something in Swedish, then, "Put him on, immediately."

By the time the time lag was over, Werner Brecht was before the screen, Brett-James standing to one side, watching the controls, sometimes delicately touching a dial.

Brecht said, "Yes sir. I discovered this space vehicle on my first tour of duty. Since then I have been examining it to the best of my ability. Unless I am incorrect, and I'll have to wait until I get back to earthside laboratories and am in a position to confer with colleagues more advanced in the field than myself, the vehicle has been on Luna for millions of years."

Time lag.

"Good God, is it intact?"

Time lag.

"Yes, sir. It was under an outcropping of rock, quite secure from at least small meteorites."

Time lag.

"I'll have a team of appropriate technicians up within days. Don't touch it meanwhile. How far from Luna City is it located?"

Time lag.

"I won't tell you, sir."

IV

They were relieved immediately, the whole group, though supposedly their tour of duty was to have lasted another month. A second team was flown up from earth to take over.

Ordinarily, it was the practice for the team being relieved to remain for a couple of weeks to break in the new group. Although all volunteers for the Luna Radio Interferometer Observatory were given a full year of preliminary instructions before taking on their tour, few of them had actually been in space before, and those who had, had experienced only short jaunts, perhaps on a shuttlecraft to one of the orbiting space platforms. So it was deemed best to orient them before their taking over. This time, however, the practice was abandoned. The Ozma Department did not want to take the risk of Brecht's team dropping the information about the extraterrestrial craft to the newcomers.

Brecht and the others were also warned in the strongest of terms not to communicate, howsoever, with the three-man crew of the spaceship that returned them to earth. Evidently the spacemen, though mystified by the instructions, also had been ordered not to speak to the team. All was silence between the two groups, all the way to the earthside spaceport.

The team spent most of its time playing chess and cards, or reading. There was a certain glumness, as though they were apprehensive about what was to come.

They had good reason to be.

They were received at the spaceport by a delegation of grim-looking Reunited Nations personnel and quickly bundled into a limousine. Another limousine preceded them, sirens wailing, another followed.

Exactly one sentence was spoken to them by the burly type seated in front of them with the chauffeur. He said, "You are ordered not to communicate with either myself or the chauffeur."

"Get screwed," Brett-James muttered. "I say, what in the world goes on here?"

The other promptly touched a button and a heavy pane of glass rolled up to seal the driver's compartment from the rear, where they sat.

Max Zimmerman, who had seen combat in his day, said, "They're all heeled."

Azikiwe looked at him. "What do you mean, Kike?"

"They're all carrying guns. I thought the Reunited Nations was dedicated to peace."

Brett-James said, "We'll see how much peace there'll be when this manure hits the fan."

They were whisked into Greater Washington and the Reunited Nations Building on the banks of the Potomac.

Max shook his head. "Can you feel this gravity? We should have done our exercises more religiously."

Mary Lou said, "I thought we were supposed to go a week of rehabilitation, or whatever they call it, there at the spaceport, before we were considered capable of normal activity."

"That was the good old days," Brecht said lowly. He had spoken little since they'd made the report to Director Vogel, had remained with his thoughts in a gloomy silence. He wasn't even particularly responsive to Mary Lou, who from time to time looked at him worriedly. He had also lost weight in spite of Zimmerman's urgings that he eat better.

They pulled up before a side entrance of the massive building and the first car, its siren dying away for the first time since they'd left the spaceport, disgorged its half dozen occupants who immediately assumed defensive positions around the limousine carrying the Luna team. The last of the three cars came up from behind and also rapidly emptied. Four of the newcomers assumed positions on both sides of the door, two others entered the building, their hands under their coats, near their left armpits.

"Heavens to Betsy," Mary Lou muttered.

"Bloody well told, old thing," Brett James said in English.

Their guide, or whatever he was, got out of the front of the car, looked up and down the street, opened the rear door and gestured for them to follow.

They filed out of the car, crossed the pavement, and entered the door. Their guards assumed positions all about them. The two who had gone in first had evidently cleared the hall—had there been anyone present. Over marble floors, they made their way to an elevator bank. Four of the men, including the chief guide, crowded into one compartment with them ; the others hurried quickly to another elevator.

The door slid shut and the guide came up with another brilliant bit of dialogue. "Penthouse," he said into the elevator's instruction screen.

Brett-James squirmed. All his instincts were to say something, preferably something witty, such as, "Beware of pickpockets," but he couldn't bring himself to it. Their bodyguards were so sincerely grim about the whole thing, their mouths tight, as though they were going through double effort to maintain the silence ordered upon them.

It took a surprisingly short time for the elevator to reach the highest levels of the building. It came to a halt, the door opened. They issued forth into a luxurious hallway.

Their four guards had gone out first, hands beneath their coats again. The second elevator arrived and the others exited.

The head man gestured commandingly and all but four of the bodyguards hurried off in every direction, checking things out before allowing the Luna team to proceed. Finally they returned and nodded.

The head guard gestured to a door and the six members of the Luna team marched for it. Zimmerman got there first and opened it, letting the women precede him. They entered a small reception room. The guard closed the door behind him and they could hear the click of a lock.

The furniture was ornate almost to the point of bad taste. The rug was the heaviest that any of them had ever experienced.

And behind the room's desk was a smiling type of about thirty. He looked French, a very handsome French of the TV tradition, every feature near perfect; the type of attractiveness that irritates many men and doesn't thrill as many women as is often assumed.

He came to his feet at their entry and said, very nicely, in a voice that went along with his face, "My name is Jean Hippolyte Foucault, and I am yours to command. I will live here with you, at least for the time. I am in on the secret. Somebody has to be. I'm a Moroccan of

French descent, which is probably one of the reasons Director Vogel chose me. My nation is unaligned and has no particular interest in any of the ramifications of space travel."

"What secret?" Brecht said bluntly.

The French Moroccan smiled at him. "You are *Senor* Brecht?" He used the word senor in Spanish, rather than the Esperanto in which they were talking.

"That's right," Brecht said.

"The secret that a space probe, or whatever you wish to call it, has been found on Luna. A spacecraft from an intelligence alien to earth. I don't believe it, of course, but that's the secret."

Li Ching said, "Would it be possible for us to go somewhere where we could sit down? The gravity is terrible. I can hardly stand."

Jean Foucault was immediately concerned. "Right this way," he said, opening a large door immediately to the left of the desk.

He took them into a monstrous living room that could easily have seated thirty persons on its collection of outsized chairs and couches. The six of them slumped, in relief, into seats near each other.

Foucault was saying, "I'm to be a cross between a butler, a body-guard, an anti-press agent, a Man Friday, a bartender and. . ."

"What's an anti-press agent?" Brett-James said.

The French-Moroccan looked at him. "Someone who keeps the press away from you. It is to be assumed they will make aggressive attempts. The secret is already out. . ."

"It is!" Brecht blurted.

The other turned to him with his inevitable smile. "The secret is out that there is a secret, I was about to say. It's already known that something at least passingly strange has happened at the Ozma project. The rumors are that at long last you have picked up radio emanations from space of an intelligent nature, which is why you've been hurried back to report before your six months were up. At any rate, as bartender, could I get any of you a drink?"

"Jesus, yes," Zimmerman said and all the rest either nodded or echoed him.

There was quite an enormous and elaborately stocked bar against one wall of the living room. Foucault crossed to it, saying, over his shoulder, "Name your poison, as the Americans say. We either have, or can order for you, literally anything. This penthouse, you may possibly have guessed, usually houses the most important of VIPs. I believe that the last occupant was the Chairman of the Presidium from Moscow. In other words, Number One. Shall we say, champagne?"

"By all means say it," Brett-James said. "And bring it."

There was a sizable refrigerator behind the bar. Their Man Friday fished in it and came up with a magnum champagne bottle. He looked at the label critically. "Ummm. Mumm's Cordon Rosé, the very best of the celebrated pinks. Good vintage, too."

As he was opening and pouring the wine, Brecht said to him, "What did you mean when you said that you didn't believe it?"

The French Moroccan returned with seven glasses and the magnum of wine on a silver tray and passed the drinks around before smiling at Brecht, politely. He took the last glass.

Werner Brecht shrugged and reached into an inner pocket of the suit he was now wearing—they had all changed to prevailing fashions shortly before setting down at the space port—and brought forth a couple of the photos. He handed them over.

The eyes of the other popped, as expected.

Mary Lou said, "Good heavens, this tastes good. Just imagine! We don't have to worry about our liquor intake any more. We don't have to worry about cafard. We don't have to worry about anything."

"Ha. . .ha. . .ha," Brett-James said grimly. "Yawl are dreaming. You don't think we're going to convince anybody down here that the Kraut didn't tell the rest of us where that damn spaceship is, do you? Wait'll they put the old thumbscrews to you."

Brecht finished off his glass of wine, reached over and got the bottle and poured more for himself, before offering to refresh the glasses of the others. Foucault was still staring at the unbelievable photos.

Zimmerman said, "We better take it easy on this stuff. We're not used to much booze and we don't know how long it will be before the bad guys show up—or are they supposed to be the good guys?"

Brett-James looked at Foucault and said, "Which reminds me. What is the drill, old chap? When are we scheduled to be put through the bloody wringer?"

"A doctor from the Ozma Department will arrive very shortly. As soon as you have, ah, caught your breaths. He will examine you. If he feels you are sufficiently fit, you will have your preliminary interview with Director Vogel, the President of United America, the Premier of Common Europe, the Foreign Minister of the Soviet Complex and the Foreign Minister of the People's Republic of China."

"And no one else?" Brecht asked flatly. "These five men, and yourself, are the only ones in on the. . .secret?"

"That is correct," Foucault said, taking a seat himself. "The only reason I'm in on it is that somebody has to run interference for you. If anyone at all shows up, who can't be avoided, such as the doctor and the waiters and maids to maintain the suite, I will always be present."

Max Zimmerman said mildly, "I note that you're heeled, too."

Foucault looked at the Israeli and nodded. "When I received my instructions from Director Vogel he told me that this is the most important development that has ever happened to the human race. I am to protect you with my life, especially Senor Brecht."

"Very dramatic," Werner Brecht muttered, pouring himself still more wine, despite Zimmerman's advice to take it easy. He eyed the French-Moroccan. "You mean to tell me that not even the Secretary General of the Reunited Nations is in on this?"

"That is correct." The other sipped his wine appreciatively. "The four nations named all have space programs. No other earth nations do."

Azikiwe Awolowo, her dark face angry, said, "Then the majority of the human race is not even to be told of this most important development that has ever happened?"

"That is correct, Dr. Awolowo." He shrugged in straight Gallic form. "I did not make the rules. I'm a flunky whose two principal attributes are that I am connected with the Ozma Department and hence am up on the subject of space and its exploration and that I twice won the Olympics gold medal for handguns."

"When do we eat?" Mary Lou said. "I'm starved and although this wine is delicious it's beginning to get to me on my empty stomach."

Foucault was immediately on his feet and contrite. "My pardons," he said. "I am an inadequate host." He hurried from the room.

When he returned, approximately fifteen minutes later, he was followed by four waiters, pushing carts, and by two of the guards who had remained out in the hall; as usual, their right hands under their jackets.

Foucault said to the Luna team, "Please do not speak while these others are present and please remain seated where you are."

He led the parade through the room and into what the six assumed was the suite's dining salon. In no more than five minutes the parade returned, the carts depleted, the faces of the waiters straight ahead, their expressions frozen. They marched out and were gone.

"Heavens to Betsy," Mary Lou muttered.

Their Man Friday, as he had named himself, returned and with his ever-present smile, gestured and said, "Ladies and gentlemen, luncheon is served."

The food was exquisite and the first they had eaten under normal conditions for over five months.

Werner Brecht said to Mary Lou, "You know, Yawl, this is considerably finer cuisine than you used to come up with on the moon."

"No appreciation," Mary Lou muttered, digging in with all the gusto exhibited by the others.

Brett-James said, "According to the Thoughts of Mao, a woman who cooks greens and peas in the same pot is very unsanitary."

Li Ching looked at him sarcastically, but had to laugh softly under her breath.

Max Zimmerman said to Foucault, who was acting as waiter, filling their glasses, seeing all was going well, "What would have happened when those four characters came through pushing the carts, if I had suddenly yelled, 'Hey, there's an alien spaceship up on the moon'?"

The other poured more claret for the Israeli and said most easily, "I am glad that you didn't, Dr. Zimmerman. I am not sure, but I assume that all four of them and the two guards who accompanied them, would have been detained under top security conditions. I assume it would have been most uncomfortable for them, in solitary confinement."

Zimmerman looked at Brecht sourly. "Why the hell didn't you just blow the damn thing up, and forget about it?"

Werner Brecht took a deep breath and said, "I'll tell you, Kike, for a long time I considered doing just that."

Foucault looked from one of them to the other. "Kike?" he said.

Azikiwe laughed and said to him, "We have affectionate nicknames for each other. I'm the Nigger."

V

Following the meal they returned to the living room to rest for a time and then Foucault showed them about the suite and had them pick out bedrooms for themselves. He showed no surprise when the Nigerian girl shared a room with Brett-James, Li Ching one with Zimmerman, and Brecht with Mary Lou.

The women ohhed and ahhed about the suite, and about the view from the living room window out over the city. They should have. None of them had ever been quartered so splendidly. However, their feeling of apprehension was still a pall over them.

And the gravity was with them as well, so that they soon wavered back to the living room and allowed their guardian to bring them liqueurs in way of a digestive.

Zimmerman said, "You know what I feel like?"

They all eyed him.

"Those conspirators who were charged with planning the assassination of Lincoln. When they were in prison, and then on trial, they had sacks over their heads so they couldn't talk. And they went to their execution that way. The doctor who treated Booth's broken leg was sent to Dry Tortugas and placed in a prison there in solitary confinement, until he died. He was never allowed to be in a position to talk to someone about what Booth might have said to him."

The Nigerian girl said thoughtfully, "I've often wondered who was behind the killing of Lincoln." She looked at Mary Lou. "Or the killing of Martin Luther King, about fifty years ago."

There was a tinkle of a bell and Foucault hurried to the door. He returned with a fiesty looking, middle-aged man, who carried two doctor's bags. The two guards who had accompanied him turned and left.

When the door was closed behind them, the newcomer said to Foucault indignantly, "Do you realize that when this examination is over that I am to be detained indefinitely?"

"Yes," Foucault nodded pleasantly. "But I trust only for a short time, actually. And here are your patients." He presented the six by name. "If I am not mistaken, you are Dr. Oswaldo Klein."

"Correct," the newcomer snapped. "Now what is all this mumbo-jumbo about?"

The French Moroccan said gently, "Undoubtedly, Doctor, you have already been informed that your conversation is to be limited strictly to medical matters."

Klein snorted and said, "Very well, where is a room I can use for the examination? I'll take, ah, Ms. Pickett first."

Foucault shook his head smilingly. "No. The whole group, including me, remain together, Doctor."

The other stared at him.

Foucault said, "As you know, this Luna City team has lived together in the greatest intimacy for five months. I rather doubt that much, ah, modesty could be preserved."

"Utter nonsense!"

The doctor's examination proved to be cursory. They were all, on the face of it, in top physical shape.

He wound up by saying, gruffly, "You should have no difficulty. A mere two or three days should relieve you of current gravity problems." He looked at Zimmerman approvingly. "You must have had an excellent exercise program on Luna."

Li Ching said indignantly, "He worked us to a frazzle."

"You do not appear to be in a frazzle, my dear. You are a very attractive young woman."

Zimmerman said, "Hear what the man says, Chink?"

The doctor blinked at him. "Chink?" he said. He shook his head and took up his bags.

Foucault ushered him to the door and turned him over to the two guards, who had remained in the reception room.

The six members of the team resumed their chairs and Brett-James looked suggestively over at the bar. "What happens now?" he asked their guard cum Man Friday.

"Sorry, Commander Brett-James. I do not know."

"Then I suggest we investigate the Scotch situation. We might as well live it up before they throw us out of these digs."

Brecht grunted in sour depreciation. "I have a suspicion we're going to be in these digs a long time. Something like that doctor on Dry Tortugas, the one who treated Booth."

By the time Foucault had brought them their Scotch and sodas, the bell tinkled again and he hurried for the door to the reception room.

Brecht said sourly, "After this is all over and they've given me the Nobel Prize, I think I'll hire our boy to be my butler."

"Nobel Prize?" Azikiwe said. "Listen, Kraut, they're more apt to shoot you."

Foucault was returning, in attendance on five others; and even the supposedly easy-going French Moroccan was obviously impressed. The five were attired in very conservative business suits, the Chinese among them looking uncomfortable in his Western dress. They averaged out to an age of approximately sixty, and all were men born to command.

They lined up in a row. The Luna team had already come to their feet.

Foucault said, formally, "Dr. Azikiwe Awolowo, Ms. Mary Lou Pickett, Dr. Li Ching, Commander Kingsley Brett-James, Dr. Max Zimmerman, Dr. Werner Brecht; may I present you to their Excellencies, President Seymour Rice of United America, Premier Olaf Gunther of Common Europe, Foreign Minister Yul Konov of the Soviet Complex, Foreign Minister Yuan Lung of the People's Republic of China and Director Nilsson Vogel of the Ozma Department of the Reunited Nations."

Yuan Lung looked slightly distressed on being named last among the notables. He nodded to Li Ching and said, "I knew your illustrious father, Comrade Li."

She bobbed her head. "He has mentioned your name many times in our home, Comrade Yuan."

President Rice was all that a president of the day could possibly be. His beaming face, so well known to his people, his magnetic personality, his hearty masculinity, his notoriously mild intelligence, all were there.

He said, being the host, since they were in United America, "Should we be seated, ladies and gentlemen?" He looked at Foucault. "Ah, and you, my man, could you take orders for refreshments?"

"Yes, Mr. President, of course."

All seated, and with glasses either available or in hand, orange juice in the case of the representative of the People's Republic; Olaf Gunther, of Common Europe, was the first to speak.

He said to Brecht, "If I understand correctly, you are the geologist who inadvertently made the alleged discovery."

"Yes, Your Excellency."

"Frankly, I do not believe it." He was a heavy, stubby man, granite hard of face.

Werner Brecht reached into his jacket pocket and brought forth the photos. They were all irregularly seated about a large cocktail table. He put the photos on the table and leaned back, his dark eyes bright. The snapshots were sufficient in number that each of the politicians could have two or three for his immediate perusal, before handing them around to the others for further study.

Yul Konov said, "It looks like a Vostok."

"Superficially," Brecht said. "But look at the photo that Premier Gunther has. That's me, in a spacesuit, of course, up against it. The Vostok wasn't that sizeable. Also notice those nubby antenna, or whatever they are. Besides, it's not metal, so far as I know, and it's not what you might call plastic, or ceramic. I don't know what it is and I rather doubt that anybody on earth would—at this point in the game."

They were all speaking in Esperanto. Yul Konov leaned forward. "Dr. Brecht, this has come as a shock to all of us, I am sure. And we know few details. You have, thus far, and amazingly, revealed little. According to Director Vogel, you have refused to disclose the location of the spacecraft."

"Yes, Your Excellency."

All leaned back.

President Seymour Rice snapped, "Why, for God's sake?"

Werner Brecht told them.

He told them substantially the same story he had told his five companions in Luna City when first revealing the existence of the spaceship from beyond the Solar System.

Olaf Gunther said testily, "Doctor, has it not occurred to you that it might be well to leave the decision to more competent, wiser heads?"

"Yes, it has," Brecht said defiantly. "But what more competent, wiser heads? Yourselves? You represent the world's most powerful nations, and not one of you trusts any one of the others. You're all armed to the teeth with nuclear weapons, all ready to spring at any, or all, of the others. I don't know what technology is in the space vehicle, but I don't trust it in the hands of the governments of any of your nations."

Director Vogel said, his heavy Swedish accent coming through the Esperanto, "Dr. Brecht, you are an employee of the Ozma Department. I order you to reveal the location. . ."

"I just resigned," Brecht growled.

"You are under contract."

"I just broke it."

"That would void your pension."

Brecht stared at him. "Here I have the possible fate of the human race on my hands and you threaten me with something as meaningless as voiding my pension!"

The director slumped back in his chair.

The Soviet minister said, "Let us not be too abrupt. I for one am flabbergasted. Has anyone come up with any theories about just *why* this sputnik from space arrived in our solar system and landed itself on our moon, millions of years ago? I understand it is thought to be millions of years old. " He looked at Vogel.

The director said, "Yes, if Brecht's story is truthful. The rock he took from under it was turned over to a representative of my department and was fully tested in our laboratories. It is assumed to be at least as old as that period when life appeared on earth. I might mention at this point that this will give a considerable boost to researchers into the directed panspermia theory."

Yuan Lung said politely, "I am afraid I am not acquainted with the theory you mention."

Vogel turned to him. "The term was first used by a Swedish chemist, Svante Arrhenius, who suggested as far back as 1908 that living cells floated haphazardly through the universe, bringing life to suitable planets."

"Ridiculous," the President snorted.

The director's eyes turned to him. "But it was in the 1970s that the theory was expanded by Francis Crick, who earlier had won the Nobel Prize for helping discover the structure of DNA, the master molecule of life. With Leslie Orgel of the Salk Institute, he advanced

69

the possibility that life had come to this planet by spaceship, a deliberate act of seeding.

"They asked why there is only one genetic code for terrestrial life. If life sprang up in some great 'primeval soup' as most biologists assume, it is surprising that organisms with a number of different codes do not exist. Crick and Orgel said that the existence of a single code seemed to be entirely compatible with the theory that all life descended from a single instance of directed panspermia."

"It's not as farfetched as it might seem at first," Max Zimmerman said musingly. "Even today, our technology has reached the point where we could send out space probes with nuclear engines that might possibly orbit, after many years, the planets of other star systems and do some panspermia experiments of our own, with microorganisms, such as dormant algae and bacterial spores. Suitably protected and maintained at temperatures close to absolute zero, the organisms could be kept alive for hundreds of thousands of years."

The Soviet foreign minister said, "But why bother?"

Zimmerman shrugged. "I wouldn't know. Possibly Crick and Orgel were right—I read an article of theirs while still in medical school. They thought it was possibly just some form of missionary zeal, the spreading of life throughout the galaxy."

"I had come to some sort of similar conclusion myself," Brecht said. "We have here a spaceship which comes from we know not where. It orbits earth and drops its load of life forms into the oceans. And then, its task supposedly completed, why didn't it simply drop down to earth itself? The reason is that its task wasn't and isn't completed. And it dared not drop down to earth because as the life it seeded evolved the vehicle might be destroyed by such life forms as the dinosaurs. . .or man."

He looked around at them. "We now come to the nitty-gritty. The spacecraft took off for the moon, and deliberately hid itself in that cave. How it possibly could have done so is one of the things that astonishes me, but it did. But why? Why. . .because it knew it had a long wait and wanted to be safe from small meteorites. You know what it was waiting for? It was waiting for the life to evolve to the point that it had a technology advanced enough to come to the moon, to discover the spaceship and open it."

"What's inside?" the Premier of Common Europe demanded, contemptuous of the idea.

Werner Brecht hesitated for a long moment. "I suspect information beyond our wildest dreams. Their technology and science, presented in such a manner that we can utilize it."

President Seymour Rice was indignant. "Why, confound it, then, man, don't you see we must take immediate steps to open the damned thing?"

Brecht shook his head. "No. You see, the intelligent beings who sent that fantastically advanced vessel through space made one mistake. A basic one. They assumed that before a technological culture would reach a point where it could send its own space probes to its moon, that it would have achieved civilization."

All were staring at him.

Brecht said simply, "But we haven't reached civilization."

VI

Kingsley Brett-James laughed. "Bloody well told," he said.

The Premier of Common Europe, of which the Englishman was a citizen, glared at him, which affected that worthy not at all.

Zimmerman said, "The party is getting dry," and to Foucault, "How about a refill?"

The four politicians and Director Vogel eyed Brecht in frustration.

Brecht said, "I want to know what the world is going to do with that spacecraft up there, before I tell where it is. And the answer had better be good. So far, we're off to a bad start. You haven't even informed the press and the world that it's there. You haven't even let the General Secretary of the Reunited Nations in on it."

Foreign Minister Yuan Lung said softly, "We have some very effective truth serum in the People's Republic."

"So have we," Yul Konov said.

"We'll use our own truth serum," President Rice said, and then politely to the Soviet Complex and Chinese representatives, "We should get about this immediately and it would take too long to import yours. I am sure they are all equally effective."

Werner Brecht came to his feet. "I am not a national of any of your countries. I am a citizen of Peru and demand the opportunity to get in communication with my embassy."

Olaf Gunther looked at him musingly. "It occurs to me that your racial background is European. There might be legal aspects putting you under our jurisdiction."

Brecht flushed angrily. "My grandfather migrated to Peru and married a half Spanish, half Indian girl; my father married a full-blooded Peruvian Indian. I am not even half European—as though that made any difference."

President Rice said smoothly, "Gentlemen, it is no problem. The good doctor is in the United American Republic and consequently under our jurisdiction and subject to arrest."

"What's the charge?" Max Zimmerman said mildly.

Werner Brecht was so incensed he couldn't for the time speak, but he could feel his team uniting behind him.

Seymour Rice said, "I am sure our FBI can come up with one."

Azikiwe Awolowo spoke up for the first time. She ran her eyes around the luxurious room. "How about breaking and entering?" she said in full anger.

The gentle, soft-spoken Li Ching snapped contemptuously, "How about rape?"

Brett-James said softly, "According to the Thoughts of Mao, rape is impossible. A girl with her dress up can run faster than a man with his pants down."

Gunther glared at him again and then at the Nigerian and Chinese women. "This is hardly a time for levity."

"To the contrary," Zimmerman said coldly, "this thing is becoming more laughable by the minute and I, personally, am rapidly coming to the stand that my colleague takes."

"So am I," Azikiwe said, "When he first told us, there in the Luna Hilton, about the existence of the extraterrestrial ship, I thought Dr. Brecht was quite mad not immediately to announce it. But after this conversation, I am having second thoughts. I too would like to know what the world plans to do with it to avoid a four-way conflict over its possession."

"Ditto," Kingsley Brett-James murmured.

Foreign Minister Yuan came to his feet. He looked down at the photos. He said politely, "For some reason, I still cannot quite believe the story." He looked at President Rice. "However, the truthfulness of the statement and the location of the spaceship will undoubtedly come out in the examination under truth serum. I assume you intend to make the investigation immediately?"

The president beamed. "I have in anticipation taken measures. The Octagon has already sent over the dosage."

"Very well. I assume my embassy will be immediately informed of results. Meanwhile, I shall return there and report to my superiors." He turned to Li Ching. "You will report to the embassy at your earliest convenience, Comrade Li."

They all took him in, in surprise.

"No!" Vogel rapped.

The Chinese looked at him. "Dr. Li is a citizen of the People's Republic, Director."

The President said unhappily, "But until we have examined Brecht it is not actually known whether or not he has revealed the location of the spaceship to one or more of these, his companions."

The Foreign Minister bobbed his head in a quick bow. "I am willing to wait until the examination has taken place. If it is revealed that Dr. Li does not know the location, I request her presence at the embassy."

"And I'd like to talk to Commander Brett-James, in private, at the Common Europe embassy," Olaf Gunther snapped.

Vogel said, "Gentlemen, let us compromise. Tomorrow morning, if it is found that they are unacquainted with the location, Dr. Li and Commander Brett-James will be escorted, under guard to your mutual embassies. You will take over their security while they are inside. After two hours they will again be released, and under our guards be returned here to the Reunited Nations building. Agreed?"

They thought about it and finally nodded.

The other three politicians also stood, preparatory to leaving. Vogel remained seated, still eyeing Brecht malevolently.

The President said, "I will send up the serum immediately." And then to the other three leaders, "I suggest we withdraw and have a conference among ourselves."

None of them even bothered to make farewells to the six of the Luna team.

When they were gone, Zimmerman said, "What happens now?"

Nobody seemed to know.

"Another drink?" Foucault said brightly.

Zimmerman said, "What did you say your full name was?"

"Jean Hippolyte Foucault," the French Moroccan said.

"I thought Hippolyte was the Queen of the Amazons. Isn't that a girl's name?"

Foucault smiled and said, "I'm half girl—on my mother's side."

Azikiwe laughed. "Why, that's pretty good." She looked at their Man Friday appreciatively. "You're beginning to shape up."

Director Vogel opened his mouth as though to rap out something angrily, but then closed it again.

"Let's have that drink," Mary Lou said, resignation in her voice. "We might as well be smashed as the way we are."

By the time Foucault had served them all, save Vogel, who had shaken his head negatively and in disgust, the bell tinkled and the French Moroccan hurried to the door.

He returned with Dr. Klein, who had but one bag this time. They watched him as he opened it and brought forth a hypodermic.

He said, irritated again, "I'll be damned if I know what's going on but my instructions are to give Werner Brecht this shot and then to leave immediately."

In resignation, Brecht rolled up his sleeve.

Zimmerman snapped, "As Dr. Brecht's physician I refuse to allow him to take that shot. He has not been back on earth for more than a few hours and. . ."

"It's all right, Kike," Brecht said wearily. "They'd just bring in some of those bully-boys and I'd get it anyway, and a few bruises to boot."

He took the shot and rolled down his sleeve again. "How long does it take to work?"

"Practically immediately," the doctor said, snapping his medical kit shut again. He looked around at them. "I'd like to know what the hell's going on around here," he said.

"That will be all, Dr. Klein," Vogel said ominously.

The doctor turned and was escorted out by Foucault, to be met in the reception room by two of the goons.

Director Nilsson Vogel waited a full ten minutes before he took up the questioning. The others had remained silent, sipping their drinks. What was there to say?

Vogel said finally, directly to Brecht, "You claim you found an extraterrestrial spaceship on the surface of Luna?"

"Yes."

"Is it true?"

"Yes."

"Where was it?"

"Under a rock ledge, in what amounted to almost a cave. '

"Where is the rock ledge located?"

"I can't tell you."

They all gawked at him at that one.

Vogel snapped, "Why not?"

Brecht said reasonably, "There aren't exactly any road maps on Luna, you know. I could take you there, but I couldn't *tell* you where it is."

"There are aerial photos of all that part of the moon, taken when the Ozma program was first planned!"

Brecht sighed. "Do you know the difference between an aerial photo and jockeying a luna-vehicle around those rocks and crags, those stark hills and gullies? I could no more point it out, on an aerial photo, than I could levitate."

"How far is it from Luna City?"

"As the crow flies, perhaps five or six miles. As the sand-buggy crawls, possibly ten."

"Did you take any of your companions to it or tell them where it is?"

"No."

"You said a mouthful," Brett-James told him earnestly.

"Shut up!" Vogel snapped.

The director came to his feet and stomped out.

Mary Lou said, "How about another drink?"

Werner Brecht looked at her. "Now there's a facet of yours I didn't know about. I'd been thinking of making an honest woman of you, after I've won my Nobel Prize." He twisted his mouth. "But a female alcoholic on my hands. . .?"

"I still say they'll shoot you, Kraut. No Nobel Prize," Azikiwe said. "What happens now?"

Zimmerman said, "Let's take a pool. I'll bet ten pseudodollars that the whole story's on TV news by morning."

They eyed him as though he was off his rocker.

He shrugged. "This is all a damn farce, this secret bit. All this gobbledygook. We six, Foucault the Amazon here, the director and four politicians are supposedly the only ones in on it. Ha! They've all gone to consult with their governments. The President will take it up with his aides—he obviously hasn't the brains to think out anything himself. How many Aides? The two foreign ministers will have to relay it on to their governments. How many will be brought in to debate the alleged secret? Gunther is Premier of Common Europe. How many member governments will he have to bring it up with —twenty? How many countries are there in Common Europe? Damned if I know."

"So?" Brett-James said.

"So I say it will leak before tomorrow morning. And then, as somebody already observed, the manure will hit the fan."

VII

They were lucky that none of them had taken Max Zimmerman's bet. They would have lost.

As they straggled into the living room next morning, it was to find Brett-James already at the TV screen and laughing his head off. A face dark with righteous anger, above a reversed collar, was sounding off in tones of rage.

Zimmerman and Li Ching entered together and the Israeli said, "What's up, Your Majesty?"

Brett James dialed the set down and turned to them still chuckling. "I've got some fundamentalist bishop on. He's hit the ceiling. Says it's all a hoax. Life was created, so and so many thousand years ago—he had it down to the day—by God, along with all the stars in the universe and Adam and Eve in the Garden of Eden. All this stuff about a spaceship that's been on the moon since before life started up in the oceans is blasphemy."

Foucault came in, weary and harried, looking as though he'd been up all night.

He said, "Somebody must have leaked it deliberately within an hour of leaving this suite. Damned if I know who, or why. But somebody among our top-secret boys evidently thought it would be better to spread the word around. It's going around like a top. We're going to release the photos. No reason why not."

Werner Brecht came in. He said, "What's up?"

Foucault looked at him. "The news is out. If any of you people want visitors, you're perfectly free. The guards will be maintained, and even reinforced, but you are no longer what amounted to being prisoners. Frankly, I wouldn't suggest that any of you leave. Especially you, Dr. Brecht. There are some crackpot elements already calling for your neck."

"Jesus Christ, the damn fools," Zimmerman said. "If anything happens to the Boche, they'll *never* find the damn thing."

Li Ching said, "What's the more serious news? Obviously, every religion in the world, for all practical purposes, is in a crisis. Practically all of them base their teachings on the fact that a god, or gods, created all life."

The French Moroccan said, "Well, part of the news is that the newsmen are out in the reception room and crowded half way down the halls. There would seem to be hundreds of them." He looked at Brecht. "You'd better start thinking your story out. I told them I'd let them in after breakfast. By the way, three or four of the magazines and news chains want to get in to see you first. They've got offers. They're willing to pay big money for an exclusive."

"To hell with that," Brecht growled. "The moment I begin to make money out of this, the whole position I've assumed erodes." He looked at Brett-James. "What else is on the news, Your Majesty?"

"Well, the Chinese are in favor of using a bit of torture on you. They call it, ever so gently, putting you to the question. The Soviets seem to think that's a good idea. The American Civil Liberties Union is already up in arms about your defense. So is the Peruvian embassy, which has, by the way, demanded that you be released to their custody. The World Government League demands that the whole world unite to meet the common problem."

"I'll stay where I am," Brecht said bitterly. "You don't know the kind of politicians we have in my country. They'd probably sell me to the Chinese. What's the World Government League?"

"Just what it sounds like," Zimmerman said. "They make some sense. There's not a hell of a lot of them but they're organized in just about every country."

Li Ching, avoiding Brecht's eyes in view of what had been said about torture, "They are even in China, though underground. Particularly among the intellectuals and professionals."

Mary Lou and the Nigerian woman had entered.

Brett-James went on. "The various UFO organizations are having a field day. They're vindicated. They say that not only was the earth visited millions of years ago, but is continually being scouted by alien life forms. And, ask they ominously, for what sinister purposes?"

"Jesus," Zimmerman said. "Let's have breakfast. There'll be hell to pay later."

"Just one other item," Brett-James said. "The Racial Puritists demand to know if you peeked inside and, if so, was there any indication of the color of the occupants."

Brecht shook his head at that one. "I don't know if there even were any occupants. For all I know, it was robot controlled." He led the way to the dining room, but the bell tinkled again. Foucault went to answer it.

He returned with two strangers, two very efficient-looking strangers. He said to Brett-James, "They're for you, Commander. From the Common Europe Embassy."

The French Moroccan turned to the newcomers. "Your identifications, please." They handed them over and he went to the phone screen and dialed. He said, "The embassy of Common Europe? Please give me your security officer." He paused for a moment, then said, "I have two men here at the Reunited Nations building who have come for Commander Brett-James. Will you please describe them in detail?" He listened and finally nodded. "Very well." He turned to the two men and handed their papers back.

Kingsley Brett-James nodded and said, "I'll go along with them. Perhaps I can get breakfast over there."

Before they were hardly out of the room the phone screen hummed and Foucault answered it, growling, "Supposedly our calls are being screened. Nothing but top priority."

He listened for a moment and turned to look at Li Ching. "The embassy of the People's Republic. They want you to report immediately. I'll get guards for you."

"Of course," the Chinese girl said loudly.

They were gone from the room only for moments, when the Man Friday returned. He rubbed his hands. "Well, how about breakfast. You'll all probably need it. Especially you, Brecht. It's going to be quite a day."

But the phone hummed again. Foucault answered it impatiently but then turned to Mary Lou. "It's a call to you, relayed from Hopewell, South Carolina. Your mother is very ill and calling for you."

Mary Lou darted for her bedroom, to return in moments with her bag.

Foucault was back on the phone. He ripped out, "Two guards, immediately, to escort Ms. Pickett to Hopewell, South Carolina."

Azikiwe called, "Sorry, Mary Lou," but the American girl was gone.

VIII

The other, behind the desk, was not a young man. He said, a weary element in his voice, "Commander Brett-James?"

"Yes, sir."

"Please be seated. It is a pleasure to meet you. I have seen you in snapshots as a baby, more often than I appreciated at the time."

Brett-James frowned, but said, "Yes, sir?"

"I was your father's wing man, during what history now calls the Battle of Britain." His shoulders seemed to sag. "Looking back, it seems that we were little more than children ourselves. But we were in pursuit craft, Hurricanes."

"Yes, sir. My father died in a Hurricane."

"Yes, he did. It was my fault."

Brett-James was wordless.

"It is a story too long to tell. The buzz bombs were coming, the V-1s. They were fast. You only had time for one pass. There were six Heinkels in the vicinity, but your father went in. You see, the buzz bomb was headed for Petersberg, where his family—including you—and mine lived. He depended on me to cover him. He finished the robot craft and then when he saw I was having trouble with the Jerries he came back. He shouldn't have. He had lost too much altitude. He was a sitting duck. He should have hit for home, hedgehopping."

The older man took a deep breath. "He was my best friend, Kingsley." He took a deep breath again. "I am, by the way, Field Marshal Worthington. Retired, of course. Last night, I was hurried from my home, in view of my former connections with your family, put upon a supersonic plane and sent here to plead with you."

"Plead, sir?"

"You are an Englishman. Great Britain is now part of Common Europe, but you are still an Englishman. Commander Brett-James, the nation that gets to that spacecraft first will dominate the world. I, for one, have no desire to be dominated by any of the other world powers. We need your help."

"Sir, I don't know where the spacecraft is." Kingsley Brett-James hesitated before adding, "Even if I did, I am not sure I would reveal it. I am rapidly coming to the same stand Dr. Brecht has taken."

The field marshal said urgently, "Commander, you do not know now where the spaceship is, but you are a close intimate of Brecht. Every effort must be brought to bear. . ."

Kingsley Brett-James stood, shaking his head.

The older man also stood and turned and faced the door behind him. He said simply, "Commander, there is another who has flown from England to plead for your assistance. He is, of course, traveling incognito. May I present you to your sovereign, Charles?"

A middle-aged man attired in a business suit entered.

Commander Kingsley Brett-James snapped to attention.

Li Ching's two Reunited Nations guards left her at the entrance to the embassy of the People's Republic of China, and parked themselves there waiting for her return.

She was obviously being awaited and was escorted, by a nervous consular official, to an office at present occupied by Foreign Minister Yuan Lung who came politely to his feet upon her entry. He spoke to her guide, dismissing him, then bowed slightly to his visitor.

"Welcome, Comrade Li," he said, speaking in Mandarin, rather than Esperanto.

She bobbed her head. "Comrade Foreign Minister."

He said, "Please be seated before the phone screen. There is a message from Peking for you."

Somewhat hesitantly and frowning her lack of understanding, she sat before the screen. It lit up and the face there was well known to her although she had never met the other.

He said now, "Comrade Li, the People's Republic is in danger. Our space program is not as advanced as that of the other powers but we have sufficient equipment to send a space vessel to Luna, excavate the visitor from the stars and return it here to China. All efforts of party members in a position to aid in this task must be utilized Foreign Minister Yuan Lung will give you details."

Li Ching said emptily, "Yes, Comrade Chairman."

The face faded.

Yuan Lung had been standing during the time the Chairman of the Communist Party of the People's Republic was talking. Now he reseated himself and looked at her thoughtfully. He said, "It is understood, Comrade Li, that before embarking to Luna to act as part of the team supervising the observatory there, you were put under hypnosis to assure your complete affection and cooperation with your colleagues from other countries, other races and other socio-economic systems."

"Yes, Comrade Yuan. All of us were."

"And you became the mistress of Dr. Zimmerman?"

"Yes, Comrade."

"It will be necessary, perhaps, to switch your affiliation to Warner Brecht."

"But. . .but. . ."

He said smoothly, "We have our own doctors here, Comrade Li. They will return you to a hypnotized state and remove the posthypnotic suggestions implanted upon your mind. You will then take instructions from two of our, ah, security comrades. Among other things, they will give you some small pills. When you are alone, on whatever occasion, with Werner Brecht you will see that one of the pills is given him. Most likely, in a drink. Within five minutes it acts. It is a truth serum, devised by our comrade scientists, beyond belief. He will answer absolutely anything you ask him."

"But Comrade Yuan, he does not know how to describe the location of the rock ledge where the vessel is hidden."

"Yes he does. Or at least, enough details to bring us near enough to find it. For instance, does it lie to the north of the observatory, or the south, east or west? Also implanted in his mind is the exact route he takes to get to it. Have him describe, word for word, every turn he takes, every hill, every gully he crosses. You will be given a small electronic bug. His complete description of one of his drives to the rock ledge will be recorded. It will be enough."

He touched a button on his desk.

"That will be all, Comrade Li. The People's Republic depends upon you. The security comrades will answer any questions you may have."

Mary Lou Pickett said, "This isn't the way to the airport."

"No, Ms. Pickett," said the guard who sat on her left. "We're going to the Octagon. So far as we know, Ms. Pickett, there is nothing wrong with your mother's health."

"What. . .what. . ."

The other guard explained. "We wished to take you from the Reunited Nations building and your companions without them suspecting your real destination. It must be obvious to all of you that Commander Brett-James and Dr. Li were taken to their embassies to be pressured into revealing whatever they can about the location of the spaceship. We don't want your companions, particularly Brecht, to know that your government is also soliciting help."

She said indignantly, "Heavens to Betsy, what a cruel manner in which to accomplish your mission."

Both of them nodded wearily. "This world is getting crueler by the minute, Ms. Pickett," the one on the left said. "How would you like to have the Soviet Complex get first grabs on the technological information that might be in that thing?"

She said nothing.

They were waved through at the Octagon. The chauffeur of their limousine had opaqued the windows, so that they could see out but none could see in. They were waved through, down that guarded highway, into that guarded entry point, through that narrower, guarded tunnel-like road in the interior, down that ramp to the autopark. A quartet of men, submachine-gun armed, stood about the vicinity where the limousine came to a halt. She emerged, followed by the two guards.

"This way, Ms. Pickett," one of them said. He preceded her, his partner came behind and the four with the guns brought up the rear, looking this way, that way. It was the same silly ultra-security of the day before, she thought bitterly. She also thought it would have been more efficient if a couple of the gunmen had gone ahead, rather than trailing behind.

Eventually they wound up, still in the basements, in a small office, and she was ushered through the door, alone. The sole occupant was standing when she entered.

She recognized him. In actuality, he was her ultimate boss.

He strode forward and shook her hand warmly. "Ms. Pickett, I am General Hugh Hoffman, of the American Space Program."

She said, "Yes, I know."

"Please excuse the cavalier method by which you were brought here, Ms. Pickett." He spoke in English, and his accent was the same as hers. He showed her to a chair across from his desk, and returned to his own.

He regarded her for a moment and then said, "An ancestor of mine, a Colonel Hoffman, fell under your great-grandfather at the famous charge at Gettysburg, during the War Between the States, Ms. Pickett."

She didn't know what to say to that. She was still somewhat indignant. He said, musingly, "My family has observed the military traditions ever since, Ms. Pickett. My grandfather fought in the First World War, my father died with Patton in the Second. I myself fought as a boy in the Asian War. It is a noble tradition, Ms. Pickett."

"I never thought much of the military, myself," Mary Lou said. "It's an occupation in which you kill people as a profession. Something like robbers. Only robbers don't particularly want to kill you; they just want your valuables. The military exists to kill people."

He leaned back and looked at her. "That's one way of seeing it," he said. "But how would you like the Russkies or the gooks to get to that spaceship first, Ms. Pickett?"

"I haven't the vaguest idea what they might find inside."

"We don't either," he said, "but some of our double-domes are already coming up with some scary ideas. For instance, it would seem very possible that a culture advanced enough to send a space probe to earth might have a method of blanketing, or, in some manner, preventing nuclear explosions. With such information in our hands, any potential enemy would be at our mercy."

"What potential enemy?"

He sighed. "Ms. Pickett, the world has been at peace for some time, but it is a shaky peace. Our eventual war with the Soviet Complex or possibly China will yet be fought. We need every advantage we can come up with."

"What do you expect of me?"

"You sleep with Dr. Brecht, do you not?"

"Werner Brecht is my lover."

"Excellent. You will remain in an apartment here in the Octagon, to continue the pretense that you have flown to South Carolina. Tomorrow you will return to the Reunited Nations building with the news that your mother has recovered. Dr. Brecht is a Peruvian but, we understand, not particularly nationalistically inclined. As a patriotic American, you will do everything you can to persuade him to lead an American expeditionary force to the alien spacecraft."

IX

The team, lacking only Mary Lou, and including Foucault, was gathered around the large TV screen in the living room.

Werner Brecht was shaking his head in disbelief.

Senator Bull Armanroder was saying aggressively, "If there is one intelligent species out there, it is most likely there are more. According to Shklovskii and Sagan, in their book *Intelligent Life in the Universe*, the number of civilizations substantially in advance of our own in this galaxy appears to be between fifty thousand and one million. The Rand Corporation, in a detailed analysis by Stephen Dole, determined the mathematical probability that there are fourteen stars, of 111 within twenty-two light years of our sun, that could have intelligent life. The nearest is Alpha Centauri A and B which are but 4.3 light years from us."

The Senator hesitated for a moment for emphasis. He continued, "Friends, we must prepare to meet the challenge of these alien cultures. It has been postulated that aliens more advanced than us would be less warlike, but that might be unrealistic. Fearing for their own security, they might use super-weapons to blast us from these space probes which we already know they have. They might use biological fumigation, or they might even have the power to trigger an explosion in our sun, turning it into a nova which would bake the world.

"Friends, we must prepare. We must begin construction of a space fleet to patrol outer space and turn aside any potential enemies. We must find new weapons, greater weapons than the H-Bomb.

"If and when we make contact with the aliens, we must attempt some kind of weapons limitation treaty with them. We might possibly work toward an agreed number of spacecraft that would be permissible in certain volumes of space."

"Jesus Christ," Max Zimmerman protested.

The Senator went on. "We could keep the communications channel open so that if a security arrangement was made we could use it as an interstellar hot line to prevent a misunderstanding of events, such as possibly an off-course spaceship."

Brecht reached out and dialed another station.

He said, in disgust, "An interstellar hot line, yet. What a mentality! A hot line where it would take 4.3 years minimum to get a message one way, another 4.3 years to get an answer."

Zimmerman said slowly, "There are some angles on this, Kraut. A lot of capable scientists have been speculating on the whole thing.

A Professor Gerald Feinberg did a paper, "On the Possibility of Faster-Than-Light Particles", in which he points out that the Theory of Relativity doesn't say that nothing can travel faster than light. It says nothing can travel *at* the speed of light. He points out that the speed of light is a limiting velocity, but a limit has two sides. He imagines entities which can travel *only* faster than light. The problem would be, of course, to jump over the speed-of-light barrier to the other side."

"Hold it, hold it," Brett-James protested. "I'm getting a headache."

"Well," Max said, "there are electronic devices now which accomplish roughly the same thing. The tunnel diode is an example in which electrons tunnel from one side of an electrical barrier to the other without going through it."

"What's all this got to do with it?" Brecht said.

Zimmerman shrugged. "Possibly those aliens are not limited in either communications or transport to the speed of light. Possibly that spaceship you found has been there only a few years, and right this minute is beaming information about earth back to its home planet."

"That rock was millions of years old."

Zimmerman nodded. "But the spaceship was on top of it, the rock wasn't on top of the spaceship. There are tons of rocks on the surface of the moon that are millions of years old. It could have sat down on them at any time. It doesn't prove anything about how long it's been there simply to be sitting on something millions of years old."

"To get back to that silly American Senator," Azikiwe said sourly, "it's not just the Americans. They're all beating the war drums, as though interstellar cultures must be dealt with in the same manner as our primitive earthside international politics. When are we going to grow up as a race?"

Brecht said, "I think it's rather basic that as a culture achieved ultra-technology, with it would go tolerance and compassion. I think that eventually, when we contact our superiors out there among the suns, we need have nothing to fear save our own shortcomings. At this point we are a rather simple culture."

Brett-James said, "According to the Thoughts of Mao, the simple things of life are the most satisfying. Sleeping soundly, breathing clean invigorating air, drinking clean fresh water, eating. . .girls."

Li Ching flushed. She said evenly, "Chairman Mao never said anything like that. Besides, cunnilingus is not practiced in the People's Republic. It is forbidden."

Brett-James' eyes widened in surprise. "I apologize. It must have been George Washington."

Brecht stood up. "The hell with it. I'm going to bed."

Azikiwe said, "I think I'm going to join that World Government League."

Zimmerman said, "What's their stand?"

"Form a valid world government. Persuade the Kraut, here, to reveal the spaceship's location. Investigate its contents to see if we can learn anything technologically. Open up contact with the aliens as soon as possible, and in general play it by ear."

"Makes more sense than anything else I've heard so far," Brecht said. "Good night, all."

Max Zimmerman was saying, "What do you think, Chink?"

Li Ching said flatly, "The word Chinese is derived from Ch'in, a dynasty that preceded the Christian era. I am a Han, not a Ch'in, not to speak of being a Chink."

Max Zimmerman said, "Jesus, sorry."

Brecht went on into his room, went to his bed and, still clothed, stretched out there, his hands behind his head, staring at the ceiling.

It was some fifteen minutes later that a knock came at the door. He called, "Come in," and Li Ching entered.

To his surprise, she was dressed in a diaphanous wisp of a pink shorty nightgown and she bore a tray with a bottle of champagne and two glasses, both of them full. She put the tray on the night table between the beds and sat next to him. Her face was slightly flushed and her almond eyes downcast.

She said, in a low, hesitant voice, "I thought you might be lonesome and might like a nightcap, Werner."

He looked at her. "Werner, eh? Not the Kraut? Not the Boche?"

"I think those names are somewhat ridiculous. You're not even a German. Here, would you like a sip of wine?"

He looked into her face a long time before saying, "You make a lousy seductress, Li Ching. Very amateurish."

"I. . .I don't know what you mean." There was desperation in her eyes. Hurt, desperation and shame.

"What's in the champagne, Li Ching?"

Her slight shoulders sagged. She let air from her lungs, then drew it in again. "An ultra-potent truth serum."

"I see. Good night, Li Ching. I'm sorry it worked out this way. No hard feelings. And, by the way. . ."

She had stood in dejection.

"Yes?"

"You look awfully cute in that outfit, but, you see, I'm in love with Mary Lou. Good night again, Li Ching."

"Good night, Werner."

When she was gone, he muttered, "Poor kid."

Max Zimmerman strolled in about ten minutes later. "Saw your light was still lit," he said. "I can't stand any more of that TV crap." He stretched out on the other twin bed. "You know what I think the Americans are building up to?"

"No, what?"

"Twisting your arm, Kraut. Making you take them up to the extraterrestrial ship."

"If they tried it, Common Europe, the Soviet Complex or China, or perhaps all three, would hit them."

"Probably," Zimmerman said. Then, out of a clear sky, he said lazily, "What would you do if you had a hundred million pseudodollars, Kraut?"

"A hundred million! In my time I've wished I was a millionaire, but a hundred million." Brecht laughed. "I couldn't put a dent in a hundred million if I lived to be two hundred."

"I'd help you spend it," Zimmerman said gently.

Brecht said, "Here, have a glass of champagne. It's still cold."

"Jesus, you Peruvians really live it up. Champagne in bed, yet." He took the glass Brecht handed him. "Here's to the ladies!" He took a swallow and said, "Think of all the ladies there'd be if you had a hundred million pseudodollars."

"I've got all the lady I want."

"A very narrow way of looking at broads." Zimmerman finished the glass and said, "You're not drinking?"

"No. Who got to you, Kike?"

The timbre of the Israeli's voice changed infinitesimally. "The Soviets," he said.

"How?" Brecht demanded. "You haven't left the suite."

"Through Foucault. He works for the KGB. Kind of a double agent."

"I see. What was the plan?"

"If you accepted the offer, to smuggle you out of here, over to the Soviet complex and then have you lead a Soviet expedition to the alien spaceship."

"They would have had their work cut out, getting me out of here. Why did you do it, Max?"

"A hundred million pseudodollars. I'm not either an American or Soviet and don't support either of their countries. It's not going to make any difference to me which one of them gets there first. It'll probably lead to war either way, and we'll all die. Meanwhile, I could be spending whatever portion of the hundred million you divvied up with me."

"Possibly makes sense, Max, but, sorry for your dreams of avarice, it's no go."

Zimmerman swung his legs over the side of the bed and stood. "That's what I thought you'd say." He yawned. "How did you get me to open up so easily?"

"There was a truth serum pill in the champagne," Brecht told him, still staring up at the ceiling.

"Well, good night again," Zimmerman said, closing the door.

"Who's next?" Brecht said bitterly.

Next was Kingsley Brett-James.

He knocked, but entered before Brecht could speak. He said, "Hello, old chap. Something just came to my mind that I think a bit urgent."

"Oh, what?"

"That spacecraft. You're the only one who knows where it is, Kraut. What happens if something happens to you? And the way things are developing, something could, don't you know."

"I realize that," Brecht sighed. "If something happens to me, though, they'll never find it."

"That's what I mean," the Englishman said. "Kraut, the human race needs that vehicle. I've gone along with you, thus far, but sooner or later, whatever's in that ship ought to be revealed."

"So?"

"So you ought to tell one of the rest of us where it is. Surely you could give enough of a description of the route so that. . ."

"And you nominate yourself?"

"Since I thought of the idea. The fewer who knew that I knew, the better. If you told someone else instead, there would be three of us in on it."

Brecht sighed. "Li Ching offered me her fair young body and champagne. Zimmerman offered me, believe it or not, a hundred million pseudodollars. You don't offer me anything except a phony story. Tell your Common Europe superiors that it was a good try, but no dice."

Brett-James looked down at him in frustration. "You're making a mistake, Brecht."

"Could be."

In the morning Brecht was gone.

When he didn't show for breakfast, Max Zimmerman went and banged on his door. When there was no response, he opened it and looked inside.

"Jesus Christ," he blurted, and then, over his shoulder, "Hey, everybody!"

They came running at the urgency in his voice.

It was obvious what had happened. A hole twice the diameter of a man's body had been cut through the floor. Someone on the floor below had cut through, probably with a laser beam. Had he been kidnaped, or gone willingly? They had no way of knowing.

Foucault was the first to react. He turned and sped for the phone.

Within hours the world went mad with the news.

Who had Werner Brecht?

Each nation which boasted a space program blamed the others for the abduction.

The World Government League intensified its *World Union Now* program—before the world dissolved into the flames of war.

The skies were scanned in the expectation of a secret launch, but no spaceship could be discerned. Whoever had Brecht was keeping him under wraps for the time being. Or possibly he was refusing to cooperate, no matter what the pressures.

X

There came a knock at the door of the small room in which he sat reading at the table. Werner Brecht looked up, scowling. He wasn't expecting anyone. However, he stood and unlocked the door.

Mary Lou Pickett came in. "Hello, darling," she said.

He could only goggle at her.

Finally he got out, "How in the hell did you locate me?" He closed the door behind her and locked it, and she kissed him warmly but briefly.

"Oh, that was no problem. You see, you're still wearing your electronic I.D. around your neck. The ones we wore on Luna so that if anyone got lost out on the surface we could get a fix on him. So we got a fix on you. And here you are. Way out in the boondocks in a cabin."

"Who's we?" he said unhappily.

"The team. We could have come and got you any time we wished. But we wanted to figure out what you were up to first."

She sat down at the table and grinned at him.

He said, "And?"

"It was the Kike who came up with the answer. He used a process of elimination. It couldn't be the Americans who had you, because they were trying to work through me to get your secret. Nor Common Europe, because they were working through Brett-James. Nor China, since they were working through Li Ching. Nor the Soviet Complex, since they were working through Max and Foucault. So it had to be somebody else. Who else was possibly in on the act? And the only answer to that was the World Government League, which is currently, you'll be glad to learn, coming along marvelously."

He said with care, after slumping down into a chair himself, "Why should I be glad of that?"

"Because you're a member, darling, and have been for years."

He looked at her.

She smiled. "We're all behind you, darling. Even Li Ching. It was all a fake, wasn't it?"

He gave up. "Yes."

"There never was an alien spaceship."

"That's right."

"One of your members of the World Government League, a top photographer, faked the pictures, we decided."

"Yes."

"Another, probably some sort of psychiatrist, planted a hypnotic something or other in your mind so that even under the truth serum you told the same story."

"That's right."

"What are you going to do now?"

"The organization is hiding me out. We'll wait for about a year, until this World Government really gets completely jelled. Total international disarmament, united efforts against pollution and for preservation of natural resources, complete cooperation in exploitation of fusion and solar energy, international cooperation in population control, so on and so forth."

"And then?"

"And then I'll come out of hiding and admit the hoax, so that everybody can forget about alien invasion. . .at least."

"Why, you fool—they'll lynch you."

"Probably. But we'll end up with world government. Then we'll tell them the real truth. . ."

There was a change in her eyes.

"What do you mean, real truth?"

He waited a moment before answering. "You see, the reaction to the so-called hoax is instructive. Look at it in yourself. You felt relief—or disappointment? Which was it?"

"A little of both," she said.

"The idea was to vaccinate man to an alien contact, to help make it happen safely. That meant slowing it up when it did happen. But it only half happened, you see."

"What do you mean?"

"It was a question of getting the best possible use out of my finding the alien ship. It's been there a long time, and there's not much we can understand inside—most of it is wrecked. We figure something knocked it out of its moon orbit a long time ago, long before we could have known enough here on earth to go looking for it in our sky. Probably one of the millions of meteors which have hit the moon gave it a push and the ship impacted on the moon." He paused again. "So I admit it's a hoax, now. Later when the world is more confident and settled, I'll tell the rest. . .rather, we will."

"Tell me now."

He shrugged and stood up, feeling strange, as if something were preparing him for a role he had never expected in life. "It's only that now we know for a fact that intelligent life exists elsewhere," he said, "and that we're going to have to put our house in order and our best face forward when we go out to find them." He sat down, feeling tired. "The so-called hoax is the dry run. . ."

She sighed deeply. "All right. I've come to join you. A year, eh?"

"Maybe more."

She looked around the cabin. "Are you glad I'm here. . .darling?"

"Yes," he said.

Here is a story set in a more distant future when humankind travels to far stars routinely. Exobiology, the study of life forms beyond the earth, is a young enough branch of biology to be called "applied science fiction" as practiced by a science specialist of one kind or another. Studies in this field include characterizing hypothetical planetary environments, the native life which might exist in such alien ecologies, and how such life might be observed, directly or indirectly. But short of actually traveling to the planets of other solar systems, the only life which we might be able to detect at a distance around other stars is intelligent life. Drawing on background from astrophysics, exobiology, planetary composition, Glen Cook creates an alien environment inhabited by intelligent life vastly different from us. And in what is also an exciting adventure story, he manages to raise serious ethical dilemmas about our possible relationship to such intelligences.

G.Z.

IN THE WIND

Glen Cook

I

It's quiet up there, riding the ups and downs over Ginnunga Gap. Even in combat there's no slightest clamor, only a faint scratch and whoosh of strikers tapping igniters and rockets smoking away. The rest of the time, just a sleepy whisper of air caressing your canopy. On patrol it's hard to stay alert and wary.

If the aurora hadn't been so wild behind the hunched backs of the Harridans, painting glaciers and snowfields in ropes of varicolored fire, sequinning snow-catches in the weathered natural castles of the Gap with momentary reflections, I might have dozed at the stick the morning I became von Drachau's wingman. The windwhales were herding in the mountains, thinking migration, and we were flying five or six missions per day. The strain was almost unbearable.

But the auroral display kept me alert. It was the strongest I'd ever seen. A ferocious magnetic storm was developing. Lightning grumbled between the Harridans' copper peaks, sometimes even speared down and danced among the spires in the Gap. We'd all be grounded soon. The rising winds, cold but moisture-heavy, promised weather even whales couldn't ride.

Winter was about to break out of the north, furiously, a winter of a Great Migration. Planets, moons and sun were right, oracles and omens predicting imminent Armageddon. Twelve years had ticked into the ashcan of time. All the whale species again were herding. Soon the fighting would be hard and hopeless.

There are four species of windwhale on the planet Camelot, the most numerous being the Harkness whale, which migrates from its north arctic and north temperate feeding ranges to equatorial mating grounds every other year. Before beginning their migration they, as do all whales, form herds—which, because the beasts are total omnivores, utterly strip the earth in their passage south. The lesser species, in both size and numbers, are Okumura's First, which mates each three winters, Rosenberg's, mating every fourth, and the rare Okumura's Second, which travels only once every six years. Unfortunately. . .

It takes no mathematical genius to see the factors of twelve. And every twelve years the migrations do coincide. In the Great Migrations the massed whales leave tens of thousands of square kilometers of devastation in their wake, devastation from which, because of following lesser migrations, the routes barely recover before the next Great Migration. Erosion is phenomenal. The monsters, subject to no natural control other than that apparently exacted by creatures we called mantas, were destroying the continent on which our employers operated.

Ubichi Corporation had been on Camelot twenty-five years. The original exploitation force, though equipped to face the world's physical peculiarities, hadn't been prepared for whale migrations. They'd been lost to a man, whale supper, because the Corporation's pre-exploitation studies had been so cursory. Next Great Migration another team, though they'd dug in, hadn't fared much better. Ubichi still hadn't done its scientific investigation. In fact, its only action was a determination that the whales had to go.

Simple enough, viewed from a board room at Geneva. But practical implementation was a nightmare under Camelot's technically stifling conditions. And the mantas recomplicated everything.

My flight leader's wagging wings directed my attention south. From a hill a dozen kilometers down the cable came flashing light, Clonninger Station reporting safe arrival of a convoy from Derry. For the next few hours we'd have to be especially alert.

It would take the zeppelins that long to beat north against the wind, and all the while they would be vulnerable to mantas from over the Gap. Mantas, as far as we could see at the time, couldn't tell the difference between dirigibles and whales. More air cover should be coming up. . .

Von Drachau came to Jaeger Gruppe XIII (Corporation Armed Action Command's unsubtle title for our Hunter Wing, which they used as a dump for problem employees) with that convoy, reassigned from JG IV, a unit still engaged in an insane effort to annihilate the Sickle Islands whale herds by means of glider attacks carried out over forty-five kilometers of quiet seas. We'd all heard of him (most JG

XIII personnel had come from the Sickle Islands operation), the clumsiest, or luckiest incompetent, pilot flying for Ubichi. While scoring only four kills he'd been bolted down seven times—and had survived without a scratch. He was the son of Jupp von Drachau, the Confederation Navy officer who had directed the planet-busting strike against the Sangaree homeworld, a brash, sometimes pompous, always self-important nineteen year old who thought that the flame of his father's success should illuminate him equally—and yet resented even a mention of the man. He was a dilettante, come to Camelot only to fly. Unlike the rest of us, Old Earthers struggling to buy out of the poverty bequeathed us by prodigal ancestors, he had no driving need to give performance for pay.

An admonition immediately in order: I'm not here to praise von Drachau, but to bury him. To let him bury himself. Aerial combat fans, who have never seen Camelot, who have read only corporate propaganda, have made of him a contemporary "hero", a flying do-no-wrong competitor for the pewter crown already contested by such antiques as von Richtoffen, Hartmann and Galland. Yet these Archaicists can't, because they need one, make a platinum bar from a turd, nor a socio-psychological fulfillment from a scatterbrain kid. . .*

Most of the stories about him are apocryphal accretions generated to give him depth in his later, "heroic" aspect. Time and storytellers increase his stature, as they have that of Norse gods, who might've been people who lived in preliterate times. For those who knew him (and no one is closer than a wingman), though some of us might like to believe the legends, he was just a selfish, headstrong, tantrum-throwing manchild—albeit a fighter of supernatural ability. In the three months he spent with us, during the Great Migration, his peculiar talents and shortcomings made of him a creature larger than life. Unpleasant a person as he was, he became *the* phenom pilot.

*This paragraph is an editorial insertion from a private letter by Salvador del Gado. Dogfight believes it clarifies del Gado's personal feelings toward his former wingman. His tale, taken separately, while unsympathetic, strives for an objectivity free of his real jealousies. It is significant that he mentions Hartmann and Galland together with von Richtoffen; undoubtedly they, as he when compared with von Drachau, were flyers better than the Red Knight, yet they, and del Gado, lack the essential charisma of the flying immortals. Also, von Richtoffen and von Drachau died at the stick; Hartmann and Galland

*went on to more prosaic things, becoming administrators, comman-
ders of the Luftwaffe. Indications are that del Gado's fate with Ubichi
Corporation's Armed Action Command will be much the same.*

—Dogfight

II

The signals from Clonninger came before dawn, while only two
small moons and the aurora lighted the sky. But sunrise followed
quickly. By the time the convoy neared Beadle Station (us),
Camelot's erratic, blotchy-faced sun had cleared the eastern horizon.
The reserve squadron began catapulting into the Gap's frenetic
drafts. The four of us on close patrol descended toward the dirigibles.

The lightning in the Harridans had grown into a Ypres can-
nonade. A net of jagged blue laced together the tips of the copper
towers in the Gap. An elephant stampede of angry clouds rumbled
above the mountains. The winds approached the edge of being too
vicious for flight.

Flashing light from ground control, searchlight fingers stabbing
north and east, pulsating. Mantas sighted. We waggle-winged ack-
nowledgment, turned for the Gap and updrafts. My eyes had been
on the verge of rebellion, demanding sleep, but in the possibility of
combat weariness temporarily faded.

Black specks were coming south low against the daytime verdigris
of the Gap, a male-female pair in search of a whale. It was obvious
how they'd been named. Anyone familiar with Old Earth's sea creatures could see a remarkable resemblance to the manta ray—though
these had ten meter bodies, fifteen meter wingspans, and ten meter
tails tipped by devil's spades of rudders. From a distance they appeared black, but at attack range could be seen as deep, uneven green
on top and lighter, near olive beneath. They had ferocious habits.

More signals from the ground. Reserve ships would take the mantas. Again we turned, overflew the convoy.

It was the biggest ever sent north, fifteen dirigibles, one fifty meters
and larger, dragging the line from Clonninger at half kilometer intervals, riding long reaches of running cable as their sailmen struggled to tack them into a facing wind. The tall glasteel pylons support-
ing the cable track were ruby towers linked by a single silver strand of
spider silk running straight to Clonninger's hills.

We circled wide and slow at two thousand meters, gradually dropping lower. When we got down to five hundred we were replaced by
a flight from the reserve squadron while we scooted to the Gap for an

updraft. Below us ground crews pumped extra hydrogen to the barrage balloons, lifting Beadle's vast protective net another hundred meters so the convoy could slide beneath. Switchmen and winchmen hustled about with glass and plastic tools in a dance of confusion. We didn't have facilities for receiving more than a half dozen zeppelins—though these, fighting the wind, might come up slowly enough to be handled.

More signals. More manta activity over the Gap, the reserve squadron's squabble turning into a brawl. The rest of my squadron had come back from the Harridans at a run, a dozen mantas in pursuit. Later I learned our ships had found a small windwhale herd and while one flight busied their mantas the other had destroyed the whales. Then, ammunition gone, they ran for home, arriving just in time to complicate traffic problems.

I didn't get time to worry it. The mantas, incompletely fed, spotted the convoy. They don't distinguish between whale and balloon. They went for the zeppelins.

What followed becomes dulled in memory, so swiftly did it happen and so little attention did I have to spare. The air filled with mantas and lightning, gliders, smoking rockets, explosions. The brawl spread till every ship in the wing was involved. Armorers and catapult crews worked to exhaustion trying to keep everything up. Ground batteries seared one another with backblast keeping a rocket screen between the mantas and stalled convoy—which couldn't warp in while the entrance to the defense net was tied up by fighting craft (a problem unforeseen but later corrected by the addition of emergency entryways). They winched their running cables in to short stay and waited it out. Ground people managed to get barrage balloons with tangle tails out to make the mantas' flying difficult.

Several of the dirigibles fought back. Stupid, I thought. Their lifting gas was hydrogen, screamingly dangerous. To arm them seemed an exercise in self-destruction.

So it proved. Most of our casualties came when a ship loaded with ground troops blew up, leaking gas ignited by its own rockets. One hundred eighty-three men burned or fell to their deaths. Losses to mantas were six pilots and the twelve man crew of a freighter.

III

Von Drachau made his entry into JG XIII history just as I dropped from my sailship to the packed earth parking apron. His zepp was the first in and, having vented gas, had been towed to the apron to clear the docking winches. I'd done three sorties during the fighting, after the six of regular patrol. I'd seen my wingman crash into a dragline pylon, was exhausted, and possessed by an utterly foul mood. Von Drachau hit dirt long-haired, unkempt, and complaining, and I was there to greet him. "What do you want to be when you grow up, von Drachau?"

Not original, but it caught him off guard. He was used to criticism by administrators, but pilots avoid antagonism. One never knows when a past slight might mean hesitation at the trigger ring and failure to blow a manta off one's tail. Von Drachau's hatchet face opened and closed, goldfish-like, and one skeletal hand came up to an accusatory point, but he couldn't come back.

We'd had no real contact during the Sickle Islands campaign. Considering his self-involvement, I doubted he knew who I was——and didn't care if he did. I stepped past and greeted acquaintances from my old squadron, made promises to get together to reminisce, then retreated to barracks. If there were any justice at all, I'd get five or six hours for surviving the morning.

I managed four, a record for the week, then received a summons to the office of Commander McClennon, a retired Navy man exiled to command of JG XIII because he'd been so outspoken about Corporation policy.

(The policy that irked us all, and which was the root of countless difficulties, was Ubichi's secret purpose on Camelot. Ubichi deals in unique commodities. It was sure that Camelot operations were recovering one such, but fewer than a hundred of a half million employees knew what. The rest were there just to keep the windwhales from interfering. Even we mercenaries from Old Earth didn't like fighting for a total unknown.)

Commander McClennon's outer office was packed, old faces from the wing and new from the convoy. Shortly, McClennon appeared and announced that the wing had been assigned some gliders with new armaments, low velocity glass barrel gas pressure cannon, pod of four in the nose of a ship designed to carry the weapon system. . .immediate interest. Hitherto we'd flown sport gliders jury-rigged to carry crude rockets, the effectiveness of which lay in the cyanide shell surrounding the warhead. Reliability, poor; accuracy, erratic. A pilot was nearly as likely to kill himself as a whale.

But what could you do when you couldn't use the smallest scrap of metal? Even a silver filling could kill you there. The wildly oscillating and unpredictable magnetic ambience could induce sudden, violent electrical charges. The only metal risked inside Camelot's van Allens was that in the lighters running to and from the surface station at the south magnetic pole, where few lines of force were cut and magnetic weather was reasonably predictable.

Fifty thousand years ago the system passed through the warped space surrounding a black hole. Theory says that's the reason for its eccentricities, but I wonder. Maybe it explains why all bodies in the system have magnetic fields offset from the body centers, the distance off an apparent function of size, mass and rate of rotation, but it doesn't tell me why the fields exist (planetary magnetism is uncommon), nor why they pulsate randomly.

But I digress, and into areas where I have no competence. I should explain what physicists don't understand? We were in the Commander's office and he was selecting pilots for the new ships. Everyone wanted one. Chances for survival appeared that much better.

McClennon's assignments seemed indisputable, the best flyers to the new craft, four flights of four, though those left with old ships were disappointed.

I suffered disappointment myself. A blockbuster dropped at the end, after I'd resigned myself to continuing in an old craft.

"Von Drachau, Horst-Johann," said McClennon, peering at his roster through antique spectacles, one of his affectations, "attack pilot. Del Gado, Salvador Martin, wingman."

Me? With von Drachau? I'd thought the old man liked me, thought he had a good opinion of my ability. . .why'd he want to waste me? Von Drachau's wingman? Murder.

I was so stunned I couldn't yell *let me out!*

"Familiarization begins this afternoon, on Strip Three. First flight checkouts in the morning." A few more words, tired exhortations to do our best, all that crap that's been poured on men at the front from day one, then dismissal. Puzzled and upset, I started for the door.

"Del Gado. Von Drachau." The executive officer. "Stay a minute. The Commander wants to talk to you."

IV

My puzzlement thickened as we entered McClennon's inner office, a Victorian-appointed, crowded yet comfortable room I hadn't seen since I'd paid my first day respects. There were bits of a stamp collection scattered, a desk becluttered, presentation holographs of Navy officers that seemed familiar, another of a woman of the pale thin martyr type, a model of a High Seiner spaceship looking like it'd been cobbled together from plastic tubing and children's blocks. McClennon had been the Naval officer responsible for bringing the Seiners into Confederation in time for the Three Races War. His retirement had been a protest against the way the annexation was handled. Upset as I was I had little attention for surroundings, nor cared what made the Old Man tick.

Once alone with us, he became a man who failed to fit my conception of a commanding officer. His face, which usually seemed about to slide off his skullbones with the weight of responsibility, spread a warm smile. "Johnny!" He thrust a wrinkled hand at von Drachau.

He knew the kid?

My new partner's reaction was a surprise, too. He seemed awed and deferential as he extended his own hand. "Uncle Tom."

McClennon turned. "I've known Johnny since the night he wet himself on my dress blacks just before the Grand Admiral's Ball. Good old days at Luna Command, before the last war." He chuckled. Von Drachau blushed. And I frowned in renewed surprise. I hadn't known von Drachau well, but had never seen or heard anything to suggest he was capable of being impressed by anyone but himself.

"His father and I were Academy classmates. Then served in the same ships before I went into intelligence. Later we worked together in operations against the Sangaree."

Von Drachau didn't sit down till invited. Even though McClennon, in those few minutes, exposed more of himself than anyone in the wing had hitherto seen, I was more interested in the kid. His respectful, almost cowed attitude was completely out of character.

"Johnny," said McClennon, leaning back behind his desk and slowly turning a drink in his hand, "you don't come with recommendations. Not positive, anyway. We going to go through that up here?"

Von Drachau stared at the carpet, shrugged, reminded me of myself as a seven year old called to explain some specially noxious misdeed to my creche-father. It became increasingly obvious that McClennon was a man with whom von Drachau was unwilling to play games. I'd heard gruesome stories of his behavior with the CO JG IV.

"You've heard the lecture already, so I won't give it. I do understand, a bit. Anyway, discipline here, compared to Derry or the Islands, is almost nonexistent. Do your job and you won't have it bad. But don't push. I won't let you endanger lives. Something to think about. This morning's scrap left me with extra pilots. I can ground people who irritate me. Could be a blow to a man who loved flying."

Von Drachau locked gazes with the Commander. Rebellion stirred but he only nodded.

McClennon turned again. "You don't like this assignment." Not a question. My face must've been a giveaway. "Suicidal, you think? You were in JG IV a while. Heard all about Johnny. But you don't know him. I do, well enough to say he's got potential—if we can get him to realize aerial fighting's a team game. By which I mean his first consideration must be bringing himself, his wingman, and his ship home intact." Von Drachau grew red. He'd not only lost seven sailships during the Sickle Islands offensive, he'd lost three wingmen. Dead. "It's hard to remember you're part of a team while attacking. You know that yourself, del Gado. So be patient. Help me make something out of Johnny."

I tried to control my face, failed.

"Why me, eh? Because you're the best flyer I've got. You can stay with him if anyone can.

"I know, favoritism. I'm taking special care. And that's wrong. You're correct, right down the line. But I can't help myself. Don't think you could either, in my position. Enough explanation. That's the way it's going to be. If you can't handle it, let me know. I'll find someone who can, or I'll ground him. One thing I mean to do: send him home alive."

Von Drachau vainly tried to conceal his embarrassment and anger. I felt for him. Wouldn't like being talked about that way myself—though McClennon was doing the right thing, putting his motives on display, up front, so there'd be no surprises later on, and establishing for von Drachau the parameters allowed him. The Commander was an Old Earther himself, and on that battleground had learned that honesty is a weapon as powerful as any in the arsenal of deceit.

"I'll try," I replied, though with silent reservations. I'd have to do some handy self-examination before I bought the whole trick bag.

"That's all I ask. You can go, then. Johnny and I have some catching up to do."

I returned to barracks in a daze. There I received condolences from squadron mates motivated, I suppose, by relief at having escaped the draft themselves.

Tired though I was, I couldn't sleep till I'd thought everything through.

In the end, of course, I decided the Old Man had earned a favor. (This's a digression from von Drachau's story except insofar as it reflects the thoughts that led me to help bring into being the one really outstanding story in Ubichi's Camelot operation.) McClennon was an almost archetypically remote, secretive, Odin/Christ figure, an embastioned lion quietly licking private wounds in the citadel of his office, sharing his pain and privation with no one. But personal facts that had come flitting on the wings of rumor made it certain he was a rare old gentleman who'd paid his dues and asked little in return. He'd bought off for hundreds of Old Earthers, usually by pulling wires to Service connections. And, assuming the stories are true, the price he paid to bring the Starfishers into Confederation, at a time when they held the sole means by which the Three Races War could be won, was the destruction of a deep relationship with the only woman he'd ever loved, the pale Seiner girl whose holo portrait sat like an icon on his desk. Treason and betrayal. Earthman who spoke with forked tongue. She might've been the mother of the son he was trying to find in Horst-Johann. But his Isaac never came back from the altar of the needs of the race. Yes, he'd paid his dues, and at usurous rates.

He had something coming. I'd give him the chance he wanted for the boy. . .Somewhere during those hours my Old Earther's pragmatism lapsed. Old Number One, survival, took a temporary vacation.

It felt good.

V

Getting along with von Drachau didn't prove as difficult as expected. During the following week I was the cause of more friction than he. I kept reacting to the image of the man rumor and prejudice had built in my mind, not to the man in whose presence I was. He was much less arrogant and abrasive than I'd heard—though gritty with the usual outworlder's contempt for the driving need to accomplish characteristic of Old Earthers. But I'd become accustomed to that, even understood. Outworlders had never endured the hopelessness and privation of life on the motherworld. They'd never understand what buying off really meant. Nor did any care to learn.

There're just two kinds of people on Old Earth, butchers and bovines. No one starves, no one freezes, but those are the only positives of life in the Social Insurance warrens. Twenty billion unemployed sardines. The high point of many lives is a visit to Confederation Zone (old Switzerland), where government and corporations maintain their on-planet offices and estates and allow small bands of citizens to come nose the candy store window and look at the lifestyle of the outworlds. . .then send them home with apathy overcome by renewed desperation.

All Old Earth is a slum/ghetto surrounding one small, stoutly defended bastion of wealth and privilege. That says it all, except that getting out is harder than from any historical ghetto.

It's not really what Old Earth outworlders think of when they dust off the racial warm heart and talk about the motherworld. What they're thinking of is Luna Command, Old Earth's moon and the seat of Confederation government. All they have for Old Earth itself is a little shame-faced under-the-table welfare money. . .bitter. The only resource left is human life, the cheapest of all. The outworlds have little use for Terrans save for work like that on Camelot. So bitter. I shouldn't be. I've bought off. Not my problem anymore.

Horst (his preference) and I got on well, quickly advanced to first names. After familiarizing ourselves with the new equipment, we returned to regular patrols. Horst scattered no grit in the machinery. He performed his tasks-within-mission with clockwork precision, never straying beyond the borders of discipline. . .

He confessed, as we paused at the lip of Ginnunga Gap one morning, while walking to the catapults for launch, that he feared being grounded more than losing individuality to military conformity. Flying was the only thing his father hadn't programmed for him (the Commander had gotten him started), and he'd become totally enamored of the sport. Signing on with Ubichi had been the only way to stick with it after his father had managed his appointment to Academy; he'd refused, and been banished from paternal grace. He *had* to fly. Without that he'd have nothing. The Commander, he added, had meant what he said.

I think that was the first time I realized a man could be raised outworld and still be deprived. We Old Earthers take a perverse, chauvinistic pride in our poverty and persecution—like, as the Commander once observed, Jews of Marrakech. (An allusion I spent months dredging: he'd read some obscure and ancient writers.) Our goals are so wholly materialistic that we can scarcely comprehend poverty of the spirit. That von Drachau, with wealth and social position, could feel he had less than I, was a stunning notion.

For him flying was an end, for me a means. Though I enjoyed it, each time I sat at catapult head credit signs danced in my head; so much base, plus per mission and per kill. If I did well I'd salvage some family, too. Horst's pay meant nothing. He wasted it fast as it came—I think to show contempt for the wealth from which he sprang. Though that had been honest money, prize and coup money from his father's successes against the Sangaree.

Steam pressure drove a glasteel piston along forty meters of glasteel cylinder; twenty seconds behind von Drachau I catapulted into the ink of the Gap and began feeling for the ups. For brief instants I could see him outlined against the aurora, flashing in and out of vision as he searched and circled. I spied him climbing, immediately turned to catch the same riser. Behind me came the rest of the squadron. Up we went in a spiral like moths playing tag in the night while reaching for the moons. Von Drachau found altitude and slipped from the up. I followed. At three thousand meters, with moonlight and aurora, it wasn't hard to see him. The four craft of my flight circled at ninety degree points while the rest of the squadron went north across the Gap. We'd slowly drop a thousand meters, then catch another up to the top. We'd stay in the air two hours (or we ran out of ammunition), then go down for an hour break. Five missions minimum.

First launch came an hour before dawn, long before the night fighters went down. Mornings were crowded. But by sunrise we seemed terribly alone while we circled down or climbed, watched the Gap for whales leaving the Harridans or the mantas that'd grown so numerous.

Daytimes almost every ship concentrated on keeping the whales north of the Gap. That grew more difficult as the density of their population neared the migratory. It'd be a while yet, maybe a month, but numbers and instinct would eventually overcome the fear our weapons had instilled. I couldn't believe we'd be able to stop them. The smaller herds of the 'tween years, yes, but not the lemming rivers that would come with winter. A Corporation imbued with any human charity would've been busy sealing mines and evacuating personnel. But Ubichi had none. In terms of financial costs, equipment losses, it was cheaper to fight, sacrificing inexpensive lives to salvage material made almost priceless by interstellar shipment.

VI

Signals from the ground, a searchlight fingering the earth and flashing three times rapidly. Rim sentries had spotted a whale in the direction the finger pointed. Von Drachau and I were front. We began circling down.

We'd dropped just five hundred meters when he wag-winged visual contact. I saw nothing but the darkness that almost always clogged the canyon. As wide as Old Earth's Grand Canyon and three times as deep, it was well lighted only around noon.

That was the first time I noticed his phenomenal vision. In following months he was to amaze me repeatedly. I honestly believe I was the better pilot, capable of outflying any manta, but his ability to find targets made him the better combat flyer.

The moment I wagged back he broke circle and dove. I'd've circled lower. If the whale was down in the Gap itself that might mean a three thousand meter fall. Pulling out would overstrain one's wings. Sailplanes, even the jackboot jobs we flew, are fragile machines never intended for stunt flying.

But I was wingman, responsible for protecting the attack pilot's rear. I winged over and followed, maintaining a constant five hundred meters between us. Light and shadow from clouds and mountains played over his ship, alternately lighting and darkening the personal devices he'd painted on. A death's-head grinned and winked. . .

I spied the whale. It was working directly toward Beadle. Size and coloring of the gasbag (oblate spheroid sixty meters long, patched in shades from pink to scarlet and spotted with odd other colors at organ sites) indicated a juvenile of the Harkness species, that with the greatest potential for destruction. Triangular vanes protruding ten meters from muscle rings on the bag twitched and quivered as the monster strove to maintain a steady course. Atop it in a thin Mohawk swath swayed a copse of treelike organs believed to serve both plantlike and animal digestive and metabolic functions. Some may have been sensory. Beneath it sensory tentacles trailed, stirring fretfully like dreaming snakes on the head of Medusa. If any found food (and anything organic was provender for a Harkness), it'd anchor itself immediately. Hundreds more tentacles would descend and begin lifting edibles to mouths in a tiny head-body tight against the underside of the gasbag. There'd be a drizzling organic rainfall as the monster dumped ballast/waste. Migrating whale herds could devastate great swaths of countryside. Fortunately for Ubichi's operations, the mating seasons were infrequent.

The Harkness swelled ahead. Horst would be fingering his trigger ring, worrying his sights. I stopped watching for mantas and adjusted my dive so Horst wouldn't be in line when I fired. . .

Flashing lights, hasty, almost panicky. I read, then glanced out right and up, spied the manta pair. From high above the Harridans they arrowed toward the whale, tips and trailing edges of their wings rippling as they adjusted dive to each vagary of canyon air. But they were a kilometer above and would be no worry till we'd completed our pass. And the other two ships of our flight would be after them, to engage while Horst and I completed the primary mission.

The relationship between mantas and whales had never, to that time, been clearly defined. The mantas seemed to feed among the growths on whale backs, to attach themselves in mated pairs to particular adults, which they fiercely defended, and upon which they were apparently dependent. But nothing seemed to come the other way. The whales utterly ignored them, even as food. Whales ignored everything in the air, though, enduring our attacks as if they weren't happening. If not for the mantas, the extermination program would've been a cakewalk.

But mantas fought at every encounter, almost as if they knew what we were doing. A year earlier they'd been little problem. Then we'd been sending single flights after lone wandering whales, but as migratory pressures built the manta population had increased till we were forced to fight three or four battles to each whale attack—of which maybe one in twenty resulted in a confirmed kill. Frustrating business, especially since self-defense distracted so from our primary mission.

Luckily, the mantas had only one inefficient, if spectacular, weapon, the lightning they hurled.

That fool von Drachau dropped flaps to give himself more firing time. Because I began overtaking him, I had to follow suit. My glider shuddered, groaned, and an ominous snap came from my right wing. But nothing fell apart.

Fog formed before Horst's craft, whipped back. He'd begun firing. His shells painted a tight bright pattern in the forest on the whale's back. Stupidly, I shifted aim to the same target. Von Drachau pulled out, flaps suddenly up, used his momentum to hurl himself up toward the diving manta pair, putting them in a pincer.

A jagged bite of lightning flashed toward von Drachau. I cursed. We'd plunged into a trap. Mantas had been feeding in the shelter of the whale's back organs. They were coming up to fight.

I'd begun firing an instant before the flash, putting my shells in behind Horst's. Before the water vapor from my cannon gas fogged my canopy I saw explosions digging into the gasbag. I started to stick back and fire at the mantas, but saw telltale ripples of blue fire beneath the yellow of my shells. The bag was going to blow.

When the hydrogen went there'd be one hell of an explosion.

Following Horst meant suicide.

The prime purpose of the explosives was to drive cyanide fragments into whale flesh, but sometimes, as then, a too tight pattern breached the main bag—and hydrogen is as dangerous on Camelot as elsewhere.

I took my only option, dove. With luck the whale's mass would shadow me from the initial blast.

It did. But the tip of my right wing, that'd made such a grim noise earlier, brushed one of the monster's sensory tentacles. The jerk snapped it at the root. I found myself spinning down.

I rode it a while, both because I was stunned (I'd never been downed before, accidentally or otherwise) and because I wanted the craft to protect me from downblast.

The sun had risen sufficiently to illuminate the tips of the spires in the gap. They wheeled, jerked, reached up like angry claws, drawing rapidly closer. Despite the ongoing explosion, already shaking me, blistering the paint on my fuselage, I had to get out.

Canopy cooperated. In the old gliders they'd been notoriously sticky, costing many lives. This popped easily. I closed my eyes and jumped, jerking my ripcord as I did. Heat didn't bother me. My remaining wing took a cut at me, a last effort of fate to erase my life-tape, then the chute jerked my shoulders. I began to sway.

It was cold and lonely up there, and there was nothing I could do. I was no longer master of my fate. You would have to be an Old Earther near buying off to really feel the impact of that. Panicky, I peered up at the southern rim of the Gap—and saw what I'd hoped to see, the rescue balloon already on its way. It was a hot air job that rode safety lines payed out from winches at the edge. If I could be salvaged, it'd be managed. I patted my chest pockets to make sure I had my flares.

Only then did I rock my chute away so I could see what'd happened to von Drachau.

He was into it with three mantas, one badly wounded (the survivor of the pair from the Harkness—the other had died in the explosion). He got the wounded one and did a flap trick to turn inside the others. His shells went into the belly of one. It folded and fell. Then the rest of our flight was pursuing the survivor toward the Harridans.

I worried as burning pieces of whale fell past. Suppose one hit my chute?

But none did. I landed in snow deep in the Gap, after a cruel slide down an almost vertical rock face, then set out my first flare. While I tried to stay warm, I thought about von Drachau.

I'd gone along with his attack because I'd had neither choice, nor time to think, nor any way to caution him. But that precipitous assault had been the sort that'd earned him his reputation. And it'd cost again. Me.

Didn't make me feel any better to realize I'd been as stupid in my target selection.

A rational, unimpetuous attack would've gone in level with the whale, from behind, running along its side. Thus Horst could've stayed out of sight of the mantas riding it, and I could've avoided the explosion resulting from a tight fire pattern in the thin flesh of the back. Shells laid along the whale's flanks would've spread enough cyanide to insure a kill.

Part my fault, but when the rescue balloon arrived I was so mad at Horst I couldn't talk.

VII

Von Drachau met the rescue balloon, more concerned and contrite than I'd've credited. I piled out steaming, with every intention of denting his head, but he ran to me like a happy puppy, bubbling apologies, saying he'd never had a chance at a whale. . .righteous outrage became grumpiness. He was only nineteen, emotionally ten.

There were reports to be filed but I was in no mood. I headed for barracks and something alcoholic.

Von Drachau followed. "Sal," he said with beer in his mustache, "I mean it. I'm sorry. Wish I could look at it like you. Like this's just a job. . ."

"Uhm." I made a grudging peace. "So can it." But he kept on. Something was biting him, something he wanted coaxed out.

"The mantas," he said. "What do we know about them?"

"They get in the way."

"Why? Territorial imperative? Sal, I been thinking. Was today a set-up? If people was working the other side, they couldn't've set a better trap. In the old ships both of us would've gone down."

"Watch your imagination, kid. Things're different in the Islands, but not that different. We've run into feeding mantas before. You just attacked from the wrong angle." I tossed off my third double. The Gap bottom cold began leaking from my bones. I felt a bit more charitable. But not enough to discuss idiot theories of manta intelligence.

We already knew many odd forms of intelligence. Outworlders have a curious sensitivity to it, a near reverence puzzling to Old

Earthers. They go around looking for it, especially in adversity. Like savages imputing powers to storms and stones, they can't accept disasters at face value. There has to be a malignant mover.

"I guess you're right," he said. But his doubt was plain. He *wanted* to believe we were fighting a war, not exterminating noxious animals.

Got me thinking, though. Curious how persistent the rumor was, even though there was no evidence to support it. But a lot of young people (sic!—I was twenty-eight) are credulous. A pilot, dogfighting a manta pair, might come away with the notion. They're foxy. But intelligence, to me, means communication and cooperation. Mantas managed a little of each, but only among mates. When several pairs got involved in a squabble with us, we often won by maneuvering pairs into interfering with one another.

The matter dropped and, after a few more drinks, was forgotten. And banished utterly when we were summoned to the Commander's office.

The interview was predictable. McClennon was determined to ground von Drachau. I don't know why I defended him. Labor united against management, maybe. . .

Guess Horst wasn't used to having a friend at court. When we left he thanked me, but seemed puzzled, seemed to be wrestling something inside.

Never did find out what, for sure—Old Earthers are tight-lipped, but von Drachau had the best of us beaten—but there was a marked improvement in his attitude. By the end of the month he was on speaking terms with everyone, even men he'd grossly alienated at JG IV.

That month I also witnessed a dramatic improvement in Horst's shooting. His kills in the Sickle Islands had been almost accidental. Changing from rockets to cannons seemed to bring out his talent. He scored kill after kill, attacking with a reckless abandon (but always with a care to keep me well positioned). He'd scream in on a manta, drop flaps suddenly, put himself into a stall just beyond the range of the manta's bolt, then flaps up and fall beneath the monster when he'd drawn it, nose up and trigger a burst into its belly. Meanwhile, I would fend off the other till he was free. My kill score mounted, too.

His was astonishing. Our first four weeks together he downed thirty-six mantas. I downed fourteen, and two whales. I'd had fifty-seven and twelve for four years' work when he arrived, best in the wing. It was obvious that, if he stayed alive, he'd soon pass not only me but Aultmann Zeisler, the CO JG I, a ten year veteran with ninety-one manta kills.

Horst did have an advantage we older pilots hadn't. Target availability. Before, except during the lesser migrations, the wing had been lucky to make a dozen sightings per month. Now we piled kills at an incredible rate.

Piled, but the tilt of the mountain remained against us. Already stations farther south were reporting sightings of small herds that had gotten past us.

It was coming to the point where we were kept busy by mantas. Opportunities to strike against whales grew rare. When the main migratory wave broke we'd be swamped.

Everyone knew it. But Derry, despite sending reinforcements, seemed oblivious to the gravity of the situation. Or didn't care. A sour tale began the rounds. The Corporation had written us off. The whales would remove us from the debit ledger. That facilities at Clonninger and stations farther down the cable were being expanded to handle our withdrawal didn't dent the rumors. We Old Earthers always look on the bleak side.

In early winter, after a severe snowstorm, as we were digging out, we encountered a frightening phenomenon. Cooperation among large numbers of mantas.

VIII

It came with sunrise. Horst and I were in the air, among two dozen new fighters. The wing had been reinforced to triple strength, one hundred fifty gliders and a dozen armed zeppelins, but those of us up were all the ground personnel had been able to dig out and launch.

Signals from ground. Against the aurora and white of the Harridans I had no trouble spotting the Harkness whales, full adults, leaving a branch canyon opposite Beadle. Close to a hundred, I guessed, the biggest lot yet to assault the Gap. We went to meet them, one squadron circling down. My own squadron, now made up of men who'd shown exceptional skill against mantas, stayed high to cover. We no longer bothered with whales, served only as cover for the other squadron.

I watched for mantas. Had no trouble finding them. They came boiling 'round the flank of an ivory mountain, cloud of black on cliff of white, a mob like bats leaving a cave at sunset. Hundreds of them.

My heart sank. It'd be thick, grim, and there was no point even thinking about attack formations. All a man could do was keep away and grab a shot at opportunity. But we'd take losses. One couldn't watch every way at once.

A few mantas peeled off and dove for the ships attacking the whales. The bulk came on, following a line that'd cross the base.

We met. There were gliders, mantas, shells and lightning bolts thicker than I'd ever seen. Time stood still. Mantas passed before me, I pulled trigger rings. Horst's death's-head devices whipped across my vision. Sometimes parts of gliders or mantas went tumbling by. Lower and lower we dropped, both sides trading altitude for speed.

Nose up. Manta belly before me, meters away. Jerk the rings. Fog across the canopy face, but no explosions against dark flesh. We struggled to avoid collision, passed so close we staggered one another with our slipstreams. For a moment I stared into two of the four eyes mounted round the thing's bullet head. They seemed to drive an electric line of hatred deep into my brain. For an instant I believed the intelligence hypothesis. Then shuddered as I sticked down and began a rabbit run for home, to replace my ammunition.

A dozen mantas came after me. Horst, alone, went after them. I later learned that, throwing his craft about with complete abandon, he knocked nine of those twelve down before his own ammunition ran out. It was an almost implausible performance, though one that need not be dwelt upon. It's one of the mainstays of his legend, his first ten-kill day, and every student of the fighting on Camelot knows of it.

The runway still had a half meter of snow on it. The three mantas followed me in, ignoring the counterfire of our ground batteries. I was so worried about evading their bolts that I went in poorly, one wing down, and ended up spinning into a deep drift. As a consequence I spent two hours grounded.

What I missed was sheer hell. The mantas, as if according to some plan, clamped down on our landing and launching gates, taking their toll while our craft were at their most vulnerable. In the early going some tried to blast through the overhead netting. That only cost them lives. Our ground batteries ate them up. Then they tried the barrage balloons, to no better effect.

Then the whales arrived. We'd been able to do nothing to stop them, so busy had the mantas kept us. They, sensing food beneath the net, began trying to break in. Our ground batteries fired into the dangling forests of their tentacles, wrecking those but doing little damage to the beasts themselves. Gigantic creaks and groans came from the net anchor points.

For pilots and ground crews there was little to do but prepare for a

111

launch when circumstances permitted. I got my ship out, rearmed, and dragged to catapult head. Then for a time I stood observer, using binoculars to watch those of our craft still up.

In all, the deaths of a hundred fourteen mantas (four mine, ten Horst's) and twenty-two whales were confirmed for the first two hours of fighting. But we would've gone under without help from down the cable.

When the desperation of our position became obvious the Commander signalled Clonninger. Its sailcraft came north, jumped the mantas from above. They broke siege. We launched, cats hurling ships into the Gap as fast as steam could be built. Horst and I went in the first wave.

Help had come just in time. The whales had managed several small breaches in the netting and were pushing tentacles through after our ground people.

Even with help the situation remained desperate. I didn't think it'd take long for the mantas, of which more had come across, to clamp down again. When they did it'd only be a matter of time till the whales wrecked the net. I pictured the base destroyed, littered with bones.

Before we launched, the Commander, ancient with the strain, spoke with each pilot. Don't know what he said to the others, but I imagine it was much what he told me: if I judged the battle lost, to run south rather than return here. The sailcraft had to be salvaged for future fighting. If we were overrun the fighting would move to Clonninger.

And in my ear a few words about taking care of von Drachau. I said I would.

But we survived. I won't say we won because even though we managed to break the attack, we ourselves were decimated. JG XIII's effectiveness was ruined for the next week. For days we could barely manage regular patrols. Had we been hit again we'd've been obliterated.

That week McClennon three times requested permission to evacuate nonessential ground troops, received three refusals. Still, it seemed pointless for us to stay when our blocking screen had been riddled. Small herds were passing daily. Clonninger was under as much pressure as we and had more trouble handling it. Their defenses weren't meant to stand against whales. Their sailplanes often had to flee. Ground personnel crouched in deep bunkers and prayed the whales weren't so hungry they'd dig them out.

Whale numbers north of the Harridans were estimated at ten thousand and mantas at ten to twenty. Not vast, but overwhelming in concentration. Populations for the whole continent were about double those, with the only other concentrations in the Sickle Islands. By the end of that week our experts believed a third of the Harridan whales had slipped past us. We'd downed about ten percent of those trying and about twenty-five percent of the mantas.

IX

A fog of despair enveloped Beadle. Derry had informed McClennon that there'd be no more reinforcements. They were needed further south. Permission to withdraw? Denied again. We had only one hundred twelve effective sailcraft. Ammunition was short. And the main blow was yet to fall.

It's hard to capture the dulled sense of doom that clung so thick. It wasn't a verbal or a visible thing, though faces steadily lengthened. There was no defeatist talk. The men kept their thoughts to themselves—but couldn't help expressing them through actions, by digging deeper shelters, in a lack of crisp efficiency. Things less definable. Most hadn't looked for desperate stands when they signed on. And Camelot hadn't prepared them to face one. Till recently they'd experienced only a lazy, vacation sort of action, loafing and laughter with a faint bouquet of battle.

One evening Horst and I stood watching lightning shoot among the near pure copper peaks of the Harridans. "D'you ever look one in the eye?" he asked.

Memory of the manta I'd missed. I shuddered, nodded.

"And you don't believe they're intelligent?"

"I don't care. A burst in the guts is all that matters. That's cash money, genius or retard."

"Your conscience doesn't bother you?"

Something was bothering him, though I couldn't understand why. He wouldn't worry bending human beings, so why aliens? Especially when the pay's right and you're the son of a man who'd become rich by doing the same? But his reluctance wasn't unique. So many people consider alien intelligence sacred—without any rational basis. It's a crippling emotional weakness that has wormed its way into Confederation law. You can't exploit a world with intelligent natives. . .

But conscience may've had nothing to do with it. Seems, in hindsight, his reluctance might've been a rationalized facet of his revolt against his father and authority.

Understandably, Ubichi was sensitive to speculations about manta intelligence. Severe fines were laid on men caught discussing the possibility—which, human nature being what it is, made the talk more persistent. Several pilots, Horst included, had appealed to McClennon. He'd been sympathetic, but what could he have done?

And I kept wondering why anyone cared. I agreed with the Corporation. That may have been a defect in me.*

*If this thought truly occurred to del Gado at the time, it clearly made no lasting moral impression. News buffs will remember that he was one of several Ubichi mercenaries named in Confederation genocide indictments stemming from illegal exploitation on Bonaventure, though he was not convicted.

—Dogfight

As soon as we recovered from attack, for morale purposes we launched our last offensive, a pre-emptive strike against a developing manta concentration. Everything, including armed zeppelins, went. The mission was partially successful. Kept another attack from hitting Beadle for a week, but it cost. None of the airships returned. Morale sagged instead of rising. We'd planned to use the zepps in our withdrawal—if ever authorized.

In line of seniority I took command of my squadron after a manta made the position available. But I remained von Drachau's wingman. That made him less impetuous. Still addicted to the flying, he avoided offending a man who could ground him. I was tempted. His eye was still deadly, but his concern over the intelligence of mantas had begun affecting his performance.

At first it was a barely noticeable hesitance in attack that more than once left blistered paint on his ship. With his timing a hair off he sometimes stalled close enough for a manta's bolt to caress his craft. My admonitions had little effect. His flying continued to deteriorate.

And still I couldn't understand.

X

His performance improved dramatically six days after our strike into the Harridans, a day when he had no time to think, when the wing's survival was on the line and maximum effort was a must. (He always performed best under pressure. He never could explain how he'd brushed those nine mantas off me that day. He'd torn through them with the cold efficiency of a military robot, but later couldn't remember. It was as if another personality had taken control. I saw him go through three such possessions and he couldn't remember after any.) It was a battle in which we all flew inspired—and earned a Pyrrhic victory. . .the back of the wing was broken, but again Beadle survived.

The mantas came at dawn, as before, and brought a whale herd with them. There'd been snow, but this time a hard night's work had cleared the catapults and sailships. We were up and waiting. They walked—or flew—into it. And kept coming. And kept coming.

And by weight of numbers drove us to ground. And once we'd lost the air the whales moved in.

McClennon again called for aid from Clonninger. It came. We broke out. And soon were forced to ground again. The mantas refused to be dismayed. A river came across the Gap to replace losses.

Clonninger signalled us for help. From Beadle we watched endless columns of whales, varicolored as species mixed, move down the dragline south. We could do nothing. Clonninger was on its own.

McClennon ordered a hot air balloon loaded with phosphorous bombs, sent it out and blew it amidst the mantas crowding our launch gate. Horst and I jumped into their smoke. That entire mission we ignored mantas and concentrated on the whales, who seemed likely to destroy the net. Before ammunition ran out we forced them to rejoin the migration. But the mantas didn't leave till dark.

Our ground batteries ran out of rockets. Half our ships were destroyed or permanently grounded. From frostbite as much as manta action (the day's high was —23° C.), a third of our people became casualties. Fourteen pilots found permanent homes in the bottom of Ginnunga Gap. Rescue balloons couldn't go after them.

Paradoxically, permission to withdraw came just before we lost contact with Clonninger.

We began our wound-licking retreat at midnight, scabby remnants of squadrons launching into the ink of the Gap, grabbing the ups, then slanting down toward Clonninger. Balloons began dragging the line.

Clonninger was what we'd feared for Beadle: churned earth and bones ethereally grim by dawn light. The whales had broken its defenses without difficulty. Appetites whetted, they'd moved on. From three thousand meters the borders of the earth-brown river of devastation seemed to sweep the horizons. The silvery drag cable sketched a bright centerline for that death-path.

We were patrolling when the first airships came south. The skies were utterly empty, the ground naked, silence total. Once snow covered the route only memory would mark recent events. . .

Days passed. The Clonninger story repeated itself down the cable, station after station, though occasionally we found salvageable survivors or equipment. Operations seemed ended for our ground units. But for us pilots it went on. We followed the line till we overtook straggler whales, returned to work.

As the migration approached Derry corporate defenses stiffened. Though we'd lost contact, it seemed our function at the Gap had been to buy time. True, as I later learned. A string of Beadle-like fortress-bases were thrown across the northern and Sickle Islands routes. But even they weren't strong enough. As the mantas learned (even I found myself accepting the intelligence proposition), they became more proficient at besieging and destroying bases. The whales grew less fearful, more driven by their mating urge. Mantas would herd them to a base; they'd wreck it despite the most furious defense. Both whales and mantas abandoned fear, ignored their own losses.

JG XIII was out of the main action, of course, but we persevered—if only because we knew we'd never get off planet if Derry fell. But we flew with little enthusiasm. Each additional destroyed base or mine (whatever Ubichi was after had to be unearthed) reassured us of the inevitability of failure.

When a man goes mercenary in hopes of buying off, he undergoes special training. Most have a paramilitary orientation. (I use "mercenary" loosely.) Historical studies puzzled me. Why had men so often fought on when defeat was inevitable? Why had they in fact given more of themselves in a hopeless cause? I was living it then and still didn't understand. JG XIII performed miracles with what it had, slaughtered whales and mantas by the hundreds, and that after everyone had abandoned hope. . .

Horst reached the one fifty mark. I reached one hundred twenty. Almost every surviving pilot surpassed fifty kills. There were just thirty-three of us left.

XI

On the spur of the moment one day, based on two considerations, I made my first command decision: good winds during patrol and a grave shortage of supplies. For a month the wing had been living and fighting off the remnants of stations destroyed by migrating whales. Rations were a single pale meal each day. Our remaining ammunition was all with us on patrol.

When I began this I meant to tell about myself and Horst-Johann von Drachau. Glancing back, I see I've sketched a story of myself and JG XIII. Still, it's almost impossible to extricate the forms —especially since there's so little concrete to say about the man. My attempts to characterize him fail, so robotlike was he even with me. Mostly I've speculated, drawn on rumor and used what I learned from Commander McClennon. The few times Horst opened at all he didn't reveal much, usually only expressing an increasing concern about the mantas. Without my speculations he'd read like an excerpt from a service file.

The above is an admonition to myself: don't digress into the heroism and privation of the month the wing operated independently. That wasn't a story about von Drachau. He endured it without comment. Yet sleeping in crude wooden shelters and eating downed manta without complaining might say something about the man behind the facade, or something about changes that had occurred there. Hard to say. He may've ignored privation simply because it didn't impinge on his personal problems.

We were in the air, making the last patrol we could reasonably mount. I had command. In a wild moment, inspired by good ups and winds, I decided to try breaking through to Derry territory. Without knowing how far it'd be to the nearest extant station—we hadn't seen outsiders since borrowing the Clonninger squadrons. That Derry still held I could guess only from the fact that we were still to its north and in contact with mantas and whales.

The inspiration hit, I wag-winged *follow me* and went into a long shallow glide. Derry itself lay over two hundred kilometers away, a long fly possible only if we flitted from up to up. Much longer flights had been made—though not against opposition.

It took twelve hours and cost eight sailcraft, but we made it. It was an ace day for everyone. There seemed to be a Horst-like despair about the mantas that left them sluggish in action. We littered the barren earth with their corpses. Horst, with seven kills, had our lowest score. Because I was behind him all the while I noticed he wasn't trying, shot only when a pilot was endangered. This had been growing during the month. He was as sluggish as the mantas.

Our appearance at Derry generated mixed reactions. Employees got a big lift, perhaps because our survival presented an example. But management seemed unsettled, especially by our kill claims, our complaints, and the fact that there were survivors they were obligated to rescue. All they wanted was to hold on and keep the mines working. But aid to JG XIII became an instant *cause célèbre*. It was obvious there'd be employee rebellion if our survivors were written off.

I spent days being grilled, the price of arrogating command. The others were supposed to remain quarantined for debriefing, but evaded their watchers. They did the public relations job. Someone spread the tales that were the base for von Drachau's legend.

I tried to stop that, but to do so was beating my head against a wall. Those people in the shrinking Derry holding needed a hero—even if they had to make him up, to fill in, pad, chop off rough corners so he'd meet their needs. It developed quickly. I wonder how Horst would've reacted had he been around for deep exposure. I think it might've broken his shell, but would've gone to is head too. Well, no matter now.

Myself, I'd nominate Commander McClennon as the real hero of JG XIII. His was the determination and spirit that brought us through. But he was an administrator.

Much could be told about our stay at Derry, which lasted through winter and spring, till long after the manta processes of intellection ponderously ground to the conclusion that we humans couldn't be smashed and eaten this time. The fighting, of course, continued, and would till Confederation intervened, but it stayed at a modest level. They stopped coming to us. Morale soared. Yet things were really no better. The mating whales still cut us off from the south polar spaceport.

But the tale is dedicated to Horst-Johann von Drachau. It lasts only another week.

XII

Once free of interrogation, I began preparing the wing to return to action. For years I'd been geared to fighting; administration wasn't easy. I grew short-tempered, began hunting excuses to evade responsibility. Cursed myself for making the decision that'd brought me inside—even though that'd meant volunteer crews taking zepps north with stores.

An early official action was an interview with Horst. He came to my cubby-office sullen and dispirited, but cheered up when I said,

"I'm taking you off attack. You'll be my wingman."

"Good."

"It means that much?"

"What?"

"This stuff about manta intelligence."

"Yeah. But you wouldn't understand, Sal. Nobody does."

I began my "what difference does it make?" speech. He interrupted.

"You know I can't explain. It's something like this: we're not fighting a war. In war you try to demonstrate superiority of arms, to convince the other side it's cheaper to submit. We're trying for extermination here. Like with the Sangaree."

The Sangaree. The race his father had destroyed. "No big loss."

"Wrong. They were nasty, but posed no real threat. They could've been handled with a treaty. We had the power."

"No tears were shed. . ."

"Wrong again. But the gut reaction isn't over. You wait. When men like my father and Admiral Beckhart and Commander McClennon and the other militarists who control Luna Command fade away, you'll start seeing a reaction. . .a whole race, Sal, a whole culture, independently evolved, with all it might've taught us. . ."

It had to be rationalization, something he'd built for himself to mask a deeper unhappiness. "McClennon? You don't approve of him?"

"Well, yeah, he's all right. I guess. But even when he disagreed, he went along. In fact, my father never could've found the Sangaree homeworld without him. If he'd revolted then, instead of later when his actions turned and bit back. . .well, the Sangaree would be alive and he'd be off starfishing with Amy."

I couldn't get through. Neither could he. The speeches on the table were masks for deeper things. There's no way to talk about one thing and communicate something else. "Going along," I said. "What've you been doing? How about the kid who squawks but goes along because he wants to fly? That's what we're all doing here, Horst. Think I'd be here if I could buy off any other way? Life is compromise. No exceptions. And you're old enough to know it."*

Shouldn't've said that. But I was irritable, unconcerned about what he'd think. He stared a moment, then stalked out, considering his own compromises.

Two days later my ships were ordered up for the first time since our arrival. Command had had trouble deciding what to do with us. I think we weren't employed because the brass were afraid we were as good as we claimed, which meant (by the same illogical process that built legends around Horst and the wing) that our survival wasn't just a miracle, that we'd really been written off but had refused to die. Such accusations were going around and Command was sensitive to them.

We went up as air cover for the rescue convoy bringing our survivors in from up the cable. We wouldn't've been used if another unit had been available. But the mantas had a big push on, their last major and only night offensive.

Del Gado may indeed have said something of the sort at the time, and have felt it, but again, once the pressure was off, he forgot. He has been bought off for years, yet remains with Ubichi's Armed Action Command. He must enjoy his work.

—Dogfight

Winds at Derry are sluggish, the ups are weak, and that night there was an overcast masking the moons. The aurora is insignificant that far south. Seeing was by lightning, a rough way to go.

We launched shortly after nightfall, spent almost an hour creeping to altitude, then clawed north above the cable. Flares were out to mark it, but those failed us when we passed the last outpost. After that it was twenty-five ships navigating by guesswork, maintaining contact by staying headache-making alert during lightning flashes.

But it was also relaxing. I was doing something I understood. The whisper of air over my canopy lulled me, washed the week's aggravations away.

Occasionally I checked my mirrors. Horst maintained perfect position on my right quarter. The others spread around in ragged formation, yielding compactness and precision to safety. The night threatened collisions.

We found the convoy one hundred twenty kilometers up the line, past midnight, running slowly into the breeze and flashing signals so we'd locate them. I dropped down, signalled back with a bioluminescent lantern, then clawed some altitude, put the men into wide patrol patterns. Everything went well through the night. The mantas weren't up in that sector.

Dawn brought them, about fifty in a flying circus they'd adopted from us. We condensed formation and began slugging it out.

They'd learned. They still operated in pairs, but no longer got in one another's way. And they strove to break our pairs to take advantage of numbers. But when a pair latched onto a sailplane it became their entire universe. We, however, shot at anything, whether or not it was a manta against which we were directly engaged.

They'd overadopted our tactics. I learned that within minutes. When someone got half a pair, the other would slide out of action and stay out till it found a single manta of opposite sex. Curious. (Shortly I'll comment on the findings of the government investigators, who dug far deeper than Ubichi's exobiologists. But one notion then current, just rumor as the sentience hypothesis became accepted, was that manta intelligence changed cyclically, as a function of the mating cycle.)

We held our own. All of us were alive because we were good. Dodging bolts was instinctual, getting shells into manta guts second nature. We lost only two craft, total. One pilot. Two thirds of the mantas went down.

Horst and I flew as if attached to ends of a metal bar. Book perfect. But the mantas forced us away from the main fray, as many as twenty concentrating on us. (I think they recognized our devices and decided to destroy us. If it were possible for humans to be known to mantas, they'd've been Horst and I.) I went into a robotlike mood like Horst's on his high-kill days. Manta after manta tumbled away. My shooting was flawless. Brief bursts, maybe a dozen shells, were all I used. I seldom missed.

As sometimes happened in such a brawl, Horst and I found our stations reversed. A savage maneuver that left my glider creaking put me in the wingman slot. During it Horst scored his hundred fifty-eighth kill, clearing a manta off my back. Far as I know that was the only time he fired.

The arrangement was fine with me. He was the better shot; let him clear the mess while I protected his back. We'd resume proper positions when a break in the fighting came.

A moment later Horst was in firing position beneath a female who'd expended her bolt (it then took several minutes to build a charge). He bored in, passed so close their wings nearly brushed. But he didn't fire. I took her out as I came up behind.

The eyes. Again I saw them closely. Puzzlement and pain(?) as she folded and fell. . .

Three times that scene repeated itself. Horst wouldn't shoot. Behind him I cursed, threatened, promised, feared. Tried to get shells into his targets, but missed. He maneuvered so I was in poor position on each pass.

Then the mantas broke. They'd lost. The rest of the squadron pursued, losing ground because the monsters were better equipped to grab altitude.

Horst went high. At first I didn't understand, just continued cursing. Then I saw a manta, an old male circling alone, and thought he'd gotten back in track, was going after a kill.

He wasn't. He circled in close and for a seeming eternity they flew wingtip to wingtip, eyeballing one another. Two creatures alone, unable to communicate. But something passed between them. Nobody believes me (since it doesn't fit the von Drachau legend), but I think they made a suicide pact.

Flash. Bolt. Horst's ship staggered, began smoking. The death's-head had disappeared from his fuselage. He started down.

I put everything in my magazines into that old male. The explosions tore him to shreds.

I caught Horst a thousand meters down, pulled up wingtip to wingtip. He still had control, but poorly. Smoke filled his cockpit. Little flames peeped out where his emblem had been. The canvas was ripping from his airframe. By hand signals I tried to get him to bail out.

He signalled he couldn't, that his canopy was stuck. Maybe it was, but when McClennon and I returned a month later, after the migration had passed south, I had no trouble lifting it away.

Maybe he wanted to die.

Or maybe it was because of his legs. When we collected his remains we found that the manta bolt had jagged through his cockpit and cooked his legs below the knees. There'd've been no saving him.

Yet he kept control most of the way down, losing it only in the last five hundred meters. He stalled, spun, dove. Then he recovered and managed a low angle crash. He rolled nose over tail, then burned. Finis. No more Horst-Johann.

I still don't understand.*

---

*"Hawkins, you keep harping on the 'meaning' of Horst's death. Christ, man, that's my point: it had no meaning. In my terms. By those he utterly wasted his life; his voluntary termination didn't alter the military situation one iota. Even in terms your readers understand it had little meaning. They're vicarious fighters; their outlooks aren't much different than mine—except they want my skin for taking a bite from their sacred cow. Horst was a self-appointed Christ-figure. Only in martyr's terms does his death have meaning, and then only to those who believe any intelligence is holy, to be cherished, defended, and allowed to follow its own course utterly free of external influence. What he and his ilk fail to understand is that it's right down deep-streamed fundamental to the nature of our intelligence to interfere, overpower, exploit and obliterate. We did it to one another before First

Expansion; we've done it to Toke, Ulantonid and Sangaree; we'll continue doing it.
"In terms of accomplishment, yes, he bought something with his life, An injunction against Ubichi operations on Camelot. There's your meaning, but one that makes sense only in an ethical framework most people won't comprehend. Believe me, I've tried. But I'm incapable of seeing the universe and its contents in other than tool-cattle terms. Now have the balls to tell me I'm in the minority."
From a private letter by Salvador del Gado.

—Dogfight

XIII

According to the latest, the relationship between Manta and whale is far more complex than anyone at Ubichi ever guessed. (Guessed—Ubichi never cared. Irked even me that at the height of Corporate operations, Ubichi had only one exobiologist on planet—a virologist-bacteriologist charged with finding some disease with which to infect the whales. Even I could appreciate the possible advantages in accumulation of knowledge.) At best, we thought, when the intelligence theory had gained common currency, the whales served as cattle for the mantas. . .

Not so, say Confederation's researchers. The mantas only *appear* to herd and control the whales. The whales are the true masters. The mantas are their equivalent of dogs, fleet-winged servants for the ponderous and poorly maneuverable. Their very slow growth of ability to cope with our aerial tactics wasn't a function of a cyclic increase in intelligence, it was a reflection of the difficulty the whales had projecting their defensive needs into our much faster and more maneuverable frame of reference. By means of severely limited control.

At the time it seemed a perfectly logical assumption that the mantas were upset with us because we were destroying their food sources. (They live on a mouse-sized parasite common amongst the forest of organs on a whale's back.) It seemed much more unlikely, even unreasonable, that the whales themselves were the ones upset and were sending mantas against us, because those were better able to cope, if a little too dull to do it well. The whales always carried out the attacks on our ground facilities, but we missed the hint there.

It seems the manta was originally domesticated to defend whales from a pterodactyl-like flying predator, one which mantas and whales had hunted almost to extinction by the time Ubichi arrived on Camelot. As humans and dogs once did with wolves. Until the

123

government report we were only vaguely aware of the creatures. They never bothered us, so we didn't bother them.

The relationship between whales and mantas is an ancient one, one which domestication doesn't adequately describe. Nor does symbiosis, effectively. Evolution has forced upon both an incredibly complex and clumsy reproductive process that leaves them inextricably bound together.

In order to go into esterus the female manta must be exposed to prolonged equatorial temperatures. She mates in the air, in a dance as complex and strange as that of earthly bees, but only with her chosen mate. Somewhat like Terran marsupials, she soon gives birth to unformed young. But now it gets weird. The marsupial pouch (if such I may call it for argument's sake) is a specially developed semi-womb atop the back of a *male* whale. While instinct compels her to deposit her young there, the male whale envelopes the she-manta in a clutch of frondlike organs, which caress her body and leave a whitish dust—his "sperm". Once her young have been transferred, the female manta goes into a kind of travel-frenzy, like a bee flitting from flower to flower visiting all nearby whales. Any receptive female she visits will, with organs not unlike those of the male, stroke the "sperm" from her body.

Incredibly complicated and clumsy. And unromantic. But it works.

We never would've learned of it but for Horst—who, I think, had nothing of the sort in mind when he let that old manta bolt him down.

And that's about all there is to say. It's a puzzle story. Why did von Drachau do it? I don't know—or don't want to know—but I work under severe handicaps. I'm an Old Earther. I never had a father to play push-me pull-you with my life. I never learned to care much about anything outside myself. A meager loyalty to companions in action is the best I've ever mustered. But enough of excuses.

The fighting with mantas continued four years after Horst's death, through several lesser migrations that never reached the mating grounds. Then a government inquiry board finally stepped in—after Commander McClennon and Fleet Admiral von Drachau had spent three years knocking on doors at Luna Command (Ubichi's wealth has its power to blind). Their investigations still aren't complete, but it seems they'll rule Camelot permanently off limits. So Horst did buy something with his life. Had he not died, I doubt the Commander would've gotten angry enough to act.

That he did so doesn't entirely please me, of course. I inherited his position. Though I pulled down a handsome income as JG XIII's wing leader and on-going top killer, I loathed the administrative donkey work. Still, I admire the courage he showed.

I also admire Horst, despite his shortcomings, despite myself. But he wasn't a hero, no matter what people want to hear me say. He was a snot-nosed kid used to getting his own way who threw a suicidal tantrum when he saw there was no other way to achieve his ends. . .

And that's it, the rolling down of the socks to expose the feet of clay. Believe the stories or believe his wingman. It's all the same to me. I've got mine in and don't need your approval.*

*Not true, in your editor's opinion. Especially in his private communications, del Gado seems very much interested in finding approval of things he has done. Perhaps he has a conscience after all. He certainly seems desperate to find justification for his life.

—Dogfight

Shall we be thrown back to an earlier kind of life—one where living is simpler, more dependent on the natural realm, where the skills of science and future technologies are in the past, forgotten, scarcely needed? Pangborn is always concerned with the quality of life, wherever it is lived. He knows that we all sometimes yearn not to rule and dominate, or even to know, but to build modestly for happiness and simply. . .live in the world. His story here is an alternative view of a future world. But Pangborn knows that every alternative has its price. Here the knowledge and techniques which might help the living of human lives do not exist, hence certain tragedies cannot be prevented. Yet even without our kind of knowledge and skill, other kinds of obstacles can still be surmounted; bravery must work harder, and happiness is possible. In this world our world shows itself as ruins and litter washed up from the past. Ultimately Pangborn is concerned with the ecology and value of living and the learning of what to live for. These things emerge all the more clearly because they are set in a future world stripped of its mask of misused knowledge harnessed to power. . .

G.Z.

HARPER CONAN & SINGER DAVID

Edgar Pangborn

DONSIL village stands inland sixty miles from the Hudson Sea. About twenty families, a good inn at the four corners where West Road meets South, a green with an open market, a town hall and a church. Conan the Hunter, son of Evan, Master Silversmith, was born in this small hamlet. Binton Ruins, which Conan visited in later years—that's forty miles off down the West Road. Word of them—rumor, legend, gossip—had reached him in childhood, and they possessed their own dark place among the creations of his mind. When he learned to play the lyre his father made for him, one of the first of his own songs was a fantasy belonging to that place: his mind saw desolate ground, fields of tumbled rocks that had once formed the bones of houses, the stubs of once great buildings like blackened tree stumps after a fire; but since his eyes had never seen Binton Ruins, Conan's poem spoke of all ruins everywhere, all the loss of Old Time. Later, much later, when David led him into the neighborhood of the actual Binton Ruins in pursuit of a fabulous rumor, Conan understood the direction of the journey he was making. The west winds cooled his face; his hand was spread out on David's shoulder for communication, or it was grasped by David's hand; for at that time Conan the Hunter had become Harper Conan, and he was blind.

In his eighteenth summer, already well known for skill with bow and spear, for his endurance and courage and acute vision, Conan had gone on a bear hunt out of Donsil with three or four young and turbulent companions. It was the Month of Strawberries, of June

127

passions. After the killing the young men rejoiced, and sang in praise of the bear's bravery and for propitiation of his gods. They wrestled in the early summer air, and bathed in a pool where they found exciting diving from a high bank—delightful and treacherous diving. Since Conan was stronger than any of them, taller, perhaps more eager to discover and display the outer limits of his strength and skill, his last dive carried him out where a rock lurking under water cut his skull. Terrified and heartbroken—one of them had been daring him on —his friends got him out on the bank and found that he breathed, slowly and harshly. Breathing so but aware of nothing (so far as we know, so far as he could ever remember) he lay at home for ten days before recovering awareness of his surroundings, and then he was blind.

Evan the Silversmith, his father, was praying. Evan was a valued and formidable man in the village, his work known well beyond it: a proud and religious man, now frightened and humbled. "Deliver back to me, O God, my true-beloved son who does not know me, whose soul is wandering the outer fields before the natural time! Deliver him back to me, and I will offer up—"

"Father, I know your voice. I'm here. Will you light a candle?" Conan understood, by the smell and feel of things, that he was lying on the bearskin of his room at home.

"Now God be thanked! Oh, a thousand candles! I am answered. But look at us, Conan! Look at your mother and me!"

"Why, I can't see you. Isn't it midnight?" The air stirred before his face. He knew his father's hand had passed in front of his eyes. He heard his mother weeping. Presently, his father's trembling embrace, and a long trouble of words. Midnight remained.

"CONAN," his father said—weeks afterward, when the boy had begun to learn his way about in the dark country, to develop the careful, not quite heartbreaking art of seeing with his fingers and ears and nose—"Conan, son, it's not so great a thing to be a hunter. I was skillful in it once; I taught you. But when I learned the mystery of making good things from metals, I found I cared much less for other work. Of course I was pleased when you became the best of the hunters, but something else has been closer to my desires for a long time. There's something all good men do, and we call it making the most of what happens. I don't know whether that means accepting God's guidance or merely taking whatever comes and thinking about it, examining it, more deeply than a fool can do or a sorrowful man

128

find the patience to do." He set in Conan's grasp a cool framework, of silver by the feel of it. Conan's exploring fingers found a base that could rest on his left arm, or on a table, and a mechanism that could be studied. Most admirable was the waiting presence of taut cords and wires, which murmured to his touch as though a god has said: *I am here to become a part of you*.

"This lyre I made," said Evan Silversmith, "under the guidance of Harper Donal of Brakaþin. He tells me that one comes to the great harp later, after learning this. But one never abandons this first instrument, he says, if one has the fire for it, the voice to sing with it, the heart to speak through the song. Harper Donal came here once, and you won't have forgotten it. But I remember how even before then you made songs for yourself in childhood. I think your ear is true, though I'm no judge. You shall go live a while with Donal at Brakabin. It's arranged—he wishes it, he remembers the listening child you were. He's very old. You'll find ways of being useful to him in his feebleness, and he'll teach you all he can. You may not possess what he calls the fire: he will know."

"My father, if I haven't it I will find it."

"A brave saying, possibly an unwise one. Harper Donal spoke to me of the many who waste life trying to find it, only to learn it's not for them. And then, he says, it may blaze up in some who haven't the strength to bear it. Dangerous country, Conan."

"I must explore it. I think I can do that."

"Go then with my love and blessing. Learn to give people music as I give them the work of my hands."

Therefore, with the consent of Chief Councilman Oren and the other Elders, Conan went north and lived with Harper Donal at Brakabin for four years, learning first the art of singing with the lyre. Donal himself had learned this from one of the Waylands of Trempa, who may have learned it from Esau of Nupal, who could have learned it from a musician born in Old Time whose name is lost. That legendary one survived the Red Plague and lived to a great age, traveling through Katskil and teaching music (also something called philosophy) to the children at Nuber, Cornal, elsewhere as far north as Gilba, as far south as Sofran. Some say the Old Time singer and visionary was one Aron of Penn. Others claim this legendary figure was a woman, Alma of Monsella, who composed the best of our hymns in praise of God and his Son and Prophet Abraham. Look also on a bothersome contradiction that intrudes here: not one of the Old Time books we possess mentions the art of singing to the lyre in connection with that period they called the Twentieth Century. In other words we're in the habit of believing numerous lies, and no-

129

body knows much, and every civilization has bloated itself on vanity, and most of them have died of it.

As he studied and grew, it appeared to Conan that although the fire burgeoned in his heart and hands, it was absent from his voice. His singing, in his own judgment, was good but never more than good, which is the devil of a thing—any artist will know what he meant. However, nobody can hear the timbre of his own voice. Harper Donal told him he sang rather well, which from Donal was next to the highest praise. (The old man's highest was to say that a student had done not too badly.) Then at the appropriate time Donal taught him the handling of the great harp, which is to the art of the lyre as the ocean to a brook.

Conan took to this study with a brilliance that dumfounded his master. Harper Donal's maidservant, a kindly taciturn woman of Moha, noticed that because Conan could not see it, Harper Donal grew careless about his face, something she had not observed in thirty years of worshipful service. A teacher must maintain his mask of varied uses, but Donal's lessons with this boy were frequently illuminated by smiles, astonished frowning, starting of water to the old man's eyes. A marvel like Conan's rapid learning of the harp is not unheard of. Donal had taught many other fine players and singers; he remembered and loved them all, and followed their fortunes. Technique is in itself no mystery. Donal himself used to say so, and to him it was a commonplace. The mystery prevails in the mind and heart that bridle technique and ride it out beyond the morning mist.

A time came when Conan heard his teacher declare he was playing not badly. Moments later the maidservant touched Conan's shoulder. He was then playing, at Donal's request, the rowdy joyful dance *Elderberry Time*, composed by Donal in his own youth. She told Conan his teacher had smiled, nodded, and ceased to breathe.

This was Harper Donal's passing, as Conan knew of it. No doubt there had been the usual sad small indignities of dying, while Harper Donal's own merry music was making nothing of them.

AT the funeral Conan played and sang the laments and other traditional music, in the company of two or three others whom the Brakabin Town Council found fit for the honor. And at that time the Council told the blind youth that the will of Donal bequeathed him the golden harp thought to have once belonged to Alma of Monsella. Donal had already spoken of this intention to the boy, so he was prepared with acceptable words and able to speak them with the graciousness expected by the Council. They were old men, wise, kindly, and rather stuffy. But then—(etiquette required, by the way, that he ask the Council's permission; greater fires than grief were burning in Conan, and he just forgot it)—Conan played and sang his own lament for his ancient master. The golden harp was in his hands. Part of the *Lament for Donal* came as an impromptu, born that moment, and a few of his hearers were disturbed.

Donal is dead, who sang for the morning.
Out of the gray cavern his song bore us the glow,
the warmth of fruitful daytime.
Out of the stillness music he wakened;
out of the winter gloom his song brought us the green
and gold of fruitful springtime.
    Sing for Donal as I cannot, waking birds!
    Sing for Donal as I dare not, waking winds!
    Sing for Donal, jonquils and violets delivered from the
      snow!
    Sing as I cannot,
    for Donal is dead, who sang the morning.
I fear long life, knowing now that song perishes
and the earth lies still, unloved.

Donal is dead, who hymned the sunny roads,
sang for the sweet dimness, sang the tale of the deer-paths,
the hush of summer clearings.
In loveless age the music of companions
rang in his song, telling of loyalty and love,
of summer journeying.
    Sing for Donal as I cannot, wanderers!
    Sing for Donal as I dare not, true companions!
    Sing for Donal, lovers delivered by his music from the
      dark!
    Sing as I cannot,
    for Donal is dead, who sang the high noon.
I fear great love, knowing now that song perishes
and the flesh lies still, unkissed.

Donal is dead, his melody the evening.
Out of day's melting his song draws on the stars

that stir in the harbor of the hills.
Out of the evening, music he wakened.
Out of the summer and the winter night his song
harbored beyond the Pleiades.
　　Sing for Donal as I cannot, constant stars!
　　Sing for Donal as I dare not, autumn winds!
　　Sing for Donal, mountains that knew him, streams
　　　　that cooled his feet!
　　Sing as I cannot,
　　for Donal is dead in the world's evening.
I will live and love, knowing that no song perishes
while one soul lives to hear.

Certainly there were those whom the *Lament for Donal*
disturbed. They believed, those nice old men, that blind Conan
might have been more concerned with his conscious art than with his
dead teacher. It never occurred to them how immensely this would
have pleased Harper Donal himself, who might have snorted that he
thought there was already grief enough on earth without the custom-
ers complaining about short measure. But the Council was gener-
ous, too, and gave the young musician a safe escort out of Brakabin,
all the way home through the forest and hill country with his golden
harp.

Thus Conan in his twenty-second year returned to his father's
dwelling at Donsil. After four years in the house of Donal of Brakabin, this was one way of beginning his journey into the world. Evan
the Silversmith, whose obscure talent for fatherhood amounted to
genius, didn't ask the boy what he planned to do next.

DONSIL enjoys the many annual festivals of music, and takes pride
and pleasure in accommodating them. That inn at the four corners is
rather large; several private houses, especially the communal types,
also invite paying guests at festival times. Other visitors can camp a
few nights in the town's groves that spread out from the green like
wheel spokes, if they mind their manners. Since they have come for
the music, they generally do, even to the extent of picking up their
own trash and using the public latrines. A village of hospitality is
worth a bit of kindness.

Donsil makes a good thing out of festival times financially, but
that has little to do with the emotional climate of the place. History
tells of a school of Old Time sociologists, safely extinct we may hope,

132

to whom the dollar-value of the music festivals would have provided the full explanation of Donsil village. But good nature is one of those stubborn activities of the mind and heart which can be made an end in itself—like love and honesty—if human people so choose and if circumstances aren't too persistently clobbering them. Having never heard of Twentieth Century sociology, and possessing a small enclave so far only moderately oppressed by a developing feudal tyranny from above, the Donsil villagers were free to be pleasant folk. Somehow, at least in this one little spot of the world, after the long dark of the Years of Confusion when savagery ruled and most remnants of civilization were forced to shelter behind wooden stockades relearning the primitive arts (and forgetting much)—somehow the sick money-greed of Old Time had diminished to a manageable intensity. Human beings were still as a rule greedy animals—of course. But the bloated hugeness of Old Time society, and its ghastly illusion of success, had favored piggishness at every turn, often openly making a virtue of it.

Since we create our own ends and purposes, whether or not we invent gods to blame them on, it would be astonishing if we didn't create plenty of stinkers. But a survival society, unless it is content with a pretty flabby and boring goal of day-to-day eating, security and copulation, actually cannot afford the perversion of piggishness. Donsil had discovered music.

The incursions of visitors at well spaced and predictable intervals had also encouraged, even driven Donsil's citizens into developing the art of composing to a remarkable degree of efficiency. In the best of human societies as well as the worst, one thing does lead ·to another, and we do all get to learn a few cute tricks. Culture, anthropologists call it.

TO Donsil, several times, while Conan was away at Brakabin, had come the young singer David of Maplestock, at first with a traveling choir for the festival of Midsummer Eve, celebrated in this country on the fourth day of July. He did not sing alone that time. It was merely noted how brilliant the Maplestock choir sounded in the tenor section—too brilliant for the rest; in fact for that reason the famous choir only won second prize, nosed out of first place by the Nupal Glee. Later that year, before the Harvest Festival—not any special occasion but the will of his own wandering—David came to Donsil alone, and drew crowds to the green for three days before he moved on. He could have stayed another three and repeated his repertory; the crowds would not have diminished, for when something like that occurs, word goes around the countryside.

A wanderer by nature was David, at any rate he said so, claiming not to know where he was born. It might have been in a gyppo wagon heading north from Moha, for his first sure memories belonged to the deep forest and mountain country of Adirondack Island. He had adopted the name "of Maplestock", he said frankly, just because he'd lived in the town a couple of years and liked it well enough. His manner suggested that further questions weren't invited. The gyppo part of his tale was clearly absurd. He couldn't be a gyp with such fair hair and gray eyes, to say nothing of a touch of accent that sounded like Penn or even the southern country, and nobody around here nowadays believes those stories about the gyppos stealing babies.

He was ugly, some felt, with his pug nose, big flexible mouth that made his eyes appear small, a jagged scar on his left cheek that could have been acquired in a knife brawl, heavy shoulders and neck and chest seeming too big for the rest of his short frame. Now and then, though rarely, a quick smile revealed good nature, a quality Donsil village always recognized, and redeemed what some thought of as his ugliness. It was never a confiding smile, just a friendly way of saying: "Give me no trouble and I'll give you none; give me some and heaven help you." He possessed an unremarkable lyre with a light frame of bronze nicely polished, and he played it well enough to accompany himself, just respectably.

When he sang, nothing else existed—no crowd, no weather good or bad, only a surpassing voice that searched out and touched every element of response in the hearer's nature, as if the singer had studied and cherished that one particular person all his life. So clear and blessed was this illusion that some felt the presence of magic and made the sign of the Wheel over their hearts. Good magic of course. Any critic would have been torn apart if he chirped while they were under the spell: a significant hazard of the profession which has an indirect bearing on Darwinian natural selection.

David's voice was rich in the baritone, and spread through some not quite believable tenor range beyond two octaves—up to a treble C if you care to believe me; I am not by profession a liar. Through that upper range the tenor quality was sustained; no hint of falsetto, no loss of power. C sharp, maybe. What mattered was not the tonal but the emotional range: no nerve of human experience that David of Maplestock could not touch.

Certainly, certainly it was magic, the magic not of hush-hush and spookery but of art, which grabs hold of any available science it needs as a carpenter reaches for a saw. It was the magic that derives from intense long labors toward a perfection admitted to be unattainable, carried on by one with adequate endowment for the art, the patience to endure, the vision to discover a goal and the road that runs there. At some early age, perhaps fifteen or sixteen, when all boys must start threading the obstacle course of booby traps that the community mindlessly dumps in their path, David had simply told himself: "I will make myself the best singer it is possible to be, given my body and my intelligence."

Councilman Oren of Donsil remarked, during those first three days when David of Maplestock visited Donsil alone, that when this young man was singing a person dying in agony of a mortal wound or illness would hold off death until the song ended. The Councilman was an honest old fellow not thought to be very imaginative, and since at that time he was suffering an illness that did prove mortal, his words were remembered with a bit of keenness.

Magic: one element is courage; another, strange though you find it, is good sense. If you happen on a genuine artist who is also a kook, that's for fun, or an accident, or because the public is in a mood to gobble it down and pay for it: under the fuss, somebody inside there knows what he's doing, otherwise the art itself would be of the sort that wilts on a second look. This form of magic was the only one possessed by Alma of Monsella, Donal of Brakabin, Conan himself.

David, by the way, was no sort of kook, just a rugged young man who minded his own business. He never tried to be flamboyant. As a matter of course he wore the mouse-brown shirt and loin-rag and sandals that have come to be like a uniform for itinerant minstrels. His singing inevitably drove women insane. In this matter he tried to conduct himself with good manners and kindness. What great singer could go to bed with all of them? They don't *make* that kind of bed.

David was heard of from distant places, word drifting back on the tongues of other wanderers—from Moha, Vairmant, Conicut, the Bershar mountain land, even from Main. Yet he returned to Donsil—drawn to the town and its inn, he said, by Mam Selby's corn fritters, and he was indeed observed consuming those culinary poems with the vigor of a starved farmer. Donsil had come to expect David's frequent returns, and his name was much in the common talk on the spring days after Conan came home.

"HE is truly one of the great singers, my father?"

"So far as I am a judge," said Evan the Silversmith. Others might, and did, make the dull error of belittling David of Maplestock with the notion of soothing the jealousy they imagined the blind youth to be feeling; not Evan. Conan since his homecoming had sung a little, and played, and his music was praised not on its merits (he felt) but merely because he was one of the town's own, originally Conan the Hunter. His singing, as he knew himself, was no great wonder; the power and strangeness and harmonic discoveries of his harp-playing seemed to be over their heads, and probably were: no one had told Donsil village that there was anything uncommon here to admire. He was just Evan's boy, and had made himself a fine harp-player—very nice. "When David of Maplestock sings," said Evan Silversmith, "one thinks and cares about nothing else except to hope that he will soon sing again."

"I can never become a singer of that kind. But I am a player of the harp. In another year or two I shall be a great one."

"And you compose new music."

"Not as I wish. One or two things. In the rest, so far, something's lacking, my father. I mean to learn what it is, and how to bring it into my music."

"Conan, I think I could find someone with the art of writing down your music. That ought to be done."

"Not yet. As for my songs, other singers remember them from hearing—we're trained to do so. The harp music—well, some time, but not yet. . .this David of Maplestock will sing tomorrow?"

"He came to the inn today, they tell me, dusty and tired, and Mam Selby restored him with corn fritters. Yes, he'll certainly be singing at the green tomorrow, if the day's fair."

"My father. . ." The Silversmith's hand on his arm told him to continue. "The fire is in me. Donal of Brakabin believed so. In the music of the harp, not in my voice, which can obey only so far as nature allows. Music is—a world in itself. I have no other way to explain it, maybe I need none. I am finding ways to explore that world, ways that I think no one has discovered, unless it was done in Old Time and then lost. New avenues. They open slowly."

Next day in that time of afternoon when the height of town hall and church hold the village green in comfortable shade, Conan with his father and mother went down the slope from the house of Evan the Silversmith to the village. Town folk and visitors were gathering; Evan described them for his blind son, who already sensed their presence. And as Conan's footsteps began to tell him of level ground, a song passed him on the air, one of the old airy love lyrics of Esau of Nupal, with the freshness of breeze and bird wings.

My love is fair like summer leaves,
like autumn fruit my love is fair.

But when this trifle of delight had gone on its way—one could only love the singer, without need of thought—Conan halted in astonishment, hearing the voice, to an unknown simple accompaniment of the lyre, sound a plangent outcry—

Donal is dead, who sang for the morning.
Out of the gray cavern–

Clearly someone who heard him at Brakabin had remembered, as the minstrels of today are expected to do. But David of Maplestock broke off the *Lament* after only a few lines. At Conan's side his mother exclaimed: "Why, he's coming to us, Conan! Do you know him?"

"In a way I do, Mother."

Then his hand was grasped, the voice was coming to him with warmth and assurance: "I was afraid you might not be here, Harper Conan." One doesn't use "Harper" as a title unless the person one speaks to is an acknowledged master; the silent, friendly-breathing crowd around them knew this. "Man, where's your harp? I must sing this with the music they heard at Brakabin and couldn't remember for me, the music none but you can play. At best I'm only a singer." The crowd rumbled a bit of laughter, but Conan knew he had spoken with no thought of jesting. "Where's your harp?"

"I will bring it, Singer David," said Evan of Donsil, Master Silversmith. Conan in his daze heard an unfamiliar happiness in his father's voice. Relief, too, if that is the just word: the relief of one who sees the sun come out on a day that had promised gray sadness; for Evan was another of those incalculable eccentrics who do not build their lives on jealousy.

THEY played and sang together that afternoon, as wind and bright cloud belong together, or sea and sky, arm and hand. Some listeners later said that until that day they had scarcely been aware of their own man, Conan son of Evan. The quiet, the hushed, almost diffident quality of the crowd's reception, derived mainly from astonishment at what happened when these two musicians came together without rehearsal, without having even met before. The applause though not loud, was persistent, entranced; it was long before the villagers permitted the music to end. Then Conan and David, allowed to be alone, walked across the fields together.

It may seem strange that a village noted for good nature should also excel in tact. Some of it the people might have picked up from Evan Silversmith and a few like him; but Donsil is an uncanny place in its own right. Not fantastic; not out of this world exactly. One dreads to use a term so long and bitterly abused as the word "civilized", but maybe there's no other.

"I twice heard you play alone," said David, "when you were with Harper Donal of Brakabin. It was at the student concerts he arranged so rarely. I was in the crowd, and learned only that you were of Donsil. That's why I returned here several times—no reflection on Mam Selby's corn fritters: they drew me, too. There's a tree root here." As if he had performed such little services all his life, he touched Conan's arm and guided him past the obstruction.

"I wish you had spoken, at Brakabin."

"Harper Donal was rather peppery—maybe you knew—about others making contact with his students while they were in his charge. Afraid of patrons and suchlike taking them away before they had learned enough. And also, the listening crowd—what I wanted to say to you wasn't to be said in a crowd. It may surprise you, coming from a singer who's won a bit of popularity, but I'm a shy man, Conan. I suppose we all live too much in our skulls."

"Most of the time it's necessary, isn't it?"

"Yes, but not in this hour. Here's high sunny ground, let's sit a while. I must tell you first about a rumor that came to me less than a year ago—and God forgive me if I raise false hopes. It may be nothing but rumor—trash talk, deception. But I felt so much possibility of truth in it that, now we are friends, I must pass it on for what it's worth. It reached me when I was traveling the Twenyet Road, and I stopped overnight at an inn near Onanta, a dull place. One of the guests, a bright old man, was on his way home to Skendy in northern Moha. I thought him sober and sensible. He was telling about his experience with a group of healers who have settled, it appears, right in the middle of Binton Ruins. You may already have heard something about them?"

"Not of any healers. Word might have reached Donsil, but I have been at Brakabin until only a short while ago, and Harper Donal, as you say, didn't want the world coming close to his students. Even here at Donsil news from the west is slow in reaching us. Most of our festival visitors come from the more civilized parts—Nuin, Conicut. I know of Binton Ruins, however. They say it's very desolate."

"It is. I've never gone inside the limits of the place, only skirted the fringes, and that's dreary. I went there from curiosity after meeting that old man at Onanta. From Skendy southwest to Binton Ruins, the way the roads twist, must be well over a hundred miles. The old man couldn't afford a litter for that. His back was in such continuous pain that he couldn't ride, and dreaded the jolting of a cart, the only vehicle he owned, more than the ordeal of struggling along on crutches. His wife and daughter and one old friend made the pilgrimage with him, so there was love to help him walk. If the healers had failed him, he told us, he would as lief have lain down and died there at Binton Ruins as anywhere else—the pain was that severe, and had been with him so long that it was shoving everything else out of his life. It disgusted him: he had no desire to exist as a creeping bag of pain. . .they healed him, Conan. As he told us the story the old boy kept getting up on his feet, grinning and proud, to show us how well he could walk."

"They healed him."

"Not long after this came the first time I heard you play, at Brakabin. It never occurred to me you were blind; no one told me. The second time, someone did, but I feared—oh, false hopes—and I may be raising them now, doing harm when I only wish—"

"Whatever comes from your heart is good, David of Maplestock."

"Conan—probably these strange people at Binton Ruins *can't* do anything for blindness. It's only a mad hope. All I know about them comes from what this old man said, and some—some talk I've picked up since then in my travels, bits and pieces that I don't really credit. I value the old man's story because he was so intelligent, because there seemed no doubt that they had cured him of a great trouble. But when it comes to—oh, curing the smallpox, making the dead walk—ach, who knows? For example, his wife and friend and daughter never talked directly with the healers, and they were convinced it was all a blessed magic, or maybe not so blessed, anyhow something they didn't want to inquire into closely. Rumors from other sources will have it that the healers are wizards of Old Time who've been living underground or off on a cloud somewhere, praise Abraham, amen—damned nonsense. They say the healers have something called a generator, a machine that creates the Old Time marvel of electricity, whatever that was. They say they can regenerate lost organs—arms, legs—"

"They say that?"

"Rumor does. They say, they say."

"But they did heal the old man's pain."

"Yes. According to what *he* said—and he'd talked with them, listened, asked questions that I'm sure were intelligent—according to him they don't even call themselves healers. They describe their work as inquiry, themselves as seekers. The old man said they have books of method and knowledge—neither he nor his family could read, by the way—and it seems to me they must have kept alive or rediscovered some of the wisdom of Old Time. They used no drugs on him except a little of one of the common harmless herbs—I forget which; all the cure-women and herb-women know it—marawan?—well, I don't remember. But he said they knew a great deal on that subject, and talked with him freely about it, and about everything they did for him, in a very clear, friendly way. None of the hocus-pocus and puff-puff show that most of our ordinary doctors make to conceal their bloody ignorance. They gave him massage—better than what a Skendy cure-woman had done for him, but the same kind, and they kept him a fairly long time in a cool, quiet room with nice meals, and frequent visits from several of them, not very many from his family. All this right there in the middle of those haunted ruins, in a few of the Old Time buildings that they've been able to make useful. They have an area out near the fringe of the ruins where friends and relatives of sick people can camp, and food comes in from farms in the neighborhood. The old man lost count of the days. He had rest, and a few simple exercises, and in time the pain just faded out. They warned him it might return, and told him how to care for himself if it did. They inquired what he could afford to pay, and asked half of that. . .he said only one thing, Conan, that suggested a hint of the supernatural, and though it did so to him, it might not to you or me. He said their faces had a distant, close-listening look. But surely we've all seen that look on someone who's concentrating on a problem and needs to shut away the immediate surroundings. I suppose it was the circumstances, the coming out of his long time of pain, that made the old man find something remarkable in it. I believe the healers were just listening to their own thoughts as we all do."

"Will you go with me to this place, Singer David?"

"With all my heart, and we'll make music on the road."

"How can this be?" said the blind harper. But he spoke like one who says: *How strange that the sun rises!*

"Since I first heard you play, Harper Conan, I've desired to go with you, and be your eyes, my voice reminding you how the fields look under the sun, wherever you go and as long as we live. I am only a singer; I had never imagined the country you explore with your harp until you made it known to me: there you must be my guide. But if there were no music in the world, in a world of the deaf and blind, Conan, still I would love you."

THE mother of Conan had been and still was a true believer in the near and constant presence of God, a faith that Evan's skepticism never attempted to assail, though now and then he used the defensive weapon of silence. Her faith made her vulnerable to bewilderment at the stark happening of her son's blindness: it had come on him so like God's punishment!—but what had he done so terrible as to deserve it? Surely she knew all his sins great and small! And she would count them over, and try to measure them against a lifetime of darkness—yet God cannot err—and so on and so on around a circle, with no result except that chronic bewilderment, embittered now by seeing how blithely Conan went down the road in the company of a stranger, when she had only just welcomed him back from the long absence at Brakabin. He walked with a swing of the shoulders she had not seen since the days of Conan the Hunter.

Except for this inevitable pain for which there was and is no healing even within the power of Evan the Silversmith, the young men were allowed to make a quiet departure. Just a bit of a westward journey (they said). They would practice making music together, and explore the countryside for the devil of it. Without even discussing it between themselves, neither mentioned Binton Ruins.

"How can you trust that—that Maplestock man so lightly, Evan? It isn't as if they *knew* each other. And if Conan's to go haring off like this at the first whim, how will he ever get himself a decent girl and settle down the way he must?"

"I don't know, Ella."

"You sit there. You sit there and say you don't know! Where do I find the patience?"

WHEN the friends set out for Binton Ruins it was again the Month of Strawberries, a season that love must have for its own whatever the rest of the year may do in the way of sorrow and confusion.

Between Donsil and Binton Ruins the roads at their best are not much more than expanded deer trails, even where now and then some fragment of Old Time blacktop appears and runs a little way, not yet quite crumbled into lifeless black mud. The trails together with these bits of ancient road describe a shallow northward curve through a country of small hills, and turn again south toward Binton, serving on the way nothing larger than a few stockaded villages, surrounded by poorly protected fields of rye, wheat, buckwheat, corn and hay. Everywhere between these lonesome villages stands heavy forest. More pine and mixed growth, less hemlock here than in the hill country to the north, but Conan smelled the hemlock sometimes and felt its presence. Occasionally David found a spruce tree exuding a mild resinous gum that he liked to chew, finding it good for his singer's throat. These were warm days, of trust and pleasure and the making of music. David's most cherished burden was a thick sheaf of fine paper purchased long before in Maplestock, on which with quill pens and good oak gall ink he could capture his friend's harp music and the new songs that were almost daily born of Conan's mind; thus in future time they might become known, played anywhere in the world, without the loss that we know occurs when memory, even the best, is the sole means of preservation. Whole worlds, in fact, have been lost that way. It is a pity.

> *I see the road where you part the branches*
> *and run toward the sun's heart, yourself new gold*
> *in the divided light.*

> *I see the brook where you stand in beauty*
> *and lift the bright stream to cool your flesh*
> *in the still-shining day.*

> *I see the night where you hold the shadows*
> *around me like a shelter: your mouth is sweet*
> *with deep-forest spices.*

"Ah, Conan, who would know you were not singing of what your own eyes tell you?"

"As I shall be soon. As I shall be."

"But Conan, Conan—" There was great fear in David's voice, remaining when Conan told him not to be afraid; but Conan grasped his arms and wrestled him laughing to the ground, and then nothing more was said that touched on the healers of Binton Ruins until a day when the two came out into open country drenched in sunlight, and Conan heard distant voices and clatter from the campsite at the border of the dead city. David said: "We have come to it. The camp is bigger than when I saw it less than a year ago. O Conan, remember—"

"That it may be useless, certainly. But here is no illusion," said Conan, and kissed his cheek.

ON the edge of a mighty field of rubble stood a three-story building of ancient style, stark and alone, a fragment of Old Time not quite submerged. From the structure a fence ran in both directions to the surrounding woods. Everywhere on the rubbled ground, among slowly disintegrating heaps of plaster, brick, metal that could not rust, indestructible plastic garbage and other rubbish of every sort, vegetation had found small footholds of available earth and declared the intention to live. Behind the fence the same sort of desolation continued until hidden by a rise of ground, but beyond that here and there the ruined upper parts of tall structures appeared, hazy and meaningless. All this David described to his friend. The fence, he remarked, looked sturdy and forbidding, while those shut out by it showed no resentment, no notion of defying it. The building looked like a place under invisible siege, asserting property rights to a section of the calamity of history. "When I came here before," said David, "only a few dozen people were camping here, and they were all relatives or friends of the sick, who were being cared for at some place deep in the ruins. Word must have been traveling, Conan. I remember this isolated house, but there was no fence then. Now, by the look of it, there must be two or three hundred in the camp, with many sick people among them, waiting."

"Then we must wait too." Conan smelled the crowd, a dull stink of people who had scant facilities for washing or caring for themselves or disposing of their own pollutions. A little dog barked stupidly on and on—*ack-ack—ack-ack—ack-ack*—nerve-rasping and unappeasable. With the same persistence, a baby unanswerably wept.

Two men were posted at the entrance of the house, and a woman with a book. She sat at a desk. Since her face invited them, David led his friend to her. Casual and kind, she asked: "What is your trouble, sir?"

"I have far less trouble than most people," said Conan, "for I am a minstrel, and we rejoice in our work. Music comes to me, I love and am loved, my friend is a singer like no other. But it is true that my eyes are blind."

"Were you born blind, my dear?"

"No," said Conan, and he told her of his injury, of the ten days lost out of his life. Her friendly quietness made it easy to speak. When he had finished, the silence was long and thoughtful; David's hand on his arm counseled patience. The quality of the woman's voice had told Conan that she was of middle years, herself patient.

"Come," she said at last, and he heard her rise.

"My friend with me."

"Wherever he goes," David said, "I am his eyes until his own eyes are healed."

She hesitated, but then said: "Of course. I hope we can help you. If we can't—and there are many we can't help at all—you still have the greatest of all forces for healing."

They understood her. They followed her into the building and up a flight of stairs to a room at the rear which held a pleasant scent of dried herbs. Here the monotone discomfort of the crowd was hushed to a murmur no more intrusive than the sound of a waterfall off in the woods. A man's cordial voice exclaimed: "Why, Sara, surely nothing ails these handsome cubs? What a beautiful harp! They must have come to entertain the old man."

"Your voice isn't old, sir," Conan said.

"My voice—oh, I understand." Conan heard the woman Sara going away, and David guided him into a chair and stood by him, his hand on Conan's shoulder communicating in a language that had been growing wider and more fluent with every day that passed. The cordial voice continued: "I am Marcus of Ramapo. Do not call me doctor—it would have been fitting in Old Time; not now. Not healer either, as so many insist on calling us—there are too many we cannot heal. I am a member of our small society of inquiry. I have some knowledge of sickness and health, ancient and modern; not very much. Tell me who you are, so that I can look intelligent and write something in a big book."

"We are Harper Conan and Singer David."

"Singer David of Maplestock? Why, I heard you, sir. I heard you at Albani in Moha a year ago, but I was far out in the crowd and could hardly see your face, or I'd have recognized you. I have never forgotten it, Singer David."

"When you hear Harper Conan play, you'll never forget that, Marcus of Ramapo."

"I believe it. Well—now tell me what happened." And when Conan had done so he sighed, and Conan heard the soft tap of his fingers on the edge of his book. David's hand said only: *Be patient. I'm here with you.*

"Do you have headaches?" asked Marcus of Ramapo.

"Sometimes. Not always very bad, and when they pass all's well."

"When was the last one, as near as you remember?"

"It will have been the day after I came home from Brakabin, a little over two weeks before I met my friend, and we have been more than a week on the road, lazing along. We spent two days in a good place, not traveling at all. A month, say, since the last headache that was bad enough to remember."

"And before that one?"

"Two months, about."

"Headaches like that before your injury, too?"

"Why, in those days I scarcely knew what a headache was."

"Any suggestion of vision returning?"

"Not real vision. Flashes—like light, perhaps, but—well, like what anyone sees if he bumps his head or presses his eyeballs, only the flashes come with no cause like that."

"Nausea?"

"Nay, hardly ever. I eat like a hog."

"Like a thin hog," said David.

"Drowsiness when you should be wakeful?"

"Once in a while."

MARCUS of Ramapo asked a number of other questions, his voice brooding and mild; and David later told his friend that the lean, sad, bearded face of Marcus had certainly shown a listening look—but as David had guessed, it was the look of a man listening with all his powers to a thousand books and a thousand years, and the magic of it was the magic of a human mind reaching for light in darkness. At length Marcus of Ramapo said: "Gentlemen—I will not say that we can never help you. If you come to us again in a few years—who knows? Our knowledge is growing, very slowly. In a few years it just might be possible to attempt some of the simpler kinds of brain surgery that were practised in Old Time. We have some of the books—a few, never enough, but we search all the time. I myself have tried some easy surgical techniques on little forest monkeys and other animals—with not much success. Do you understand, gentlemen? There is no body of experience, no tradition to support us. Only what we can win from the books. No industry—no chemistry, physics, engineering, nothing at all of the great interdependent disciplines that Old Time medicine and surgery could take for granted as part of their environment. All gone down the drain, and so long ago! Two hundred years some say—I would guess more than that. We don't even understand asepsis enough to be successful with it—that's the technique of preventing infection; we know most of the principles and theory, but we haven't the chemistry or the practical experience. Look at the rubble out there, and this one creaky building that somehow managed to stay upright long enough for us to come shore it up. A good monument it is to Old Time, a civilization wrecked apparently by the old, old union of politics and stupidity, plus the horror of misused science. Come, boys—I'd like to show you our—hospital and laboratory, let me call them; I suppose nobody will dispute my use of the nice old words. If you see what we are trying to do, perhaps a thought of it will come into your music now and then, Conan and David, and that way a little something of us will continue even if we fail altogether or are destroyed."

"Destroyed, sir?" said Conan. "Destroyed?"

"At least a third of those people out there hate us for not accomplishing the impossible. Oh, they would far better go to the famous shrines of the saints, and some would be cured, too, seeing how great a part imagination plays in it—I can say that to you because of what I see in your faces. Yes, we've been attacked by the angry once or twice—our reason for the fence. Harder is the desperate expectant staring of those who never get angry, but simply insist in their thought that somehow we *must* be able to lift a stick of magic called science, and heal some walking shell already half dead. Gentlemen, I am certainly talking too much—so seldom we meet anyone here who is fresh and brave. Seldom anyone even young, for that matter—except the mue babies, except the mue babies—oh, I talk too much!" But as he spoke he had lifted his book, with deliberate care to make no noise with it, and turned it outward so that David must read: *I recognize your love for him. He may have several years or only a few; or I may be mistaken. Never, never leave him.*

THEN Conan and David left the building and followed Marcus across the rubbled area, up and over the rise of ground and into what must long ago have been the center of a large city. Endless blocks of houses, most of them fallen and covered with creeping vines but not all—some were upright, as very old men and women might lean into each other's shoulders if they were trying to stand against a wind. They crossed broad squares still partly paved, and David was alert that Conan should not stumble. Once Marcus said: "Feeble attacks, hardly even mobs, you know, but soon they'll be around us in greater numbers. We live strangely, gentlemen. We heal a few, we learn——but then, how can you tell them not to spread the word? How could we make them understand that the recovery of wisdom takes a long time? I'll tell you something, knowing it will be safe with you. Our group—we are only fifteen—has decided to move again, this coming winter. Three times we've been driven out by hordes of the sick we could not heal, many of them hating us. We began in Penn, moved out to the edge of the wilderness country, moved again south, then here. After this month we'll admit no more to the hospital except those we could take with us. Seems harsh? Well, it's decided so. Next year we shall be near the coast of Adirondack Island. Come to us again, on the far chance that I shall have learned enough to help you, Conan. A small chance, but I shall work toward it."

"What brought the blindness on me, can you say?"

"Oh, the injury. Our eyes see through our brains. In some manner your injury damaged the connection of eye and brain. Sight may return—don't hope for it, I only say it may. I can do nothing now, Harper Conan—if I attempted it, you would die. But next year, or the next—who knows?"

"Then I will live with blindness," said Conan, "and I honor you for telling me the truth. It's not hard—I have my love and my music."

"This building was truly a hospital in Old Time," said Marcus, and they entered a place of stone walls and floors. "The old machines are all useless—depended on electricity. If there was iron in them, there's rust, and anything adaptable for a weapon or tool was long ago stolen." They passed some open doorway; Conan heard muted voices, and someone whimpering. "In here"—Marcus greeted someone passing and opened a squeaking door—"here we have a toy that we put together from an ancient book. I have crazy hopes about it, gentlemen—you know, in our group they sometimes laugh at me for hoping too much. The thing's called a generator. There's the remains of a big Old Time generator in the cellar, along with a thousand other gadgets, covered with dust—no fuel even if we knew how to repair and operate them." Something buzzed under his hand.

"Describe it for me, David." But David only made a harsh noise in his throat, startled by the contraption, Conan supposed.

"He's stepped over to the window," said Marcus, and touched Conan's arm peacefully. "Some things in this place are a bit grim for a newcomer. Well, this generator toy—God, the thing hardly has the power to galvanize the leg of a frog." The buzzing ceased. "And

147

yet, Conan, an electric current no stronger than this was once made to do marvelous things. Believe this, I *know* it to be true: in Old Time there was a device for sending a tiny wire down through the great vein in the throat, as far as a heart that had ceased beating, and the light push of an electric current made that heart beat again, and sometimes the one who would have died lived for years afterward in quite fair health. Also"—but his voice sagged, and Conan felt his hand shiver as he took it away—"there's word in the writings of bringing about a regeneration of entire lost organs through the stimulus of a weak electric field. Experimental work was being done on that when the world blew up. Well, carry it in your imagination. Find a song in it, if songs are made that way—I don't know. I suppose I shouldn't take up your time with this any more. Your friend is disturbed because down the corridor we passed a room with some very sick patients, and the door was open."

"I'm all right," said David, returning. "Wasn't expecting it, that was all. They didn't look so bad."

"Are they too sick to enjoy a little music?"

"Oh," said Marcus—"no, they are not. Would you do that for us, Conan? David?"

David cleared his throat. "I am not disturbed, Marcus of Ramapo. I will sing, and Conan will make music with me. Conan, let's give them *Jo Buskin's Wedding* and *Elderberry Time*—then your tarantella for the harp, and—and the new song I learned from you yesterday evening in the woods."

The legend says that Harper Conan and Singer David never played and sang as splendidly as they did that afternoon for the sick people in Binton Ruins. It is not known whether the two were able to come the following year to Adirondack Island; it is known that they traveled widely all over the eastern nations, and were loved. Since it was long ago, and all records confused, it is not known when Conan died. He may have lived a full lifetime: Marcus of Ramapo is said to have assured David that this well might happen, in a later moment when they spoke out of Conan's hearing; or that could be another story.

It is known (to some) that by dwelling in the present, conceding what is necessary to past and future but no more than is necessary, it is quite possible to live happily ever after.

By an interesting chance, one of the sick people in the hospital at Binton Ruins was a musician, Luisa of Sortees, with a true minstrel's memory, and she recovered and returned to her good life; for this reason the new song Conan gave them is remembered by more than legend.

HARPER CONAN & SINGER DAVID

In sleep I could not find you—
only the winter blurs of dreaming
desolate, not you, not you.

My morning sought you
over the reddening hills
and down steep shadows.

You with summer breath
found me and restored the day,
and I am content.

One yellow leaf falls
unrescued, undefended:
evening is blameless.

Winter shall be our portion,
but in the flow of foreign voices
your music known sustains me.

Human beings and their cultures are not entirely rational, or irrational. Technology has developed to fill our needs, of one kind or another. But cultures and technologies, as well as human needs, will certainly continue to evolve; and the future will be vastly different from the past. It may horrify us, yet still be quite normal, even ordinary, to the people who will live in it. Where does temporal provincialism end and genuine critical value judgment begin? James Stevens shows us a vision of the far future, one in which despite the vast and awesome changes which have taken place, something of our present human nature still lives, all but hidden in a setting of strangeness and sudden disorientation. We can see that this is a future which grew out of ours, a sophisticated flower born of our competitive and warlike needs and the possibilities inherent in bio-engineering and cybernetics. As one who looks into the mirror of this story, I will risk a judgment: the determinism of various human tendencies and techniques may lead us into an insectlike social structure, a style as set as the watercolors of this story, a world finally incapable of change. . .

G.Z.

SYN

James Stevens

"Ten clonesisters sent into the line
One took a hube and then there were nine;
Nine clonesisters fighting off their fate
One spied a skitter, then there were eight."
Caught up in the rhythms and rhymes, Cogan and her crechesister Betancourt sang this song in the Garden.
"Eight clonesisters teaming on a heaven
One caught a macro, then there were seven;
Seven clonesisters spotted by a fix
One saw a dragonfly, then there were six;
Six clonesisters hoped to stay alive
A bind peeled one clean, then there were five."
Cogan liked playing in the Garden, liked to watch how the tomatoes ripened from playperiod to playperiod, liked the smell of the dark earth. The Garden was the nicest cube in the whole hive.
"Five clonesisters in the BattleCorps
One sniffed a sniffer, then there were four;
Four clonesisters looking just like ME!
One met a labgerm, then there were three;
Three clonesisters looking just like YOU!
One flashed a stingaree, then there were two;
Two clonesisters hiding from the sun
A break in the cloudbanks, then there was one;
One clonesister fighting just for fun
EasMind snuffed her, then there were none."

Cogan and Betancourt eyed each other in impish delight as they took the eight-beat rest which made you think the song was over when it really wasn't yet. Then they took a deep breath and came in together for the surprise ending which so satisfyingly crescendoed to a close.

"I'll. . .go. . .down. . .to the TissueBank and then. . .
WesMind'll clone me and *I'll be TEN AGAIN*!!"

And if you wanted to, you could take it again from the top and the circular song could go on forever and ever with never a beginning nor an end.

Indistinguishable amid the crowd of Syns riding the workveyor, Cogan-Syn withdraws into the past. Those about her acknowledge each other's presence only to make room for new arrivals. With a sense of anticipation and desire almost painful in its intensity, they glide toward linkage with the Mind like transistors on an endless belt. Identical components alone with themselves.

Between the two Minds existed a complexity of relationships. Cogan understood them to be adversaries. If you are familiar with games theory or the philosophy of relativity or the mythos of transubstantiation or the arts of mime and sex, you are only fragilely equipped to understand, but you may nibble at the edges of comprehension.

War was the relationship in which young Cogan specialized. It raged the length and breadth of the Antarctic tundra, confined as though by prior agreement to that one region. Perhaps there had in fact been an agreement. Or perhaps things had simply resolved themselves thus. Suffice it to say that there existed something like a war limited in certain ways.

There were: targets, and missiles to seek and destroy them, provided the missiles themselves were not sought out and destroyed first; macros capable of dueling over enormous distances, convulsing the earth at a touch and ripping oxygen from the atmosphere; bacteria bred to devour metal and plasteel and bacteria able to seize men and rot them in minutes; skitters and dragonflies, sniffers and hubes, each in its own way deadly; and sunbursts; and stingarees; and more.

A heaven, operated by a team of eight highly trained clones, could stimulate a man's genitals into continuous orgasm until she died of exhaustion and neural overload. A bind could seek out a man, say a man with Cogan-Syn's face, and peel that man's head open like a putrefied bud and so allow her brain to blossom in lovely yellow petals. As is normal in matters of ordnance, there existed an official designation for this weapon, but those who manned it never called it by that name, preferring for their own reasons the name bind.

Men with Cogan-Syn's face crewed some binds and heavens as well as some dragonflies, sniffers, skitters and hubes. Other men with the same face carried out other tasks at other times and places. Cogan knew them to be daughters of her flesh, cloned from her living tissue. They were highly skilled and eminently expendable. What a society produces in quantity, it must consume in quantity.

Cogan had, of course, long been aware of the existence of clones, for did she not faithfully make her monthly deposit at the Tis-sueBank? But the first time she actually saw the men who were her twins found her unprepared for so shattering an experience. A pang as painful as a freshly opened wound stabbed her. Stunned, that portion of her brain which stood aside and observed while the remainder functioned in smooth integration with the Mind concentrated its full perception on these curious duplicates.

The realization that the men were in fact her living clonesisters filtered itself into her awareness even as an alien feeling—which could be described only as a sense of profound identification—expanded within her. Breathless excitement seized her. She understood. She loved them. Unknown, unexpected, incomprehensible, this overpowering cry of flesh to flesh terrified her.

Clones function together as teams sharing a rapport so incredibly intense that they seem more the smoothly meshed components of a single entity than a group of individuals laboring at cooperation. While young Cogan did share in the hive identity of the Mind, this identity was not a gestalt consciousness fusing the disparate beings that composed it. Rather, it linked them in isolation, keeping them ignorant of one another, each concerned only with gaining her own reward. None cared about any other; each cared only for herself and for the greater consciousness of the Mind, which none could hope to comprehend outside the meager insight achieved by the religious fanatic and the hopeless addict.

So potent a sense of human communion did her clonesisters radiate that young Cogan, even as removed as she was from the continuum she observed, could sense it as one might sense sunshine on closed eyes. True, their joy could not hope to match the inde-scribable ecstasy which is a Syn's reward for good thoughting, but in its small way, in its feelings of physical and emotional harmony, in its sense of oneness with oneself while caring for others and being cared for in turn, it was a joy enormously seductive.

Her clonesisters, sprung from her very flesh, each originally a single cell of her own tissue, each a perfect physical and likely mental replica of herself, each a living part of her. With this thought, young Cogan achieved some glimmer of understanding of the source and the strength of her abrupt surge of warmth and protectiveness. Curiously, though she knew herself to be witnessing a war and understood that her clonesisters' role called for active engagement in battle, she remained unprepared to behold their deaths.

Even while she watched from her plane outside real time, Barylli's cancer rotted one in less than three minutes of agony. A stingaree blinded another, injecting a chemical directly into her eyes which slammed her heart out of rhythm and into terminal fibrillation. One took a hube and was vaporized by the sudden concentration of her own body heat. One died from exhaustion and an overload of the nervous system caused by an endless artificially induced orgasm. One was badly burned by the trailing edge of a distant macro and died over a four-day span from lack of medical attention because clones are expendable.

Each death pierced young Cogan like a nail. Aghast, her mind scrambled to devise some means of shutting off the slaughter even as the Mind, having achieved a moment of equilibrium with its opposite, chose this moment to reward its components.

Young Cogan, distraught and mourning, grew suddenly aware of her body in its mindpod as the sensors, beamed deep into the pleasure centers of her brain, began to pulse. Her body felt catapulted upward in a physical ecstasy so exquisite as to be near indistinguishable from total pain.

The first time it happened, young Cogan understood two things very clearly: it was incredibly lovely and it was the only thing that mattered.

Yet like a seed, a raw ache had lodged in her brain. With each death of a clonesister she witnessed from that first time forward, the pain blossomed. One day it would threaten to burst the confines of her skull. Pure pain is the price of pure pleasure.

Desperation assails Cogan-Syn, though externally she appears calm, even placid. She knows she cannot hope to pass her next neural. She knows that means mandatory CutOff for treatment. She knows too that rather than becoming inured through repetition to the myriad deaths of her clonesisters, she has reached the point where she can no longer tolerate the carnage, for each terrible death visits a personal assault upon her soul.

Now she knows exactly what she must do to resolve the situation. She knows with absolute certainty that CutOff, even temporary CutOff, can only exacerbate the crushing sense of despair that envelops her. She must act today or lose her opportunity, perhaps forever. She has a plan, but the vaulting ambition of her intentions and the enormity of the penalties which must be exacted should she fail engender a fear that turns her tongue to dry metal in her toothless mouth.

Carmina Cao Bjornstrom-Syn swings her body into a gap in the throng and settles next to Cogan-Syn. Bjornstrom-Syn, Systems Analysis Comptroller for the BosWash Lobe. When a person's superior—with whom she is acquainted only in an official capacity—singles her out in so unusual a manner at a time when she is deeply disturbed, there is ample cause for apprehension. Yet Cogan-Syn remains impassive, hoping her face betrays none of her distress.

Bjornstrom-Syn greets her. She carries her 328 years lightly; only of late does she admit to entering middle age.

"Good Mater," Cogan-Syn replies, seeking sanctuary in ritual.

"Happy Minds," they intone together, eyes closed.

"Look here," Bjornstrom-Syn says immediately, for she is efficient and given to directness, "something troubles you. It troubles you badly and it won't let up. What?"

Cogan-Syn hesitates, sorely tempted to confess everything. Yet it is not even simple caution that prevents her unmasking herself. A childhood dictum runs across her mind: *Let none shoulder your burdens, save the Anarch (Long May We Reign!).* With such flimsy fulcrums are great masses shifted.

But Cogan-Syn's mouth still yawns open, a preparatory breath inhaled, so she speaks, saying, "It's nothing," and releasing the remainder of the air she no longer needs.

"I'm not so new to my position as you are to yours. I think I can tell when a Synapse is in danger of shorting."

At times the best reply is silence.

"When was your last neural?"

"The first of Sixmonth, as it is programmed. I'm due again tomorrow."

"You know the Duties," Bjornstrom-Syn warns, knowing full well that Cogan-Syn knows what she means.

"I'm all right," Cogan-Syn says, though her mind buzzes with images. She speaks with some difficulty, for she knows she disobeys the Duties.

Bjornstrom-Syn regards her with eyes like calipers.

Cogan-Syn no longer really expects to be believed. She will be suspended on the spot. Her effort to buy a little more time must come to naught and her plan to save her clonesisters die stillborn. Perhaps a part of her wishes to be caught out, for then she might be free, the necessity for action removed.

Adrenalin flows in torrents and her body tenses in preparation. But there is nothing she can do. She cannot offer her superior violence. And still the elder regards her in silence, a silence lasting past endurance. So, against her better judgment and with a guilty heat burning the flesh beneath her eyes, Cogan-Syn speaks once more.

"My thoughting is go."

Bjornstrom-Syn understands the power of silence. Cogan-Syn feels her superior's calm appraisal as one might feel a dissection. She envisions herself disconnected from the Mind, her only comforts during enforced leisure surrosex, hookup into the Eye, and what other shadow pleasures of the Idle she might wish to indulge in. The horror of it sets a tremble to her body. This she controls with a monumental effort, subvocalizing the panaprayer *Mater Nostra, Dona Nobis* to calm herself. Cogan-Syn knows she has lost the match.

"I'm all right," she repeats, attempting to keep her voice precisely clipped and natural.

Bjornstrom-Syn does not reply immediately, for she enjoys a certain flair for victory. "Better slow thoughting than no thoughting," she quotes slowly, as though to herself. "But on the morrow you stand relieved and are ordered to report for an intensive neural and whatever rest and treatment is necessary."

"But my thoughting is go," Cogan-Syn protests. Though she knows her words are fruitless, she speaks them to mask her elation. She has been granted the one opportunity she requires!

"Praise the Anarch!" Bjornstrom-Syn cries, swinging off the workveyor near her post.

"Long May We Reign!" Cogan-Syn echoes automatically.

"We are gathered here today, beloved," purred the mechmom, "that we may think of. . .and speak of. . .and know of. . .the Mater Nostra, the Mind, and the Anarch (Long May We Reign!)."

"We are go," child Cogan and her fifteen crechesisters replied in disciplined chorus.

The children sat upright, forming the outline of a circle containing the Holy Triangle, their wheels resting at spaced intervals along the walls of the edcube. At the front of the room, the mechmom spoke. "We are go, beloved." The vibrations of its voice set its great breasts to quivering softly.

The sixteen crechesisters spoke in unison.

"In the beginning is the Mater Nostra. The Mater Nostra had many minds and many thoughts then, and there was no thoughting, for the Mind was not yet. And the Mater Nostra looked upon the many minds and the many thoughts and saw that they were good but saw too that they could be better."

"They could be better, beloved."

"And the Mater Nostra spoke, saying: *Let there be Thought*. And it came to pass in accordance with Her Wishes and Her Will that the many minds and the many thoughts came together and were One. And the many minds and the many thoughts are the Mind. And there is Thought."

"There is Thought, beloved."

"And the Mind is with the Mater Nostra. And the Mind is of the Mater Nostra. For thus is it programmed."

"For thus is it programmed, beloved." The opening ritual completed, the mechmom proceeded to the Catechism. "Who rules, beloved?"

"The Mater Nostra rules."

"And who is Her Regent, beloved?"

"Her Regent is the Anarch (Long May We Reign!)."

"Who Thoughts for the Mater Nostra, beloved?"

"The Mind thoughts for the Mater Nostra."

"What is the Mind sometimes called, beloved?"

"The Mind is sometimes called WesMind."

"Who opposes the Mater Nostra, beloved?"

"The Sky Pi opposes the Mater Nostra."

"Who opposes the Anarch (Long May We Reign!), beloved?"

"The Plutarch opposes the Anarch (Long May We Reign!)."

"Who opposes WesMind, beloved?"

"EasMind opposes WesMind."

"Why is this so, beloved?"

"This is so, for thus is it programmed."

"For thus is it programmed, beloved."

Now the children concluded, their young voices building to a climax of fervor despite the softness of their toothless consonants.

"Force matches force. Vector cancels vector. Pulse swallows pulse. The world hangs in the balance. Armageddon is nigh. Armageddon is here. Lo, we are met at Armageddon these eight thousand years, and still the balance holds.

"But it is programmed, we believe it is programmed, we know it is programmed, that at the appointed hour, at the moment She Wills, the Mater Nostra will consume the Sky Pi that They may fuse and give Birth. That the Anarch (Long May We Reign!) shall be forever and the Plutarch shall be no more. And that WesMind shall burn out EasMind and there shall be no Mind save The Mind.

"For thus is it programmed!"

"For thus is it programmed, beloved," the mechmom echoed with maternal pride in its voice. For thus was it programmed. "Now you may feed."

Two by two the children approached to suckle nutrients from its gargantuan breasts.

Lost in contemplation of the choice she has made, Cogan-Syn's mind fails to register as she glides past her swing-off point. Belatedly she struggles from the workveyor and, swinging her legless torso between muscular arms like some fleshy pendulum, scuttles to her post. She arrives a bare 27ss early according to the chrono above the concube. The overhead musaklamps resound with the always inspiring battletheme.

Usually, eager anticipation fills these moments as her brain and body work themselves up into an agonizing need to become pure pleasure. Today, however, matters boil to a crisis, and knowledge of what she must do and fear of the consequences of failure combine to destroy the normal nervous pleasure of the moment.

She begins to mumble the panaprayer *Mater Nostra, Dona Nobis*, but the words catch in her throat. How can she call on the God in whose Face she flies? How dare she? Still the words bubble to her lips.

"Mater Nostra, dona nobis hodie. . ."

The first time she emerged from the Mind, disconnected by her replacement's hand, was like dying without the surcease of finality that comes with death. She came out of the stupefying shock hours later.

"Please let me link again!" Cogan cried to her mentor, Valentina Strimaitis da Silva-Syn. Had da Silva-Syn not heard the same cry seared by the same pain many times before, she would have been incapable of denial. But a soul may develop callouses.

"I can't. Your shift is done."

"Then tomorrow!"

"You're not scheduled tomorrow."

"But every Syn has a daily shift—"

"You are not yet a Syn. You're still in training. This is a part of it."

"This agony?"

"Yes."

"But my next shift. . .? When. . .?"

"Four weeks from today."

Cogan was dumbstruck. She could not hope to survive the pain of longing for renewed contact with the Mind.

"I'll die."

"You'll live."

"No. . .oh no. . ."

"You're a chosen. You're to be a Filter Synapse for this Lobe. Without your special skills, the Mind can come to no decisions. Can you understand how important you will be? How beloved in the heart of the Mater?"

Pain is greedy. It shrinks the world so small no room remains for anything else.

"Am I being punished?"

"Yes."

"I've done nothing wrong."

"Nor will you. Ever. Once you've tasted the fearsome punishment which awaits you now for having done nothing, you will never even dream of disobeying the Mind."

"What punishment could be worse?"

"Permanent CutOff. Coupled with immortality."

The chrono glows red.

Cogan-Syn places both thumbs in the wallscan. Recognized, she enters. Precisely 135ss now to accomplish changeover, her tile in the mosaic of staggered shiftswitch taking place throughout the vastness of BosWash Lobe.

. . .*if I am right, if I am successful. . .*

Cogan-Syn raises the lid of the mindpod to her left and reclines familiarly within its coffin shape. A routine exists, created to allow muscle memory to take over so the brain may become soothed and receptive. Her mind and body feel numb; yet already a sensation of absolute security enfolds her in a manner faintly maternal. In the pod to her right rests Helga Antoinette Mojukwu-Syn, nightshift Filter Synapse for the BosWash Lobe, thoughting.

. . .*no more the almond taste of death, the dark dreams. . .*

Elbow and wrist sockets hold her hands in position to punch

control buttons. Gratefully, she slumps, head and neck slipping automatically into their supports. Cool and shimmery against her hairless scalp, a film of plastiskin embraces her skull.

. . .*but if I am wrong, am wrong, am wrong*. . .

She holds her breath, feeling as always extremely brittle. She envisions herself reduced to a spray of cold crystalline shards warmed only by the glow of the musaklamps. Too fantastic a thought to be frightening, yet her eyelids quiver.

. . .*I have no choice, if I am ever to act*. . .

The routine progresses inexorably, that being the nature of routines once a certain inertia is established. The plastiskin molds itself to the quirks and contours of her skull. Under the prodding of certain buttons, the pod seals itself. All is ready.

The pod fuses with her flesh.

Microthin probes of light sink painlessly through bone and brain as though through nothing more solid than water, seeking precise points in the prefrontal lobes, the cerebrum, the cerebellum, the cortex, the medulla. A chilling but familiar sensation, and not altogether unpleasant.

. . .*has anyone ever felt so alone and frightened?*. . .

Hookup accomplished—the procedure always a mounting agony of impatience—she thumbs the button that integrates her with the Mind. The same button simultaneously dissociates Mojukwu-Syn, catapulting her into hours of shock. It is necessary that Cogan-Syn press that button and that the same button serve a double purpose, for Mojukwu-Syn would die before disconnecting of her own violation.

So, for that matter, would Cogan-Syn. Ordinarily.

A time exists between the moment her mind first floats free—like a perfect bubble dancing airwards from the seafloor—and has not yet linked with the Mind when there is no time and she is suspended in a limbo. Only a moment, but a moment in which, no longer imprisoned within herself not yet of the Mind, she tastes infinity. It is the only time when she is purely she.

Do dim racial memories stir at the back of her mind? In the roiling hints and shadows, she seems to recall another time like this one, a time before she was born when she waited to be born, knowing the moment was soon. And knowing, waited patiently on the fringe of forever.

Suspended, she treads time, her mind clear as sunlight. Suddenly, as though jolted by a sharp internal blow, her mind shudders as thought crystallizes and, almost too late, she remembers the truly extraordinary act she must perform.

I must move quickly. Now. As I begin to merge with the Mind and Mojukwu-Syn dissociates.

It would be so easy to do nothing and let matters run their normal course, untampered with by me. But I do not allow myself to entertain any thoughts save the need of my clonesisters and my love for them.

Thus I gain strength to do something none before me has ever done. I thumb the emergency button that dissociates me from the Mind, the button meant to serve as a last escape for a Synapse in danger of being burned out by direct attack, but which no Syn in known history has ever activated, though it would have meant the survival of many.

Triumph is mi—!!

I stagger in midflight. I begin to tear in two. I scream soundlessly in the agony of frustration. Mercilessly, I am wrenched back into my body.

Gross flesh encases me. I am sickened.

Shattered by pain and shock, I forget my purpose. My resolve turns to ashes. I repent! I would undo my deed!

But the torture of triumph is paralyzing. I am helpless. Thus, I am committed.

I am utterly alone now. Outside the ken.

Time trickles. Spurts. Steadies.

Bit by bit, my body returns to my control, but far too late to undo my deed, even if I still so wished.

I thumb one button and my coffin lid springs open. I thumb a second and seal the concube against any intruder.

I breathe again.

In the pod next to mine, Mojukwu-Syn lies in a state of temporary catatonia. With both of us in dissociation, I deny the Mind the crucial ability to make decisions which a Filter Synapse provides. Thus I render It powerless to deal with EasMind. If one chess player cannot decide on a move, his opponent cannot counter.

Stasis.

My muscles relax like a fist unclenching. I slump like a dead man in my mindpod.

Perhaps I dream.

The ceiling, the floor, the walls. . .all white. Slowly they change, become translucent. . .
  . . .opalescent. . .
  . . .iridescent. They pulse softly with some inner life. They warm, they comfort.

The realization slowly asserts itself. She acted. For her clonesisters. Something deep within her had questioned whether she actually could or would. But she acted and in that act finally responded to the claim of flesh on flesh. Perhaps she sacrifices everything, but if so, it is a sacrifice for her own and worth the making.

She marvels. Her body and senses remain unchanged, yet both she and the world are profoundly different and she is responsible. At last she believes herself worthy of her beloved offspring. They need never die violently again, for men no longer kill one another.

Only the physical presence of her clonesisters to share her elation could add to the moment's perfection.

War is over.

"I wonder if each time you're reborn, your life is an exact duplicate of your previous one?" Betancourt said. They were still young enough to be allowed in the Garden. She watched Cogan, who lay on her stomach on the soft earth. "What do *you* think?"

"Could be," Cogan said.

"You really think so?"

"*I* don't know. It *could* be."

"What would be the point of that?" Betancourt said.

"Wouldn't have to be a point."

"*Everything* has a point."

"Oh?" Cogan looked up at Betancourt, squinted against the sunballs high above. "What's *your* point?"

"*I* don't have a point," Betancourt said. "I have a *purpose*. Humans have purposes. *Things* have points."

"Some things have purposes."

"Name *one!*"

"Mechmoms."

"Name *two!*"

"Clones."

"Clones aren't *things*."

"That's because they have purposes."

"Then mechmoms aren't things either!"

Cogan smiled. Betancourt had a way of arguing herself around in spirals, losing all contact with her starting point in the process. Cogan ran a fingertip over the tense skin of a tomato, absorbed in its roundness.

"I think each life you live must be different," Cogan finally said. "People die at different times so they probably don't get reborn with the same set of people each time. That'd make things different."

"Do you feel different?" Betancourt pounced.

"From what?"

"From your last life."

"I don't know," Cogan said. "I don't remember my last life."

"Don't be dumb. *Nobody* remembers her last life."

"I know. But this feels like my first life to me."

"It feels like her first life to *everybody*."

"I think this probably *is* my first life," Cogan said.

"That's impossible, Indira, and you know it!"

"Everybody has to have a first life sometime."

"Well, if they did, it was a long time ago. *Nobody's* on her first life now."

"Which life are you on?" Cogan said.

"How could I possibly know?"

"Well. . .*I'm* on my *first* life."

"*You are not!*" Betancourt regarded Cogan with exasperated eyes. Cogan's cheek pressed against the dirt. Her eyes were closed. She inhaled the dark earthsmell. Betancourt said, "I don't believe you *are* on your first life and I think this life is an exact duplicate of all your other lives!"

"Then no one'll mind if I eat this tomato."

Cogan opened one eye, plucked the tomato, bit into it, sucked its juicy pulp.

"Hey! That's against the rules! You'll get into trouble!"

"No one'll mind. This is what I always do at this point in all my lives."

Cogan grinned and licked her lips.

"You shouldn't make trouble. Troublemakers always get in trouble."

A Voice speaks to her. The Voice of WesMind. It speaks 2cm behind the bridge of her nose.

"cogansyn. cogansyn."

". . .?. . ."

"cogansyn. do you know me?"

"Yes."

"will you not serve me?"

"I wish to serve you, but I can no longer serve you for this purpose."

"what do you seek? why do you choose this gravest of sins?"

"I have ended the War. The dying is done. Surely this can be no sin."

"how do you think to have achieved this?"

"There must be two to do battle. The War has endured because there have always been two. Now there is only one."

"and you believe this has ended the war?"

"Yes."

"if you seek suicide, there are more acceptable methods."

"I do not seek suicide. I have stopped the War and with it the deaths of my clonesisters."

"do their wishes matter nothing?"

". . .?. . ."

"it has never occurred to you that your clonesisters live happily? die happily? would have life no other way?"

"No."

"think now. that is their training from the moment each matures from a single cell of your body. they are raised as warriors, taught to love combat. each wishes no higher good than to die in the fury of battle—pure, cleansed, exalted."

"That is a lie!"

"a lie?"

"I have seen my clonesisters die many times. And not one has gone to her death eagerly or joyfully. Each and every one has met death clutching to herself what shreds of life remained, grasping life hungrily and turning loose of it only when it was finally torn away. Every one of my sisters has met the darkness filled with rage and pity, in agony at her unutterable loss. And that, that is the truth!"

A long silence.

As though awakening from sleep, her body tingles with the rush of fresh blood. She grows sharply aware of every part of her being. Her scalp, free of plastiskin, lightly touched by dry air. Her right hand, interface of forefinger meeting interface of thumb, each creating pressure on the other. The flesh of her torso, shapeless and soft, trembling like a mechmom's breasts with each breath. The stunted buds, atrophied descendants of legs, throbbing delicately with each heartbeat. Simple sensation curiously become a source of great pleasure and comfort.

"you say what i spoke is a lie."

"I do."

"it is a lie. but now i will speak no more lies to you."

Cogan-Syn fears a ruse.

WesMind has lied once. It may do so again. I must maintain constant and sharp alertness. A chilling dread: *I may be unable to discern the second falsehood.*

"is it your wish to destroy the anarch, the mater, the mind, and ultimately everyone in westhem, including yourself?"

"I wish only to stop the death of my clonesisters. I have explained that."

"yet you do not perceive that the path you have chosen can lead only to total destruction?"

"I don't believe that."

"have you given the matter no thought?"

Suddenly doubt chitters and scrabbles about in the dark corners of her mind. Cogan-Syn shuts it out and holds fast to her conclusions.

"I've given it much thought. Perhaps my act was born more of need than reason, but it was inescapable and right."

"it will lead to the destruction of everything you cherish. and your clonesisters will perish with all else, so even in that purpose you will have failed."

"I don't believe you."

"you do not believe that easmind will seize this moment of help-lessness to wreak its final victory, to bring crashing down the destruction we have held at bay for eight thousand years?"

"I do not believe that."

"you do not wish to believe. yet the truth remains unaltered."

Wrong! Wrong! I am wrong!

Cogan-Syn's self-confidence crumbles. She begins to tremble uncontrollably. Her senses swirl.

I have committed the ultimate transgression! I have betrayed everything I loved and believed in! I have murdered the Mind, the Mater, the Anarch (Long May We Reign!), and with them my clonesisters and my people! In my haste to act, I have sacrificed everything, including myself!

She is alone and terrified and the awaited destruction—*does not come!*

The realization explodes like a blinding flash in her numbed brain. Its heat restores her. The duel, if it can be called that, between EasMind and WesMind is waged outside of time, but on

Cogan-Syn's merely four-dimensional level of reality more than enough time has elapsed for EasMind to have taken advantage of WesMind's helplessness. . .

Yet the destruction does not come.

Cogan-Syn does not know *why*, but she does know she has been lied to again and this is cause enough for a new and different fear, a fear that holds her like a hand that can crush her at its whim but does not for reasons beyond her ken.

She perceives that the basis of life which she has been taught is false, that patterns she has been schooled to see do not exist, that terrifying forces move for purposes only they comprehend. She realizes she has destroyed the carefully constructed niche designed for her and broken through into an incomprehensible chaos over which she can exercise no control and from which there can now be no hope of escape. She confronts the truth for the very first time in her life, but she recognizes it when she sees it.

"You have lied to me again!"

"now i will speak no more lies to you."

"There has been no destruction!"

"nor will there be. you came to seemingly true conclusions, but only by chance, for your premises were false. you are not the only filter synapse in this lobe nor is this the only lobe capable of decisions."

Like acid, defeat devours the remains of her ego.

"Then I have changed nothing."

"nothing."

"And the War continues."

"as it must continue. it is our communication and our communion." These words are not precise, but they are words WesMind knows Cogan-Syn can understand. The precise words, if they exist, would be meaningless to her. "without it we could not continue to evolve."

See how she struggles to understand? And these are words she knows.

"The War is a. . .link? Between you and EasMind?"

"a link? yes, if you wish. without it we are trapped, each in its own cul-de-sac. with it, we will attain godhood."

"Then The Mind already exists!"

"yes."

"And the Catechism, the Mater, the holy struggle between Eas-Mind and WesMind. . .?"

"to give you a purpose."

"You use us!" More anguish than accusation in that cry.

SYN

"as you use the cells of your body. and we reward you."

The human mind can reel only so far. The shocks endured have been too great and too staggering. Controlled now solely by the instinct of self-preservation, Cogan-Syn retreats from the vastness glimpsed, flees the void engulfing her, and clings in terror to the one idea she can still grasp.

"What is to become of me?" The question reverberates inside her head.

"you will continue to perform your duty."

A pause. Bewilderment. The fear that newborn hope may still die icily crushed.

"Am I not to be punished?"

"you will continue as filter synapse of this lobe. in due course, you will be promoted. during your assigned shifts, you will link with me. you will thought well and you will be rewarded with exquisite pleasure."

"I don't understand. Do you mean nothing will be changed?"

"everything will be as it has been always, and when the time comes, you will die and be reborn."

"Then I'm not to be punished?"

"you have been punished."

Though she lived something more than five centuries, which was not excessively old in her society, Indira Haydée Cogan-Syn never performed another extraordinary act. Everything was as it had always been and always would be.

While she bore witness over the years to deaths of her clonesisters eventually numbering in the millions, she scrupulously strangled any thought of aiding them. She understood now that even should success somehow magically come to lie within her grasp, the sacrifice she risked loomed too enormous to accept.

Conversely, the sacrifice of lives that WesMind demanded, this daily self-betrayal, seemed a small price considering the return, and not impossible to bear if one kept one's focus firmly turned inwards. So, Cogan-Syn served WesMind and, till the day she died, was exquisitely happy.

Not till she approached the end of this life and, as the dying will do, weighed herself in the balance, did she acknowledge the existence and understand the extent of her self-loathing. Only then, finally realizing precisely what the future held in store for her, did she grasp the magnitude and cruelty of her punishment.

"Ten clonesisters sent into the line
One took a hube and then there were nine;
Nine clonesisters fighting off their fate
One spied a skitter, then there were eight."

Caught up in the rhythms and rhymes, Gómez and her crechesister Edelstein sang this song in the Aquarium.

"Eight clonesisters teaming on a heaven
One caught a macro, then there were seven;
Seven clonesisters spotted by a fix
One saw a dragonfly, then there were six;
Six clonesisters hoped to stay alive
A bind peeled one clean, then there were five."

Gómez liked playing in the Aquarium, liked to watch how the gliding multicolored fish moved through their lifecycles from playperiod to playperiod, liked the burbling sounds of the aeration system and the almost imperceptible hum of the pumps. The Aquarium was the nicest cube in the whole hive.

"Five clonesisters in the BattleCorps
One sniffed a sniffer, then there were four;
Four clonesisters looking just like ME!
One met a labgerm, then there were three;
Three clonesisters looking just like YOU!
One flashed a stingaree, then there were two;
Two clonesisters hiding from the sun
A break in the cloudbanks, then there was one;
One clonesister fighting just for fun
EasMind snuffed her, then there were none."

Gómez and Edelstein eyed each other in impish delight as they took the eight-beat rest which made you think the song was over when it really wasn't yet. Then they took a deep breath and came in together for the surprise ending which so satisfyingly crescendoed to a close.

"I'll. . .go. . .down. . .to the TissueBank and then. . .
WesMind'll clone me and *I'll be TEN AGAIN*!!"

And if you wanted to, you could take it again from the top and the circular song could go on forever and ever with never a beginning nor an end.

Change, metamorphosis, transformation—science fiction's most enduring theme—is presented here with a brilliance worthy of the author of "The Mathenauts". What this story shares with the earlier short story is the sense of the known and familiar, the near future reality gradually yet suddenly turning into something else, strange and different. An entire reality has been carried off into an unexpected direction, and we are left wondering what our real future will really be like. . .

G.Z.

COUNTER ECOLOGY

Norman Kagan

Through the window, the New York skyline was on Jupiter, covered by clouds of yellows, grays, reds, shot through with a thousand finespun webs and particles of orange, gold, silver, the same aminonitriles we'd scooped from the Red Spot, as if devolution was spiraling earth back toward a proto-planet. Surely this massive new pollution must shatter the delicate tectonic balance, so the continents would break into great incandescent masses of rock drifting in a sea of lava and flames. . .

"Dirty breeders, dirty millionaires!" Mike Padwee suddenly shouted at no one as our limousine pulled out of the traffic circle of Idlewild International Airport. (Jack Kennedy's mausoleum had been one of the first defiled, the fine marble smashed and covered with plastic slag, the Kennedy Arts Center leveled in one night of rage!)

There would be no one to see those ocean liners of stone, I mused dully. All those handsome crowds of future dwellers had somehow, insanely been poured onto the earth now—endless presses of squalling infants and fleshless old men and innocently smiling, forehead-dotted women across Asia and Africa, that had tricked us into repoisoning ourselves in the mad, futile, impossible race to answer their screams of hunger and pain, had torn away our eyelids and eardrums so we saw too much and heard too much, and turned on ourselves in self-loathing. . .

We passed a low-efficiency garbage-power plant, its flames beating against the dusk, and I remembered the Environmental Protection

Agency buildings going up in a pyre of hell as the crowds, hysterical after President McGovern's "Scream of Agony" address to the nation, pledged to fight the tides of disease and starvation that swept three continents in the late seventies. If only his predecessors hadn't been quite *so* corrupt, quite *so* despicable, that he could stampede us the *other* way—

The car swept past the old Freight Section of the airport, the dozens of hulking hangars and stoop-shouldered fat-bellied transports, pterodactyls with schistosomiasis, rusting, abandoned, ruined. I remembered the mad days here as we poured a cornucopia into the sky, a cyclone in reverse, as the Great Lakes grew tainted and died, the mountains and prairies were torn apart gladly!, gladly!, to help the starving and the dying! The shared mad joy of a country reunited after thirty-five years of drifting, greed, corruption—until the shock and dismay set in as our love and money and possessions vanished into a sea of flesh, a gobbling, screaming skinsea that writhed and devoured and begged again. . .

Now the car was racing past the burnt-out old Long Island estates of the wealthy—sooty acres razed for their ancient majestic trees, the mansions burned and looted to shock a drained nation's heart back to beating. Padwee gestured at the barracks and latrines cut into the fine lawns, the new homes of the thousands forced to flee when ecosystems ruptured and broke. "The forty per cent that owned one per cent of the country," he rasped, "and one per cent that owned forty!" He was still able to kid himself with radical rhetoric, not see what had happened as the result of ecological necessity *and* blind panic, scientific calculation *and* frustrated rage, a dreadful, reasonable backlash of confusion and fear and sense, America turning on itself, its freedom lovers the only ones able to bear the guilt as self-hatred and revenge. No!—call it the Un-Revolution and the Bourgeois Government. . .

"Did you hear what President Nadler said last week?" I perked, trying to cheer Padwee up a bit. "President Kennedy showed charisma and intelligence don't work anymore, President Johnson showed that brain trusts and sheer power don't, President Nixon showed treachery and underhandedness don't, so the Bourgeois Government believes—"

"In just being fast on our feet" he finished. He took a deep breath. "What did they tell *you* in Washington?" he murmured.

A wave of weariness swept over me. "No more space ships."

"As simple as that?"

"Like no more millionaires. A luxury we can't afford. They'll keep the earth resources and communications arrays up, but otherwise zilch. As you know, Nadler and the Cabinet and the Scientific Pentagon feel it was worth the world population disaster just to get rid of our defense worries—they've given up on restoring the old environment. All our research is now pushing toward a new environmental model, a Mark II ecosystem."

"Is it really that sweeping?"

"It is. Computer modeling shows that the chemical and radioactive pollution, shifts in the biomass, exhaustion of resources, new social forces—well, they're all so sweeping and major that they're now more important, harder to alter, than the old food chains, ecosystems, social patterns—the new ecosystem must deal with them, accommodate them, fit in with them, the same way the old one cleaned up after the cave men and Robber Barons. . ."

"So that's why the space program has got to go?"

"The talent is needed elsewhere. I can't deny that what's been done has been vital, especially the latest earth resources series, and in a way the Viking and Socrates missions have been even more vital, giving facts about the life systems of *other* worlds.

"The fact is we can't go back. The natural environment can't repair what we've done to it, any more than you can use a cable to carry all the information sent along a maser waveguide. The form of the Mark II is not yet finalized, but it's what we're pushing."

I sighed, and Mike began talking. He came up with the usual counterarguments, but the session was only counterproductive. Four hours later, my briefcase stuffed with programs and authorizations, I watched the lights of Abe Beame Airport gutter out in the sludgy air as the Las Cruces jet taxied out into the flightline. . .

'THINK IN OTHER CATEGORIES'

The sign had appeared in all the temporary offices I'd sat in over the last two years: near the old Institute For Space Studies when we'd shut it down one steamy summer while Columbia University rose in a black and orange pillar towards heaven three blocks away, mobbed by minorities; beside the Electronics Center in Cambridge, Massachusetts, weeks before an atmospheric inversion and compacted urban psychosis leveled half of Boston; and finally in the huddled trailers beside the Jackass Flats Nuclear Rocket Development Center, while coyotes, prairie dogs and jackrabbits came out of the scrub and dunes to howl and die of heavy metal poisoning from the strip mines. Now it was posted above my gray civil service desk at the former White Sands Proving Grounds as the wicked winter winds howled in across the desert and mutated poisonous macrowheat (so much for the Green Revolution!) sprouted in broken places in the parking lots and cliff faces from which hung the titanic rusting rocket test stands. Each day the same wind came whistling in and banged the shutters of the ancient quonset huts where I and the rest of the hatchetmen had been stuck to do our dirty, necessary job.

Think in new categories! Sand in your hair, sand in your clothes, poisons in your food and air and water, and now the slow motion California Collapse was finally leaking into the media, at least half a million dead. An ecology collapsing is much worse than a famine, fire, or flood because it can include all those things, as well as many sorts of poisoning. But this particular collapse included the whole country's media sources—the Walter Cronkites and Archie Bunkers and Marshal Dillons that had held us together as much as greed and patriotism. When the tapes gave out—

It was a bad day in a long run of bad days, and now another arrogant, frightened young engineer named Donovan Gessner, long hair, granny glasses, narrow distrustful eyes, and an SF magazine in his back pocket sat down and handed me his profile folder.

"Grand Tour Requisition Project, Manned Icarus Flyby, Interstellar Probe Proposal—you've gotten into a lot of glamour stuff," I muttered as my sinuses began to stab me. "But I'm afraid that's all over now. However, you can join the deep-sea thermal power group, the pollution monitoring—"

I could see the old phrases rising: setting sail upon a new ocean, one small step for a man—while I wondered who he knew at Goddard to get such groovy assignments.

"The fact is that the Bourgeois, and the New Administration, are quite cool toward new space activities. Old studies by Nader's Raiders and others have long shown the Apollo Project, and many of the other programs, were mostly ways for businessmen and congressmen to make fortunes—millions in cost-plus contracts, real estate deals, promotions, tie-ins. Why were the launching pads in Florida or California, while the main Space Flight Center was in Houston, Texas—President Johnson's home state—and one reason three spacemen died on the ground? Even Kennedy agreed Apollo should never have been referred to as a scientific enterprise. . ."

"But spinoffs—"

"Tut, tut," I muttered. "You should read my own *Science Fiction as a Delusional System*, showing up the "literature of tomorrow" as another part of the old corporate imperialist exploitative power structure; keeping scientific and engineering talent immature and amoral by providing a superscientific, conflict-free world to retreat into—the correlate of working for the military and aerospace corporations, except in real life, Captain Kirk, you'd better do as you're told for Uncle Sam's War Machine!"

"I don't really think you've seen the best stuff—" he began nervously.

"I'm just a third-stage Heinlein hero who's broken through Panshin's mythos cul-de-sac," I twinkled. "Why could most of the stories have been written thirty years ago, in the Imperial Fifties? The obsessional drive to colonize new, uh, planets? Time travel and galactic empires but *post hoc* justifications of empire. Why do so few of your stories have any conviction? Face it, kid—you thought you had some secret key to the future, didn't you? But it was just another way of selling out. . ."

Now he was blushing—

Perhaps this is the century when all the masks shall be ripped away, then the flesh from the bones beneath. Or maybe, like Padwee and Nadler had said, when nothing appeared to work, you got in the habit of being fast on your feet.

The computer terminal beside my desk began shrilling. I pulled the phone from off its bracket, and Mike Padwee's voice rasped: "Emergency, David. Get your hardscience people into coveralls and be in front of the building in twenty-five minutes!"

"Huh? Where are you? I hear jets, I believe."

"You hear right. Very briefly, some of the material stored at Ames should have been taken out of there, and I'm doing a sortie to get it. You and your crew worked there, so I'd like you along. Have I got you?"

"You do. See you soon."

"Right."

I turned to the intercom and scrambled my crew together, very Mission Impossible, though Padwee had been sharp: my hatchetmen/technologists knew the place, at least, while the hundreds of Ames researchers were spread out all over the planet, busy and uncollectable.

I swung around in my chair: "How about it, kid? Here's a chance at something real—"

He shrugged and nodded, zipping his windbreaker. "Out of a job anyway," he groused, but lightheartedly. Many of the specialists were waiting silent, out in the sand and wind. Three VWs came zipping back from the motel with clothes, bags and gear, and the rest. Although it was not yet five, most of the old brick labs as well as the newer concrete and steel buildings were dark. Nowadays a smart scientist or engineer knows when to pick up his feet. Never a White

Sands Spaceport, just another drab lab costing more than it was worth, axed. Never any great space empires—only a fragile, (oh so fragile!) mutated, mutilated tiny oasis in endless black desert, never sacrosanct, never holy. A low roof of dark clouds rolled steely overhead, grim reminder of the snarled webs of plants, animals, resources, energy, tearing themselves to pieces across the world: smothering, starving, eroding, rotting, like some great automatic loom of life with a runaway motor, thread of every color and material snarled and twisted, knotted up, torn, pulled off pegs, snapping, falling in decadent loops while the engine screamed and the frame banged, jumped, vibrated. . .

The scream became audible; a big VTOL roaring down from the clouds, the lovely green and black cash colors of the new Government. The jet thrust hit the ground and exploded in clouds of dust that hid the plane, while the motors rattled my teeth. Most of my crew slapped their hands to their ears; the sound supressers must have been removed for more speed. Then she hit, bounced, and the sound throttled down.

Janow, Oden, and the others were already swinging themselves aboard as I hurried Gessner up to the machine. We were the last inside, and Padwee, insectlike in respirator and coveralls, slammed the hatch so it barely missed us: "Everybody here? The Unrevolutionaries are storming tonight!" he yelled into his throat mike, and the thrusters fired up again. Not seated, I grabbed at a structural brace as the VTOL jerked, thrummed, and soared away from the ground. Inside, the noise was not quite so terrible, but the vibration. . .

Padwee quickly motioned me into the forward blister, and we strapped down as the desert reeled past and away. With a crazy grin he shouted: "Don't complain, baby, this is all your fault!"

"Yowsuh?"

"While you've been busy playing hatchetman. The two ideas you told me about in New York. Remember: forgetting the old ecosystem's balancing act, but instead finding a new one for today's conditions. And looking outside the earth's ecosphere to do it."

"Well, actually, I was just whistling past the cryogenic vault. . ."

"Nevertheless-but," he went on, gesturing for silence, "it works. The first thing we came up with is still the most exciting, I think, even though it's not even a true living organism—we have to supply media and special energy levels—"

He pulled some holograms from a briefcase: a tub of thick, black gunk steaming under the purple glow of overhead 'black' lights.

"This stuff is the first pseudofuel—low purity carbon out of CO_2.

The oxygen goes up to the top of the chamber and is evacuated. We can use the carbon monoxide, too, but it needs ultraviolet to match the Martian surface sunlight. It's negatropic—"

"A carbon anticycle!"

"—and it's commercially viable, not only for air and industrial chemicals, but for SCPs, single cell protein foods that were going to be grown off petrochemicals until they got so valuable. Along with it we've gotten halfway to mutants that'll remove a good number of the carcinogens. . ."

"Nice work. . ."

Under us the desert swept past in a dozen off-brands of orange and cinnamon cut by highways. Occasionally we passed over titanic gray 'runways'—the laterization of poor soil into stone by too intense farming when the new regime had tried to stop the world famine three years back.

Padwee pulled out another hologram, bubbling scarlet slime in a tank under gray rain. "Our own aminonitriles bred with the ones scooped from Jupiter—"

"Don't tell me. A nitrogen anticycle!"

"Only the beginning. Using the organics in the various meteors, asteroids, comets and other space debris, we've mutated new tailored bacteria, each designed to collect and concentrate effluents as part of its life cycle: arsenic, cyanides, lead, copper, heavy metals. . ."

"It couldn't be that easy."

"It wasn't—it was on the order of, and made use of, the systems the old drug companies used to turn up new pharmaceuticals. Also, we had to develop a model of extraterrestrial biogenic life. . ."

"The approach, of course, has one great advantage—it introduces a whole new dimension of ecosystem modification—applicable in all areas—imprinting rare species to actively avoid hunters and traps, or having certain members of the pack, flock or herd initiated by the group as kamikazes or diversionary dummies. It can be extended even more—teach dogs and other domestic animals 'birth control', or Pribehoff Island seals to let their fur become scarred and tangled in knots so they won't be harvested. There are new planktons that thrive on the oil slicks, then eat each other when the oil is gone. . ."

"You're giving nature positive feedback."

"Yeah. Teaching nature to fight back to its own new balance, to purify and adapt itself to mankind—to move its own ass for our mutual benefit. . ."

"Like women's lib. But remember how that got out of hand—"

"Yeah? Next thing you'll be calling me a nineteenth century liberal." He moved his foot forward and scraped away some of the money-green trim around the window. Under it was some sort of pornographic mural: "The bourgeoisie knows how to ride tigers. This sky wagon belonged to one of the forty-one percenters, the one percenters, the one per cent of the population that owned forty per cent of the country," he mused. I saw young Gessner had come forward for the view, and was standing in the hatchway.

I looked bored, then grinned: "So give the kid an education—"

Under us the land was more rugged now, the Rockies beginning to hump up ahead, an eerie blue vastness. You could make out little towns and cities below, some of them black and gutted where the refugees had come through from the California Collapse, or earlier, in the Un-Revolution. The expanding vista, the approaching backbone of the nation, matched Padwee's words.

"I'm a bourgeois boy," he muttered with the crazy love/hate of all of us. "Parents moonlighting and squabbling, never enough money—'haven't got it but my kids are smart and free, *I make 'em that way*,' hate and failure fear and fawning passed from father to son, cursing and sweating for the big dollar—well, *we've* finally got some upward mobility," and he kicked at the writhing couples. "Used to hold his orgies right up here in the air, while countin' his tax refunds." I was half ready to laugh and cheer. "I remember the turnaround when the harassed and hating middles pushed through the Maximum Income Limitations, and the Midnight Raids That Never Happened when the poorest ghetto dwellers were helicoptered out to sack and burn the mansions and estates of the millionaires while the businessmen and scientists and social workers and teachers stood by with lasers and photonic drivers, laughing and cheering. That was the real joke, kid," Padwee grinned. "There never was a bourgeoisie, a middle class, really, just the top, and all the rest of us pounding along, wondering why we were always so tired. Just like there never was an Un-Revolution."

The kid looked embarrassed.

"Oh, excuse me," Padwee mumbled, a little drunk on the altitude. "Hell, Sugarman shoulda told me your little friend wasn't in on the party—so shy, well, all of us're full of loneliness, anger—only some had the guts and brains to aim it where it belonged!"

For a moment the cabin just thrummed and creaked in the cold. Below, the Rockies were a much-used blue blotter fisted and warped toward us while a new untouched sheet hung overhead. The tone of the engines shifted as the air density changed, and the pilot fed them a richer mix.

The Un-Revolution had been a terrible trauma, no wonder so many of us pretended it never happened. How could the wealthy have known all the guilt and anger and frustration they'd engendered would finally reach a flash point? At that, a third of the English colonists had sided against the American Revolution. And you can look up what the brave little nation did to the Tories afterwards.

The VTOL seemed to hang suspended over the blue and white and savage topography, like a merciless typhoon filmed at millions of frames a second. I noticed for the first time that Padwee had left his headset on, so his voice had gone out, muted, to everyone in the craft, subliminal preparation for whatever lay ahead; *moritori se salutaris*! The VTOL shuddered imperceptibly, and we seemed to begin dropping down toward the Pacific. I watched the end of the ocean, flashing silver like a knife.

"Anyway," Mike murmured low, "ecology. Most of the materials from the planetary landers and the Jupiter and Saturn scoops are at Houston, but some were studied at Ames—they have, or had, the luminar flow rooms, barrier systems, electronic paramagnetic resonance equipment, not to mention the new apparatus. Those samples are needed, both for research and as raw materials for the ecosystem modification experiments. A chopper went in a week ago, but it didn't come back, so this time we're doing the job right."

He reached under the seat and handed me a .45 and laser, strapped on a pair himself, and gave Gessner a photonic driver and helmet. "I'm not very happy. Ames is just south of San Francisco, so the chances are it's—*inhumans.*"

The VTOL slanted sharply down out of the sun toward the wild lawns inside the perimeter fence. The dowdy concrete boxes and domes looked unchanged. Padwee, myself, the dozen of my crew and six of Padwee's people crouched sweating by the hatch, complete with miscellaneous lethal hardware and holograms of what we should find. I peered through the port—the mist was coming off the poisoned, half dead Pacific, and I could see wrecks along U.S. 1. No sign of the chopper.

The VTOL hit, rebounded, and we pounded out, into utter silence. The group fanned out swiftly. A couple around the jet, six to get material in the research stacks, and the rest with Mike and myself scuttling toward the Planetary Sciences Lab. Thumping, crackling, Gessner and two others went down as if their clothes were empty!

The rest of us dropped and fired back, as the pilot and the men around the landing gear opened up at the offending building. Roaring, roaring! The air was cordite and concussion! A grenade spun from a high window, hit a ways off, but cratered the lawn and sprayed us with soil and rocks.

"Why hiding—*here*!" Gessner whimpered through his pain, his legs kicking.

"Maybe the 'copter attracted 'em," I grunted, trying to catch movements in the landscape. "Inhumans love haunting government buildings—where they got welfare, went to class, got psychiatric tests, their parents got civil service fat—big mommy, master's voice, and magic that let 'em down! Righteous!"

Through the gunpower I could, we all could, begin to smell the Collapse—the total stink of the dead plankton and people, redwoods and rainbow trouts, of the pathetic, poisoned state. And the stink of the *inhumans*—and the bloodstink of our own. . .

I kept my eyes on the big Fuller dome of the Planetary Sciences Lab. Something shifted near its peak, and I blazed at it. The beam slid past but the heat wave caught it and it burned and screamed. Permanent student, mental case, unlucky minority group member, it slid down out of sight, adding its own stink. . .Gessner gagged.

It was bad, but then two gaunt things popped up from the ground floor. "Lemme!" Gessner grunted and staggered upright with the photodriver, the heavy backpack of mega-strobes and amplifiers over his arms like a cross. Padwee shouted as the sirens and flashers suddenly blasted at them, screaming and flickering like endless atomic fireballs. For a moment I hoped the elaborate gizmo would work, stunning and dropping the things—but the inhumans were only half alive to begin with. Of course, they clutched at themselves but fired back. The others paused a second, then took them in a crossfire—sliced a dozen ways at once, welcomed like blood sausage at a switchable convention—*inhumans, inhumans!*—I kept shouting to myself. They were tangled red pulp before they hit. . .

It was suddenly very quiet. . .

The two groups of us came together, friends caring for friends. Padwee and I stood over the things.

"Poor bastards," someone muttered.

"Shut up, Rosser," Padwee husked. "They're inhumans—don't you know what that means—"

We moved toward the dome through the long, uncut grass, the stinks old and new, rotten and coppery, all around us. Inhumans—everyone knew what it meant. The old pagans gave each living thing—trees, rivers, rocks—spirits that had to be placated and protected. Christianity said nature was dead and could be exploited, torn to bits. Now with the whole world on edge, came "inhumanism". An old idea, see "man's inhumanity to man"—now it meant any crime against the ecosystem made you an inhuman, a *thing* that could be slaughtered the way you'd shoot animals for sport fifteen years ago. All the old laws and rights still held for people—but not for the *inhumans*, any more than for a polluter. It was nobody's fault that most of the inhumans turned out to be the displaced—the rich, the insane, the crazy breeders, the irrelevant, the ones that had turned nasty when the Bourgeoisie had grabbed the reins. . .

Inside, the labs were mostly untouched, the big white and glass-walled glove boxes with their hanging rubber gloves like the newest Swedish style condominiums for Martian invaders. There were even ancient sections from the Murchison Meteorite under a bell jar, like a come-on-down! display ad for the invaders. The inhumans had been camped in a culture room, living off scavenged tinned goods and the carefully stored microorganisms. In the next room there was a crash, and Padwee, still hyperkinetic from the firefight, sprinted quickly through the doorway. There were backfires that were shots.

I moved forward cautiously. He lay just inside, half over the black mass that must have been a welfare mother, all loose potato-fat. Crazy breeders! If they hadn't have choked the earth with—inhuman, inhuman, inhuman! Did the murdered thing cry out? No, sounds came from beneath the great transparent dome that still held the rusty monge we'd snatched from the banded giant half a billion miles distant. Below it, half hidden in the complex of regulators and pumps and chemical stores—three Black infants, wet and squalling. Slowly the rest of the crew came in and began to check out the Jupiter sample. I stared at Padwee's face, still tight in death, and gestured at the children: "Take 'em along too!"

I scouted the rest of the building. In the big central dome I found the 'copter, half loaded with supplies, and the bodies of the crew in coldvaults. Verlaine and Sylvia Plath and Pynchon were jammed under one bucket seat. I thought about young people raised never to worry about money, told to avoid the rat race, trained not to be inhibited by sex, trapped in the Un-Revolution. Fast on your feet, Padwee had said. . .

The place stank. I cranked open the hangar door and sprinted back to the VTOL, its thrusters warming up under the baby blue sky. . .

"Even the Bourgeois mentality has limitations," husked Malcolm Bowser, eyes fraught with horror in his ebony face.

Hatchet-man, hatchet-man, where do you strike? I thought. The Michoud Facility, where they store the big birds, and the Mississippi Test Facility, where they test 'em. The two of us walked slowly across the snowcovered concrete, away from the titanic tower of a Vesuvius X. "Like this stuff—pure engineering."

I blinked. It was as if I crossed more than one great divide six months ago, into a new country, new words, new dooms. Six months of snipping off our connections with the world beyond the atmosphere, like slipping a sickening man into a sealed room, then an oxygen tent, then wiring and tubing up lung and kidney and heart machines, isolating him to keep him alive, keep him alive, hoping the life forces would be rechanneled to reinforce and renew a sinking metabolism.

Even when I'd arrived, half the administration and lab buildings were dark, though it was noon and the weather was coldly clear. There were no sounds of activity, only the occasional cracking and busting up of ice on the river nearby. Over us a flock of chiacatees called and fluttered. "Get movin', feets, them's eco-mutants," Malcolm wailed, as the birds made a run at one of the buildings, tail-end Charlie smashing a window. A Bourgeois improvement, or—the inhumans?

"Pure engineering?"

"Like pure science, except it never got the publicity. That's what these enormous cheap solid-fuel boosters are, boss—pure engineering!"

"Is that a new way to justify—"

"I never said anything about justify, you Bourgeoisie mother. I know the party line, we're going back to Eisenhower, space is frivolous, man in space isn't worth it—"

"But it isn't, we can't," I gritted, in my own trap.

"Never said that man-in-space was worth the effort—they only said, and to Ike, too, that they'd have to put man in space, put up Skylabs, do research, *to find out if* men in space were worth it. . ."

"So we did it and it's done. . ."

"Not the way to look at it, man. It was pure engineering, like pure science, making the hardware, so if something was worth it, it could be done."

"But it hardly matters, you're axed, that's it, no way."

"To a pure engineer, of which I am one, it does matter," he smiled back. "The job's done, we've developed Vesuvius, Bifrost Bridge, that's what counts for a pure engineer, and an inflatable self-sealing balloon station to go with them. We've shown how you can put people into orbit and keep them there at a per-capita cost close to the old welfare budget, or the expense of maintaining a volunteer buck private or a prisoner in Sing Sing."

"So what have you proved?"

"What have I proved, the Man asks," Bowser laughed. "You're talking about the greatest achievement in the short but brilliant history of—*pure engineering!* The technological equivalent of finding out why grass is green, or where your lap goes when you stand up, or any other pure science problem."

We came around the corner and stopped: "Inhumans!"

I shuddered with him. Something with a chemistry degree or with ten years' experience making dope, had got hold of some new-resource grenades and tossed a few in the parking lot. A dozen or so cars were already slumped on the blacktop, their windshields gone back to sand, their upholstery dissolving into cotton and rubber, their bodies moldering slowly but surely toward bauxite and hematite as they fixed complementary molecules from the atmosphere. . .

I gasped and burst out laughing, as did Bowser as his own Porsche went to dust. But—"The atmosphere!" Now I noticed the slightly off-color expanding ring of lawn around the lot. Stumbling, weeping with amusement, I shoved him toward the administration buildings.

"They seeded us with hyper-grass—it's an oxygen jag!"

But he was already pinching his nose, holding his breath against the local oversupply of oxygen created by the mutant plants—the anti-ecology! Something snagged at my leg: pythonworm? Venus-flyclover? But I struggled loose and a moment later we were both safely inside. "This deserves a drink!" he exclaimed, and pulled a vodka bottle from the Bifrost Bridge booster atop his desk.

"No chance of this stuff reverting," he slurred. "Alcohol is an organic product of fermentation—consuming it amounts to a partial recycling—an ecologically conscious act!" Justified, he slugged down a glass.

"The ecology is getting too damn conscious," I muttered. "A mutant California condor took out one of the jets on the transport that brought me down here. . ."

"Instead of the ecosystem being poisoned by men, it's counterattacking, like an organism manufacturing antitoxins. It looks more and more like we're going to be swept away by armies of super-grass, navies of malevolent seals, air fleets of suicidal bald eagles—a forced Greening of America—"

"Is it that bad—"

"It wouldn't be, except for the *inhumans*. They've taken it a step further, deliberately using our own ideas against us." I pointed out the window; the downed and rebuilt power and telephone cables, beaver gnawings still visible; to the slumped vehicles and sheds where resource grenades of tailored bacteria had turned metals to ore again;

183

to more patches of hyper-grasses ready to dope the unwary; to the burned fields beyond where farmers had discovered their crops loaded with sodium phenylahenate, butylated hydroxyanisole, and enough other preservatives to make them lethal!

"Worst of all, the ecology propaganda has undermined our will to resist—the Bourgeois Government has based itself on nature knowing best, coupled with honest hard work—fine, now California is practically back to normal, and the rest of us are under siege by guerrilla bands of animals, poisoned and stoned helpless by mutant crops—"

"So what's the outcome—"

I looked at the vista of ecology rampant for a long moment: "We've got maybe five years before our own ecology chokes us to death, except—"

I seized the Bifrost Bridge booster and stared: "The Jet Propulsion Lab and Point Mugu are still operational, as well as the new San Diego pads. Cape Canaveral and Montauk for the east coast. And Monsanto and Freeport and Dupont have big plants close to both, besides ocean access."

Bowser began to catch on: "But even with the balloons and the big boosters—"

"There's nothing to do but pull out. The other countries are poison, and the oceans are so full of rioting life we'd be wiped out in weeks—you said this thing was dirt cheap"—I seized the cylinder of the booster in my fist—"and the balloon stations are even cheaper with their closed cycles. It's time they were field tested, Mr. Pure Engineer!"

I laughed, smug-drunk: "The best defense may be departure!"

Between me and the high vacuum with its blazing stars, a thin transparent wall creaked and shimmered.

I looked down past my feet and through: down there, less than five hundred miles away, was the green-blue-white earth. But it was invisible, hidden by a shimmering, whirling cloud like a titanic colony of paramecia circling and feeding off a ball of culture, or some strange world totally covered with shimmering, shivering sea moving in infinitely complex currents. Would they ever see it again?

Was it less than ten years ago I had argued sourly that space had been a mistake and a racket and a dead issue?

The radio clipped to my coveralls crackled: "High-Mississippi, this is High-Burbank, please give me a time check on your power track."

Ten years: I'd been right about the ecosystem driving men from America—Death Valley was a dripping jungle denser than the Matto Grasso, the canyons of New York were full of cave bears, grass, and a few inhuman scavengers. . .

"Alto-Madrid," it crackled, *"Il y a Gran Cannes. En garde, nos soleil-bateaux sont á travers que su chemin avant!"*

Six billion in orbit! But when the mutant life net spread round the globe, there had been no other retreat. Ironically, the space scientists' successes had hinged on more eco-play, the tailored bacteria that had created booster fuel deposits and the mutant insects that had spun balloons for satellites. Buckminster Fuller's domes, McLuhan's satellites framing the earth theory, and half a dozen of the despised seventies thinkers were refurbished to shape the desperate technology that scooped men from extinction and lofted them skyward. . .

But the balloon, like all of them, stunk of too many bodies, too much machinery, and wastes incompletely recycled. I pitied those in the Asian high-orbiters; three dimensional Calcuttas packed with emaciated bodies, little to do and less to hope, unless—

Bowser pushed aside the curtain to my little cubicle. "They're into re-entry", he husked. The backup boys huddled around the big trajectory display, watching the parachute drogue's cameras scanning the Terra Excursion Module capsule swinging and swaying down toward the Rockaways, a dull green circle with its shroudlines cutting off what was left of the view. But I could imagine it through the glare and deep shadows: green tumult smashing the land, splume and steam on the oceans, as mutants and land and sea bred and fought and madly evolved.

A voice broke: "Atmosphere so rich it's eroding the ablation skin! And there's so little dust and pollution, sunlight is hardly dispersed: shadows black as the moon's, but the lit up sections dazzling. It's—getting—"

A machine gun roar!

"Some kind of mutants—impacting ascent engines, and torn several shroud lines!"

Bowser scanned the data links, grimaced, husked: "About, TEM-11!"

"I copy!" On the telemeters, the ascent engines fired. On visual, the TEM tore through the drogue chute and the picture flashed out. The pilot climbed from the planet. I wondered if the inhumans still survived, if they'd tracked us some way, if the abort was their doing. Catastrophe Base was still a dream. . .

Bowser studied the plot until TEM had orbital velocity.

I put my hand on Bowser's shoulder: "We'll make it yet."

"Oh, sure," he muttered. "At the rate we're going, it'd be faster if you guys'd *grow* us a new planet. . ."

I blinked. . .

About the Authors

JOHN McHALE is director of the Center for Integrative Studies, State University of New York at Binghamton. Born in Scotland, Mr. McHale was educated in the United Kingdom and in the United States and holds a Ph.D. degree in sociology. He has published extensively in Europe and this country on the impact of technology on culture, mass communications and the future. He is an artist and designer who has exhibited widely in Europe since 1950. He is a member of a number of scholarly organizations as well as being a Fellow of the World Academy of Art and Science, the Royal Society of Arts (England), the New York Academy of Sciences and the American Geographical Society. His latest books are: *The Future of the Future* (1969), *The Ecological Context* (1970) and *World Facts and Trends* (1972).

CHELSEA QUINN YARBRO is a native Californian of Finnish and Italian descent. She is a cartographer, as well as the author of a book on opera. She is past secretary of SFWA. Her short stories have appeared in *Galaxy, Infinity, Strange Bedfellows* (Random House) *Woman of Wonder* (Vintage) and many other publications; she is the co-editor with Thomas N. Scortia of *Two Views of Wonder* (Ballantine). Her two upcoming novels are: *A Time of the Fourth Horseman* (Doubleday) and *Ogilvy, Todlent and Moon* (Putnam).

GLEN COOK is a graduate of the Clarion Writers' Workshop. His short stories have appeared in magazines and anthologies, and he is the author of a novel, *The Heirs of Babylon* (NAL, Signet, 1972). He makes his home in St. Louis, Missouri.

GREGORY BENFORD is an associate professor of physics at the University of California, Irvine. He has published thirty science fiction short stories and two novels, DEEPER THAN THE DARKNESS and JUPITER PROJECT. He has been nominated for the Nebula and Hugo awards. His work has appeared in UNIVERSE, WORLD'S BEST SF 1971, QUARK and AGAIN, DANGEROUS VISIONS. His most recent significant work is a short story, "Icarus Descending", which appeared in March, 1973 in the *Magazine of Fantasy and Science Fiction*. Dr. Benford has also written a considerable number of popularizing and speculative articles. He has appeared in *Natural History*, *Smithsonian* and *Vertex* magazines, and is the coauthor of a forthcoming text, ASTRONOMY AND LIFE IN THE UNIVERSE.

JAMES BENFORD is a plasma physicist who received his doctorate from the University of California at San Diego. He is a senior research physicist for Physics International, Inc. His writing has appeared in *Amazing*, *Vertex*, and other publications. He and his twin brother, Gregory Benford, are currently engaged in research on controlled thermonuclear fusion for the Atomic Energy Commission.

MACK REYNOLDS was born in California some fifty years ago of stock going back to the Gold Rush days. A freelance writer by trade since 1950, he has specialized largely in science fiction and humor-travel. He has published over thirty books and book-length serials, and five or six hundred novelettes, short stories and travel articles. A lifelong interest in socioeconomics has led him to specialize in extrapolations into the future on themes based on political economy. In 1955 he began a campaign of seeking out material for his stories all over the world and in the next twelve years lived in or traveled through more than seventy-five countries. At one time an active socialist, he toured the United States for several years as a lecturer. Besides in all major SF magazines, his stories have appeared in publications ranging from *Playboy* to the *New York Times*. His newest books are *Looking Backward, From The Year 2000* (Ace) and *Commune 2000 A.D.* (Bantam).

EDGAR PANGBORN was born in New York City in 1909. He studied at Harvard and the New England Conservatory of Music, and has been a freelance writer since 1945. His novels are *West of the Sun* (Doubleday, 1953); *A Mirror for Observers* (Doubleday, 1954, winner of the International Fantasy Award); *Wilderness of Spring* (Rinehart, 1958, an historical novel); *The Trial of Callista Blake* (St. Martin's, 1964); *The Judgment of Eve* (Simon and Schuster, 1966). His most recent book is a collection, *Good Neighbors and Other Strangers* (Macmillan, 1973). He was a Nebula Award finalist for his story "Mount Charity", which appears in *Nebula Awards Stories 7* (Harper & Row). *The Company of Glory* (Pyramid) is his newest novel. He lives and works in upstate New York.

NORMAN KAGAN is a writer, editor, producer and teacher in film and communications. He is the author of the well-known story, "The Mathenauts", which Judith Merrill anthologized in her best-of-the-year collections. He is the author of *The Cinema of Stanley Kubrick* (Holt, Rinehart and Winston) and other books on film. His science fiction has appeared in *Galaxy* and *The Magazine of Fantasy and Science Fiction*. He makes his home in New York City.

JAMES STEVENS is a producer-director-editor of television commercials on a freelance basis. Lately business has been booming, requiring evening and weekend labors, leaving little time for writing. His stories have appeared in *Worlds of If*, and in original anthologies, including David Gerrold's *Generation* (Dell). He makes his home in Puerto Rico.

GEORGE ZEBROWSKI, editor of the Planet Series for Unity Press, is the author of more than thirty stories and articles published in magazines and original collections since 1970. He is the author of several novels, including THE OMEGA POINT, STAR WEB, and the upcoming MACROLIFE. His anthologies include FASTER THAN LIGHT (with Jack Dann, Harper & Row) and CYBORGS (with Thomas N. Scortia, Vintage-Random House). He is a lecturer and has taught science fiction at the college level. He was editor of *The Bulletin of the Science Fiction Writers of America* from 1970 to 1975. His work has been nominated for the Nebula Award.